THE AURA
OF DESTINY

Michael Brian Brussin

Michael Brian Brussin
Publications

Michael Brian Brussin Publications
Michael B. Brussin
2008 Charade Way
Redding, CA 96003
michaelbrussin@sbcglobal.net

Cover Design/Editing/Layout: Jason Crye

Agent/Project Manager: Penny Callmeyer, Tiger Lilly Enterprises

ISBN 978-0-615-77999-7

Library of Congress Control Number: 2013935921

ATTENTION:
Contact the publisher for information on quantity discounts.

Printed and bound in the United States of America
at Color House Graphics, Grand Rapids, Michigan

First Edition

For Lola   o7 July 2013

Dear Stephanie,

I look forward to seeing you next year.

Mi casa es su casa.

Best Wishes,
Love,

Lola

ACKNOWLEDGEMENTS

A big thank you to my beautiful wife, Lola, for her never-ending love and support. Special thanks to my agent and project manager, Penny Callmeyer, for such a professional contribution, and for all the fun we had in seeing the project to completion. A special thank you to Jason Crye for the superb layout and design. To departed friends – you are missed, and you are always in my thoughts, R.I.P... Peter Scholes, Peter Stang, Geoff Cooper, Bryan Behrens, John Twidle. And to my other special friends, thanks for all the years, and those yet to come... Goldie Bradbury, Reg Head, Edvart Oye, Duncan Wilson, and Heinrich Brunotte and Fred Werner – In Fussball und Freundschaft!

CHAPTER 1

Peter Matthews was exhausted and devastated and chose to end his life. All he had to do was let go of the boat's supply barrel that was keeping him afloat. He went limp. There was no pain; it was dark and peaceful. But his transition into an emotionless void suddenly sent him battling furiously against the ocean's onslaught. His desire to live overpowered his physical and mental exhaustion and found him again clinging to the supply barrel.

Ten thousand miles away at his suburban London home, Jack Matthews shuddered. He felt something crawl through him – body and soul – and it wasn't good.

"*What the…*" he said to himself. "Something's wrong…"

Jack knew that someone was in desperate trouble… someone he was close to. He instinctively tried to reach his son, Peter, who was vacationing with his wife in Tahiti, so he called his mobile phone but there was no answer; in fact, the phone didn't even ring.

Jack tried to reach Peter over the next two days, both at his hotel and on his mobile phone, but still had no success. Soon after he was notified of his son's drowning off the shores of Tahiti.

Several weeks after Jack was informed of his son and daughter-in-law's deaths, he was awakened by an early morning telephone call... a call that would catapult him into a world he could never have imagined.

"Hello," he mumbled, rubbing his eyes with his forefinger and thumb.

"Mr. Matthews?" the voice inquired.

"Yes."

"*Jack* Matthews?"

"*Yes...*"

The voice at the other end belonged to an official at the Home Office.

Jack was puzzled; he couldn't understand what business he had with Her Majesty's Government.

The official told Jack that the navy had come across a package marked for his attention, and to claim it he was required to appear at the Home Office in person.

Despite his curiosity, Jack was annoyed at the inconvenience of having to drive across London to collect this strange parcel.

Jack was a fifty-five year old attorney, and a widower, who ran his own law office. He looked younger than his years even though the tragic death of his only son often saw him spin into moments of anger, sometimes followed by a period of depression.

Jack's thoughts turned to Peter... an engaging young

man of twenty-seven. He was six feet tall and powerfully built, having gained his physique from his rowing days at university. He was also an established attorney enjoying a lucrative partnership with his father. What an injustice it all seemed to Jack that his son and daughter-in-law should be so cruelly cut down.

What Jack Matthews found when he opened the package was a stack of handwritten papers several inches thick, which appeared to be a diary. The curious thing was that each page had yellowness about it and the stack was almost brittle in places, even when handled delicately. It was obvious that Jack had a very old document in his possession. Nothing made sense to him when he scanned the writing, but rather than try to unravel the mystery of the papers there at the Home Office, he drove back to his house in Surrey where he could concentrate in comfort.

Once back at home Jack settled down in his study and examined the contents of the package with more intensity. He was suddenly jarred by the recognition of his son's hand-writing. There was no doubt about it – it was Peter's.

Jack looked closely at the worn pages, carefully examining the fading characters. He wondered how this could be from Peter as there was only one reported survivor of the ferryboat sinking – a man by the name of Heinrich Werner, but being in possession of something so compelling Jack took it seriously and began to read the manuscript...

I have directed this journal to my father, Jack Matthews, who will not be born for almost two hundred years.

I think I should begin with my intense desire to visit Tahiti. I ought to have realized there was something odd about this obsession. It was not just a simple fascination I had for the island; something beyond my control had pulled me here.

My suggestion we spend our holiday in Tahiti excited Sarah. She was thrilled over the opportunity of visiting such an exotic and far away place.

The airport was alive with tourists when Sarah and I stepped from the plane into the cool Tahitian air. I felt a tang of excitement at being here when I saw the palm trees and heard their leaves rustling in the midnight breeze.

Our hotel had all of the modern necessities required by the discriminating traveler, yet as our taxi approached the brightly lit entrance I sensed I would have been just as comfortable in a primitive native hut.

Sarah was in the bathroom when I awoke after a few hours sleep.

"What do you want to do today, darling?" she called after hearing me stir.

"I don't know, let's have breakfast and look through the paper; there should be an English edition in the lobby."

We decided to hire a car and drive around the island, which would take most of the day.

"We should be back in time for dinner and the show," I said, sipping my morning coffee.

Tahiti is comprised of two parts – Tahiti-Nui and Tahiti-Iti. A seventy-mile road encircled Tahiti-Nui, the larger and most northern part of the island. Two small roads broke off into Tahiti-Iti; one extending ten miles along the north coast into the village of Tautira, and the other about the same distance along the south coast into Tehupoo. There were no roads beyond these two villages so the normal mode of travel past these points was by motor-driven outrigger canoe.

Our first stop was going to be Papeete, the heart of Tahiti some five miles from the hotel. Then with stops further along we would drive into the Taiarapu Peninsula, or Tahiti-Iti. From there we would return to our hotel by the opposite route.

Tahiti measured only four hundred square miles, and with the road circling Tahiti-Nui and the two roads branching off into the peninsula being just one hundred miles in combined length, we estimated it would take around eight hours to complete our tour.

We parked on the Quai du Commerce in Papeete and strolled along the waterfront after stopping at several souvenir shops. Sitting outside these shops were elderly women stringing necklaces together while politely urging passing tourists to stop and buy.

I found nothing particularly captivating about Papeete; if anything this busy downtown section resembled something of a dusty border town; but when I looked at the beauty of the hills, the swaying palms, and the majestic peaks of Moorea lying ten miles out to sea, my initial disappointment went away.

Leaving Papeete, we entered the Arue district where we passed the tomb of Pomare the Fifth, the last king of Tahiti and the one who relinquished the island to France in 1880.

We continued into the district of Mahina and drove down a narrow side road leading to Point Venus, which was the site of a fifty-foot high lighthouse marking Captain Cook's 1769 expedition. It was on this expedition that Cook anchored in Matavai Bay, bringing with him a group of scientists who were sent by the Royal Geographical Society to observe the passage of Venus around the face of the sun.

We drove down the road as far as it went and stopped

the car at the edge of the grass, fifty yards from where the lighthouse stood. We were just a few miles from the bustle of Papeete yet the beauty and stillness of this spot was unmatched.

As we strolled hand in hand towards the historical beacon, Sarah asked me what it was that made me want to come to Tahiti so much. Because I couldn't essentially answer her question I shrugged it off by telling her that Captain Cook anchored in neighboring Matavai Bay and that the lighthouse was erected to commemorate his landing.

We turned towards the lagoon and came upon a monument honoring Captains Wallis, de Bougainville, and Cook, the former discovering Tahiti in 1767.

We continued to an unusually shaped piece of land that jutted into the lagoon.

"Let's sit here for a while," I said, stretching myself under a well-crowned palm tree.

With the lagoon flowing lazily to the sides of us Sarah lay her head in my lap as I started to doze.

I felt that Sarah and I were getting closer, that this holiday was exactly what we needed to begin strengthening our marriage, which had become a little strained. She was an incredibly beautiful and intelligent woman, Sarah; her shapely five foot seven form was often the object of an admiring look.

As I lay dozing I unexplainably got to my feet and walked to the water's edge, startling Sarah as her head dropped from my lap.

I stood frozen, staring into the water. Sarah came over to me puzzled about why I got up so inexplicably.

"Peter, what's the matter?" she asked with concern. I didn't move or reply. "Peter, what is it?" I still didn't respond,

I was in some sort of a trance. She finally had to pull at me. "Peter?" she inquired in an anxious tone.

"I just had the most incredible sensation," I said. "I felt like I knew this place, like I'd been here before."

Sarah stared at me, then nervously ran a hand through her hair.

"That's ridiculous," she said.

"I know it sounds crazy; I can't explain it, I just felt familiar with everything."

I couldn't remember how long I stood transfixed; I just recalled coming back to the consciousness of my surroundings when Sarah shook me.

Although I was feeling refreshed, Sarah was disturbed over my behavior and suggested moving on. She gave me a questioning look as we walked back to the car, but I laughed it off and assured her that everything was alright. We drove back towards the main road and headed next for the Blowhole of Arahoohoo in the Tiarei district.

I enjoyed driving our Peugeot, but I did nearly run into one of the slow moving buses ahead of us after speeding out of a curve and onto a straightaway. These buses were simple vehicles; they were open topped, had wooden seats and no windows, and nor was there an enclosure at the back. A small ladder protruded at the rear platform for the passengers to climb on and off, and Polynesian music echoed from a loudspeaker above the driver's seat.

We parked near the Blowhole of Arahoohoo, which was simply a large ten-foot rock with a hole in it, and because of its position, water would spout high in the air each time a wave crashed against it.

"Fascinating, isn't it?" I turned to see a towering man with thick black hair and a complementing beard talking to me. I exchanged a few words with him before he and his wife moved on.

There were no other sights on our southerly route until the other side of the Isthmus of Taravao, those being the Botanical Garden and Gauguin Museum, which we planned to visit on the way back from the peninsula.

We drove a further fifteen miles or so and stopped at a quaint restaurant in the Faaone district. While sitting outside having a coffee, I wondered out loud what was happening at the practice back home.

"Peter, that's exactly the reason for this holiday – for you to *forget* about the bloody firm. What are you worrying about? Your father's handling everything." Even though it was natural for me to think about the office, I dropped the subject not wanting to annoy Sarah any further; after all, a holiday was no place for a quarrel.

I thought about the French influence that was instilled in the Society Islands.

"I don't know how we managed to lose Tahiti and the other islands," I remarked, "especially since we were here first." Sarah asked how Tahiti came to be a French possession.

"It was because the Tahitians were afraid of a growing dissention between the British and the French, who also had a stronghold on the island, and rather than us, they asked the French to act as their protectors in case fighting broke out; that eventually led them to totally relinquish the islands to the French."

With it approaching mid-afternoon we continued on to the isthmus then drove along the northern coast of the peninsula into Tautira. It was in the village of Tautira that Robert Louis Stevenson and Zane Gray had settled and produced some of their writings.

We drove through the village, passing some of the island's many Chinese owned shops. We also passed a local school and a tiny cinema. We continued along the northern coast until the road ended then turned back toward the hotel through the isthmus and around the other side of the island.

Stopping again on the way, we found an inviting spot near the water and settled in the shade provided by several trees. There was an enchanting stillness around us; the only sounds coming from the birds chirping and the occasional barking of a dog.

"Hey, how about a swim?" I said with a burst of spirit.

We followed the exotic variety of fish as they darted in and out of the coral, then we swam out to the reef. The reef was about a mile out and the crystalline water eight or nine feet deep.

"Race you back!" Sarah challenged when we reached the reef, then teased, "If I beat you, you don't get any tonight!"

"Then I bet you lose on purpose!" I laughed before setting off after her. We didn't race but swam leisurely, enjoying the cool, serene water, but when we approached the beach I began to race while Sarah deliberately took her time, giggling, making sure I would win.

We flopped onto the grass and lay quietly for a few moments, then we turned to each other and kissed, happy that our holiday was indeed bringing us closer together.

It didn't take long before consciousness began to fade and I was asleep. It was at this time that I again behaved in a very strange way. I was in a deep sleep when Sarah shook me.

"Peter! Wake up! You're dreaming!"

"What? What's the matter?" I stammered.

"You kept mumbling… on and on; then you shouted

something. It… it sounded like gibberish, but it scared me… Peter?"

I felt momentarily lost.

"What did it sound like? I mean did it sound like anything made sense?" I asked nervously.

"I don't know, I…" Just then a native couple who were nearby approached us and asked if everything was alright as my shouting had caught their attention. I assured them I was fine and thanked them for their concern. Sarah again studied me as the couple smiled and walked away. But then the man called back to me.

"Welcome home!" I didn't grasp his meaning so I called out to him and asked what he meant, all the time sensing that something was terribly wrong. The puzzled native told me that what I had shouted so powerfully was Tahitian for *I have come home.*

This bizarre event left me thoroughly confused, and when I recalled my vivid familiarity with Point Venus earlier in the day I became inwardly alarmed.

I tried to reason how I could suddenly gain a subconscious knowledge of the Tahitian language. First I attempted to shrug my outburst off as gibberish that coincidentally sounded like the words that the man said I spoke, but coincidences like that just didn't happen. Meanwhile, Sarah had become still more disturbed over my behavior, but I was able to calm her by explaining that I had invariably picked up pieces of the language from various readings I'd done over the years as I had always had a keen interest in Tahitian history. Even though this made Sarah feel a little better I did not fool myself; I knew something strange was starting to happen to me but I couldn't unravel it. It was frightening me more and more.

We continued onward to the Botanical Garden hoping to put the sleep-talking incident behind us. We mingled among the tourists when we arrived at the garden and enjoyed the flowers' beauty and fragrances that floated around us.

Lying in the vicinity of the garden was the Guaguin Museum, which was made up of four buildings that formed a quadrangle, and it contained a display of more than a thousand of Guaguin's documents and exhibits.

We also stopped at the ruins of the Mehiatea temple after leaving the museum. The temple's altar measured some three hundred feet in length and consisted of several tiers, each tier reaching a height of approximately fifty feet. It was at such temples, or maraes as they were called, that wedding ceremonies were held, and ancient lower class natives were sacrificed to the Polynesian gods on these altars.

We sat quietly for a long time during our drive back to the hotel but my mind was by no means idle. I broke the silence when I abruptly stopped the car at the side of the road.

"I've got it!" I said.

"Got what?"

"I've been piecing this thing together; I know why I've been acting this way." Sarah looked at me curiously, waiting for me to elaborate. "*One*," I said, "why did I want to come to Tahiti so much?" I answered my own question, "I *had* to come – something was pulling me. *Two*, I had the strangest feeling of déjà vu at Point Venus, and *three*, I spoke in Tahitian while I was asleep – I said I had come home. What does it add up to?" Sarah was disturbed; she knew what I was driving at.

"Are you trying to tell me you've lived here before, in another life?"

"Why not? Can you tell me why I've wanted to come here so much? Why I had that déjà vu sensation? And why I spoke in Tahitian?" Sarah's response was shallow.

"Maybe it's just an inexplicable phenomenon."

"And what's that supposed to mean? Isn't it even remotely feasible?"

"No, it *isn't!*" she insisted, although I suspected she did feel it plausible but was afraid to say so.

Silence again dominated as I steered the car onto the road and drove the final leg to the hotel.

It was Sarah who broke the silence this time when she asked me if I really believed in reincarnation.

"I don't know; but I look at it this way, if we're born once, then die, why can't we be born again into the physical world?"

"The body decomposes when we die, so what you're saying is our soul leaves the body at the moment of death, right?"

"Right. What happens to the soul between incarnations I don't know, and what causes the soul to choose a specific body in its next life is *another* question."

"But if this is true," Sarah said, "why can't the soul – in each incarnation – remember anything of its *previous* lives?"

"I would imagine the soul, or in this case the mind, isn't developed enough; it seems that flashes of déjà vu are the only conscious links to recollection."

The sun had just set when we pulled into the hotel car park. Although I had gone through a considerable mental ordeal, I began to feel more composed and was looking forward to dinner and an entertaining evening.

We were handed a list of exotic drinks after being seated for dinner, and while deciding what I wanted Sarah asked me how I was feeling.

"Don't worry, love, I'm fine; we'll sort it out when we get home – if it's necessary," I said. Just then a voice called to us.

"Hello, would you like to join us?" I turned to the next table and recognized the man I spoke with earlier in the day at the Blowhole of Arahoohoo.

We introduced ourselves to Heinrich and Ursula Werner, who were vacationing from Canada. Heinrich presented himself as a psychiatrist, having a practice in Vancouver. The doctor, who with his wife immigrated to Canada from Germany twenty years earlier, was in his late forties and he stood about six feet three or four inches tall. Although he was a little on the stout side he appeared very fit. Ursula was an elegant and attractive woman, much smaller than her husband and less outgoing.

"So what made you come to Tahiti for your holiday?" Heinrich asked in his still prevalent German accent. Sarah and I glanced at each other in cautious amusement.

"Oh, we just wanted to go somewhere different," I said with a wink to Sarah.

We sat back over a round of drinks after dinner and waited for the entertainment to begin.

Being a psychiatrist, Heinrich liked to study people and he talked to me about behavioral characteristics, but soon the lights went dim and a dozen island girls dressed in native costumes walked briskly onto the stage followed by a group of similarly dressed male drummers. The dancers were dressed in ankle length skirts made of green leaves, and they wore plates of pearl shell over their breasts. They also wore very fetching headdresses, and each girl carried a fan in her hands. As the drummers played with rhythmic vigor the dancers went into their provocative hip motions. I had become mesmerized by the wantonness of the dance. Then the drumming stopped as abruptly as it had begun and the dancers stopped in unison with the cessation of the drums.

"This was quite a performance," Heinrich said during the applause.

"Sorry? What?" I stumbled.

"I said this was quite a dance."

"Oh, yes, it was," I agreed.

"You were very absorbed in that, Peter," Ursula remarked as Sarah watched over me. I didn't answer her; I just smiled and sipped my drink.

Another group of dancers had since taken the stage and *they* went into their frenetic movements to the sound of the drums. Then a group of men, each holding a flaming torch, leapt onto the stage. The dance reached its climax when the lights went dimmer and the men twirled their torches as the dancers continued their vigorous and hypnotic movements.

When the show was over I commented that the first performance was a fertility dance, which was danced by young girls to assure the men of their fertility and to let them know they were ready for marriage.

"How do you know this?" Ursula asked quite surprised but nevertheless impressed. Actually I was not consciously sure of the interpretation yet I knew that was what it meant.

"Oh, I just recall it from some reading I did," I answered matter-of- factly.

Remembering Heinrich Werner's conversation on behavioral characteristics earlier in the evening, I asked him what would make a person do something in a conscious state while not being aware he was doing it. The psychiatrist stroked his beard thoughtfully while Sarah and Ursula continued *their* conversation.

"Can you be more specific?" he finally said; "give me an example." I was reluctant to go into detail about my behavior as I didn't know Werner well, but I told him how at Point Venus I got up from a reclining position and walked to the water and stood transfixed, all without remembering I did it, and I went on to explain how this action was simultaneous with a sensational feeling of déjà vu.

"I don't think your behavior was so eccentric," he said, "after all, déjà vu experiences are not uncommon." I was disappointed over such a general answer and was quick to remind him that I had no recollection of getting up and walking to the water.

"Here again," a pensive Werner said, "your mind was so absorbed with this powerful sensation that when your body reacted you were not mentally aware of its movements. It is true, your actions were a little unusual; still, I believe it is all very harmless." He then gave a short laugh and said, "Why do you ask? Do you think you have lived here in a previous life?"

Before retiring for the night Heinrich asked if we would like to spend a couple of days on Moorea with him and Ursula. We happily accepted the invitation, as the four of us were becoming very good friends.

I broke into a broad smile when Sarah and I returned to our bungalow.

"You look like the Cheshire Cat," she mused. "What is it?"

"I told Heinrich what happened at Point Venus. He passed it off as a common déjà vu experience and doesn't think it's anything to worry about."

"Did you also tell him about what you said in your sleep?"

"No, I didn't. It had to be gibberish that just *happened* to sound like Tahitian," I answered emphatically and in a deliberately serious tone.

Sarah became more settled when she saw that my earlier apprehension had disappeared.

She snuggled up to me while I sat on the bed and started unbuttoning my shirt, and soon we lay naked on the sheets with the breeze blowing gently against our warm, satisfied bodies.

CHAPTER 2

The Hirondelle was a supply boat that sailed twice a day from Papeete to Moorea. She transported foodstuffs and domestic goods to the hotels and stores scattered about the island, and as a sideline the vessel also carried up to fifty passengers on each of her trips.

These crossings were known to get a little rough at times, which was why many tourists chose to take the short ten-minute flight across rather than suffer for an hour on a rolling sea.

After stowing our overnight bags Sarah and I and the Werners climbed a steel staircase to the upper deck.

The Hirondelle backed out of her berth and swung into the direction of the harbor entrance, sailing impudently past a French cruiser that lay at anchor.

I watched Papeete become smaller as we chugged into the open sea. The cruiser soon shrunk to the size of the Hirondelle while the boats lining the shorefront had disappeared and the hubbub of the Quai du Commerce fell silent.

I turned from Tahiti's shrinking hills to see the proud peaks of Moorea grow to welcome us.

We were about half way across when the swells began to get bigger and the up-down motion of the boat became increasingly more prominent.

Heinrich was enjoying a snack when he joined me at the railing. Seeing him pull out a sandwich seemed to be the undoing of one particular passenger, as having long since lost his color, the man dashed to the railing, leaned over, and threw up.

"Poor fellow," Heinrich said before taking another bite of his sandwich.

The queasy passengers welcomed the sight of the lagoon as the Hirondelle changed direction towards an opening in the reef.

Porpoises swam playfully alongside when we approached the barrier, then spurted ahead, and after letting the boat catch up with them they spurted ahead again. This game continued until we entered the lagoon when the porpoises vanished as quickly as they had appeared.

When the Hirondelle settled alongside the wharf a crew-member tossed a rope to a worker standing by who secured it around a curled iron bar fixed in the ground.

Dark green hills whose peaks were shrouded by clouds encompassed us on three sides. This particular area was so thick with brush little sunlight penetrated.

"Peter! Are you coming?" Sarah called, stirring my wondering mind. "There's a bus to take us to the hotel!"

The bus was the same kind that was driven in Tahiti. It, too, had simple wooden seats and was open all around except for the top. The crewmembers of the Hirondelle were busy unloading the supplies when we boarded the vehicle. Half of the items were stacked on our bus and were marked for delivery to places on the western part of the island, while a second bus waited to take *its* passengers and provisions to points on the eastern side.

Moorea had only one road encircling it, which was not very well paved; but we rambled on, passing through the village of Paopao, which we were told by the driver boasted a population of two hundred, and which was also the site of a school, a clinic, and a general store.

Although it was midday and the sun shone brightly, the road was so shaded by trees and hills that not only were we actually quite cool, it had the appearance of being dusk.

We next entered Cook's Bay, named after the famous captain's landing. The bay was not shadowed by growth, which made its appearance all the more beautiful from the contrasting darkness.

We rolled to a stop at the Moorea Lagoon Hotel, about five miles from where we had disembarked from the Hirondelle.

Our bungalow overhung the lagoon and it, too, was complete with all the modern day necessities. Behind a large bedroom was an open closet, a shower, and a toilet. There were no windows, just movable wooden slats which supported a handle to regulate the amount of air and light to let in. The soft sounds of rippling water below and the breeze finding its way between the openings in the slats made this the perfect romantic hideaway.

The sunset was a magnificent sight with the sky a combination of yellow, orange, and deep blue. The hills were silhouetted by the darkening sky, and the water had been given a golden glow by the sun's reflection.

At dinner it was delightfully different to see the wait-resses entertain the guests by spontaneously breaking into song and dance routines.

Seated cross-legged at the front of the dining room were some of the men whom we had seen earlier in the day con-structing the hotel's newest bungalows. One of them played a guitar while the others sang, then the waitresses would join in. Our waitress, whose name was Denise, had picked up some spoons and began tapping them between her fingers while singing with the rest of the group. The carefree mood was momentarily broken, though, when the sick man from the Hirondelle started to fuss over what he felt was the wait-resses' inattentiveness to his table. The man had evidently resented having to wait a long time to order his meal while his waitress, who happened to also be Denise, was singing and dancing. When the music was over and the waitresses went back to their work Denise was given a curt admon-ishment and a prolonged stare by the irritated man when she offered to take his order. Though Denise did not speak very much English, she nevertheless understood the man's message and responded by rolling her eyes in an amusing forbearance.

While we relaxed in the lounge after dinner Denise stopped by with a greeting.

"Est que vous voulez asseoir avec nous?" I invited her to join us in my passing French.

"Je veux bien," she said before going to the bar to fetch herself a drink.

Like the other waitresses, Denise was dressed in the smaller version of the pareu; the top was actually part of a two-piece swim suit, and the bottom was like a very short skirt. She was an exceedingly pretty girl with trimmed black hair and big almond eyes, and she had a smile to warm the heart.

"Parlez-vous francais?" she asked when she returned with her drink. Heinrich and Ursula looked at Sarah and me before I answered her.

"Je ne parle pas bien; parlez-vous anglais?"

"Yes, but I speak not so well," she said with a cute shyness, so in a flattering tone I assured her that her English was very good.

She asked if we would be coming to the tamaaraa, or the feast, that the hotel was hosting the next day. "There will be er… beaucoup de nourriture, et chant et danse; I am sorry, my English…"

"That's alright," I smiled. Then I turned to Sarah and the Werners. "She said there'll be plenty to eat, and singing and dancing."

"You will come, oui?" On behalf of us all, I told her we would be here.

I realized that Sarah had become uncomfortable over my attention to Denise, as it was evident I was captivated by her beauty and charm. Meanwhile, Heinrich asked Denise what all the fuss was about with the sick man.

"Oh, he is tres miserable; he does not know how to have, er, a good time; he is always… vit, you know, quick, in a rush," at which she made a *whooshing* sound accompanied by a fast motion of her hand to clarify her explanation of the man's impatience.

It was late in the evening when Denise said goodnight. "Do not forget, I will see you tomorrow," she reminded us when she got up to leave.

The tamaaraa was to begin in the afternoon, which left

several hours open for us. Heinrich and I had decided to rent a car and explore the island while Sarah and Ursula chose to stay at the hotel and swim and sunbathe.

Sarah was perceptibly cool towards me when we returned to our bungalow. She wouldn't talk to me, and when I said something to her she would respond with just a quick word or two, and when I touched her she moved away.

"Alright, what is it?" I said.

"Nothing," she answered curtly.

"Oh, come off it!" I snapped, "it's because I was talking to Denise."

"Well, you acted as though I wasn't even there."

"For Christ sake, Sarah, you're being ridiculous. If I can't talk to another woman without you carrying on…" The exchange went nowhere and ended on a sour note with both of us going straight to sleep. But as I lay in bed, unfairly angry with Sarah, I thought of Denise and how different she was. It was a special difference, a difference I liked.

I awoke in the morning to see Sarah sitting up in bed reading a magazine. I turned to her and smiled sheepishly.

"I'm sorry about last night."

"Me, too," she offered, then we kissed and the entire thing was forgotten. But while Sarah was showering I wondered if I might be getting progressively distant from her. Were we communicating? Did we *really* ever have an understanding or enough in common? I sensed I was falling *out* of love with Sarah. My thoughts were now very much on Denise and the intriguing characteristics of her people.

Heinrich and I rented a jeep after breakfast and left for a drive around the island.

There was little to see on the road but we enjoyed the carefree, boyish adventure of exploring a strange land.

Just before entering the village of Vaiere we came to a stream with sturdy but narrow boards slung across it. This crude bridge took Heinrich by surprise.

"Scheisse! I thought we were going to end up in the water!" he exclaimed after stopping on the other side to compose himself.

"You had *me* convinced," I breathed with relief.

We next came upon some women washing their clothes in the same stream we had crossed when we entered Vaiere. They were all dressed just from the waist down and were scrubbing their clothes on rocks before rinsing them in the water.

We drove a few more miles before stopping in Vairapu Bay, the southern part of Moorea. We spotted an islet a short distance from the bay, parked the jeep, and swam out to it.

While we rested on the tiny patch, which sprouted a lone palm tree right in its center, Heinrich posed a question to me.

"How have you felt over the past couple of days, Peter?"

"Fine…" I answered, not immediately realizing why he was asking.

As we strolled about the islet Heinrich remarked that he was looking forward to the tamaaraa.

"Did you know that the natives held these feasts hundreds of years ago?" I said. "They cooked their food in underground ovens. It was a simple process really, they heated stones in a fire which they built in a pit; the ovens were ready for the food once the wood had burned away and the stones were red hot, then the food was wrapped in banana leaves and placed over the stones." Heinrich listened curiously while I continued. "Meat and fish usually went into the himaas first, then the vegetables."

"The *what*?" Heinrich said.

"The himaas… the ovens," I clarified.

"What happened once the food was in the ovens?"

"It was covered with more banana leaves and coconut fronds, and then a layer of earth to seal in the heat… then it was left to cook." Heinrich looked amazed, almost disturbed when he asked me how I knew these things. "I don't know, I suppose from the reading I've done," I answered.

After studying me in typical psychiatrist fashion, Heinrich suggested for my own peace of mind that I consult someone to evaluate my recent behavior.

"Are you telling me that I *do* have a problem after all?" I asked somewhat alarmed.

"No, no, no," he tried to assure me, "I'm sure you are perfectly fine; all I am saying is I think it might be a good idea for you to do whatever you can to eliminate any doubt of the situation being more complicated than we both feel it is."

"You're a real diplomat, Heinrich, you know that?" I said with a bite of sarcasm.

"There is no need to get upset, Peter, but let's face it, you *have* experienced some rather strange sensations." I contemplated Werner's apparent change of opinion but still favored his initial analysis that it was all harmlessly in my mind.

"I'm sorry, Heinrich, I don't know what I should do," I sighed, "maybe I'll look into it."

We returned to the hotel early enough to see the staff prepare the ovens for the food. The process was virtually as I had described… once the stones were red hot, the cooks put the meat and vegetables into the ovens and covered them with leaves.

This was not to be a primitive feast where everyone sat on

the ground and ate with their fingers, but it was comfortably arranged with tables and benches, and plates and utensils.

The owner of the hotel spoke briefly to his guests and explained the ancient tradition of the tamaaraa before turning his hungry listeners loose.

The sun was nearing the horizon when a staff member lit the torches that had been placed in the ground.

Sarah suddenly became withdrawn after returning with a plate of food. I was about to question her when I learned why. It was Denise. My heart beat quicker as I watched her approach. I was infatuated with the young island girl, it was as simple as that, but I had to be fair to Sarah and not let it show.

"Hello, everyone," Denise greeted us, "I am late, I was helping to prepare the tamaaraa, but I work no more today, I stay with you, d'accord?"

Not long after Denise arrived a group of drummers began to play within the circle of guests, and several native girls dressed in traditional island costumes joined them in dance. At the end of their dance the girls went over to the guests where each one selected a partner and again began dancing to the vigorous beating of the drums. The men hopelessly attempted the hip and leg movements, but the harder they tried the more they laughed. While this was happening Denise got up, took my hand, and led me to the center of the circle. She then picked up a crown of flowers, known as a couronne, and placed it on my head. As she did this with an enticing deftness, the dancers and guests moved aside and Denise began her exotic step. She pulled me closer to her while provocatively moving her hips to the beat of the drums. I showed a remarkable coordination when I danced with her. I looked into her sensuous eyes, which invited me into her world of passion. Then, when she and the drummers abruptly stopped she broke into a big smile and put her arms around my neck and kissed me on both cheeks.

Sarah and the Werners applauded along with the other guests when we sat down, then Sarah locked arms with me as if to show Denise that I belonged to her.

"You dance very well, Peter," Denise said. "How do you say in English – it must be in your blood."

Sarah took me for a walk afterwards, which appeared to be a tactic to keep Denise away from me; I didn't mind, though, as I knew I wouldn't see Denise again after tonight and I recognized the fact that I had a responsibility to make my marriage a happy one.

When the evening ended Denise asked if we were leaving the next day.

"I'm afraid we must," I answered, feeling oddly dejected over our farewell. Denise then kissed us in turn before leaving our lives forever.

We boarded the Hirondelle the next morning for the return journey to Papeete.

We were all a little uncomfortable over the possibility of another rough crossing, but the weather was beautiful with a clear blue sky and an eighty-degree temperature.

Heinrich and I perched ourselves at the forward-most section of the boat and watched the porpoises play their game with the Hirondelle as she left the stillness of the lagoon and entered the ocean.

I estimated we were about midway between Moorea and Tahiti when I momentarily shivered. It was as though the sun went in and a cold wind blew right through me.

"Did you feel that?" I asked Heinrich.

"Feel what?"

"I just felt a cold wind; you didn't feel it?"

"No, I did not feel anything," he said disinterestedly.

We stayed at the forward railing watching the swells gently break against the boat when I again felt that same icy wind cut into me. This time, however, I noticed some of the other passengers look up at the sky; they, too, had sensed something.

Ominous clouds began to gather and in a matter of minutes they had engulfed the sun. Rain increasingly pelted the vessel making the passengers run for cover below the deck. The once acquiescing sea now tossed the Hirondelle as though she were a cork bouncing with no purpose or direction.

"Peter, I'm scared," Sarah whimpered as she held my arm tightly. Day had incredulously turned into night as the ocean threw us about savagely. Panic shot through everyone when the squall reached its summit. I couldn't see anything but I felt Sarah clinging to me for her life.

"*God no*," I realized, "we're going to go down…" Then I heard the screams… men screaming, women screaming, and children shrieking helplessly in fear.

I felt Sarah's terror sweep through her as the Hirondelle was flung onto her side. The ferry lurched back up only to be mercilessly flung down a second time, then she was sucked under in a gurgling whirlpool.

Hysterical, chilling screams bit into the wind when the doomed passengers felt their lives being ripped from them.

I struggled in the water praying I would find Sarah but I was made helpless by the raging sea. I gave up my struggle and let go of the supply barrel that was keeping me afloat, but my desire to live was too strong and I grabbed onto the barrel again.

It was not long before the sky began to clear. The blanket of clouds shifted submissively to let the sun shine once again onto a calming sea.

I looked around only to see Papeete's harbor a few miles to the east and in the other direction about the same distance was Moorea. I guessed I was stranded midway between the two pieces of land, alone and exhausted.

A sudden movement caught my attention. I squinted and saw another survivor.

"Hello!" I shouted. "Are you alright?"

"Yes! Are there any others!" a familiar voice called back. It was Heinrich Werner; he had managed to latch onto a crate that had also broken loose from the Hirondelle.

"Heinrich! It's me – Peter! I think everyone's lost!"

"Oh, no! Nein! Mein Gott!" Werner sobbed, coughing water.

Werner and I bobbed about hoping to be carried closer to shore.

"Hold on, Heinrich!" I shouted, "we're bound to be spotted soon!" There was probably fifty yards between us which we tried to narrow but neither of us had the strength.

Suddenly, a strange aura appeared on the water which grew progressively more brilliant and which looked to contain the colors of a rainbow. No sooner had this phantom ring encircled us when the waters again became turbulent. It seemed that this mysterious aura was the root cause of the sudden fury, as outside the ring the water remained strangely calm. While Werner and I were again thrown about in a raging sea, I saw something moving but could not discern what it was. Then I recognized a boat, three or four of them; they looked like outrigger canoes and they were coming on fast.

"Heinrich! We're alright!" I bellowed, "They've seen us!" Werner strained to see.

"Where? I do not see anything!"

"*There*! They'll reach us in a couple of minutes!" Then to my horror, when I turned back to Heinrich Werner, he was gone. Vanished. A chill shot through my cold, soaked body as I stared at the spot where I last saw him seconds earlier.

I was nearing the point of collapse when one of the canoes pulled alongside me. I faintly felt myself being lifted out of the water and remember being placed on my back in the boat, then I passed out.

CHAPTER 3

I was alone in a large empty room when I opened my eyes.

I immediately remembered the storm and Werner's sudden drowning, and I was grief-stricken over Sarah's death. Tears welled in my eyes as I cursed that we chose not to fly back to Papeete.

I was lying on what appeared to be a thick carpet and was covered with a light blanket. I assumed I was in a hospital, a rather strange hospital; there were no windows, and there was a long narrow piece of cloth hanging from the ceiling as if where a screen or a door would normally be placed.

I felt stronger after resting, and being curious where I was I got to my feet and walked outside into the afternoon sunshine.

Everything looked normal enough, but when I examined the area more closely I noticed a difference in the houses;

they were all thatched and shared a basic, common rectan-gular shape.

The people seemed to be going about their usual business; women were washing clothes in a nearby stream while others were mending a fishing net, and off in the distance some men were shaping wood from a fallen tree.

I guessed I was in a village somewhere on Tahiti or Moorea.

Several villagers approached me when I appeared. Their dress was strange and unfamiliar; the men wore cloth kilts and capes while others adorned only the kilt. Some of them wore cloth turbans or coconut leaves, which resembled the couronne that Denise had placed on my head the previous night, and they were heavily tattooed… which was another unusual characteristic.

The women were dressed in cloth skirts and they wore cloaks over their shoulders, although some went about bare-breasted. All in all, their garb was not unlike that of the ancient Romans.

I approached two men and asked them where I was but all they did was stare at me. Realizing that little or no English was spoken on this remote part of Tahiti I asked them again in French.

"Ou suis je?" All I got in return was uncomprehending looks. "Quel sort d'endroit?" I continued, but again all I got back were smiles and responses in Tahitian. I was confused, why didn't they understand French? "Damn it, where *am* I! Is this Tahiti?" I burst out with increasing frustration. A growing crowd stood silently as some of the children clutched their mothers' skirts.

"O Taheite," a gruff voice finally answered. It came from a weathered old man who had approached me slowly with two aides. He looked to be well into his seventies, perhaps older, and although he seemed feeble he carried himself with an upright dignity. He was also heavily tattooed and was dressed in a pure white kilt and a cloak that folded carefully over his shoulders. His hair was short and gray, as was his stubbly beard, and his skin was a dark healthy brown like that of his countrymen. To my astonishment, as I was about to question him, one of his aides shouted at me, ripped off my shirt, and threw me to the ground. When I got to my feet, more bewildered than afraid, the old man said to me in remarkably correct English, "It is proper to bare one's shoulders when in the presence of a chief." I stood speechless; before I could manage anything he added, "This is Tahiti; you are in Mahina, I am Matai, chief of Mahina."

I was unable to put things into perspective. The crowd had grown larger and I was now thoroughly confused. Then when I saw one of the old man's aides showing my wristwatch to some of the other men – who were curiously examining it – a strange, eerie feeling went through my body.

It became evident that the chief was the only one who spoke English, so I asked him if we could talk privately. He agreed, but his aides were always close behind as we walked.

I asked Matai who it was that pulled me from the water.

"The fishermen," he answered. "They say you came from nowhere. You must tell me where your land is and how you came to be struggling in the water." I told him of the Hirondelle being caught in the squall between Moorea and Tahiti, and of everyone drowning but myself.

The chief gave me a quizzical look and said, "You do not make sense, fair one, there has been no storm to sink the smallest boat; the skies have been clear for many days."

By this time we had approached a piece of land that

jutted into the lagoon.

"Wait!" I exclaimed, putting the chief's aides on guard. "I know this place! I was here with my wife a few days ago!" It was the same spot where I had the déjà vu sensation.

"You were here before today?" Matai asked sounding puzzled.

"Yes, with my wife."

"It is not possible, we would have known of you before now," he disputed.

"Is this Point Venus?" I then asked, almost dreading the answer. My fear was confirmed with the chief's response.

"It is so called by the white man, Cook."

I knew this was Point Venus from certain landmarks, yet there were those that were not there. Gone was the lighthouse and the Wallis – de Bougaineville – Cook monument. But Matai confirmed this was Point Venus – so called by the white man Cook. It finally hit me… I had somehow gone back in time!

I asked Matai if I could be left alone, and sensing my need for solitude he consented, but he told me I was to dine with him at sunset and explain my presence and background to him.

Matai left me mentally and emotionally spent, sitting against a palm tree that was virtually the same spot that Sarah and I had enjoyed just a few days earlier.

I was confused and afraid, and completely drained. Had I really gone back more than two hundred years in time? How was this possible?

I tried hard to put these eccentric occurrences into perspective and determine if they did indeed add up to regression. The dress of the natives was just as described in various books I had read, and the language… no one could speak

French. I recognized Point Venus but certain landmarks were not there, yet Matai said this spot was called Point Venus by the white man, Cook; who else but Captain James Cook?

I continued to struggle to put the pieces together. Captain Cook landed in Matavia Bay in 1769, which would of course make this sometime after his landing, but what year *was* it? I had gone back in time, but *how*? Through what means? What phenomenon? Then something hit me like a bolt of lightening. I realized what had happened to Heinrich. He *didn't* drown, he couldn't see the outriggers approaching because he wasn't caught in the time change, even though he was in the aura with me... or was he? No, wait! He wasn't! He was tossed backwards and over the aura's rim. The crate he was clinging to was gone as well; if he had drowned the crate would have remained afloat. Heinrich Werner didn't die; he was alive... in the twenty-first century! He must think *I* have drowned!

I got to my feet and walked to the lagoon trying to convince myself that this simply wasn't happening. But I was well aware of the truth as the realization of being thrown back more than two hundred years in time hit me both in the form of fear and fantasy.

I pondered my intense déjà vu sensation and the sleep talking incident, and the other things that suggested I had a previous affiliation with this island. It was then that I believed I must have lived a former life here, and now I had come back – as a reincarnated Peter Matthews. Who was I originally? I asked myself, and what life did I live? It couldn't have been at this time, that was not possible; it had to have been earlier, but when?

I continued to walk, collecting smiles and waves from the Indians along the way.

Suddenly I became terrified. I feared I wouldn't be able to cope with the conscious awareness of knowing I was a reincarnate.

Grief overcame me again when I thought of Sarah. But I managed to get a grip on myself and continued to tax my mind, wondering if there was a purpose to all of this. Then I felt that perhaps God had destined these events. I felt momentarily composed when I contemplated such a destiny, but I was still very much afraid of what lay ahead in this world turned upside down.

I walked back in the direction of the village thinking of a possible life of tranquility here. Perhaps I *could* adjust, if only I could be sure I wouldn't encounter any more strange forces behind my past and present lives. I felt more strongly that there was a purpose to my regression after all, that I was put here for a reason. But what *was* that reason?

I eventually came upon a grove of trees. Unable to stave off a need for rest, I lay back contemplating my situation, but with less fear, then I drifted into a deep sleep.

I must have sensed the chief's order to meet with him because the sun was setting when I awoke. I jumped to my feet and started towards the village, but after a few steps I hesitated. I had been sleeping for a long time and now wondered if I might have actually dreamt of Matai and his people. My encounter with them was so strange I thought it just possible I *did* dream it.

Starting for the village again, and hoping to find a paved road, bicycles, and automobiles along the way, my heart beat faster as I quickened my pace.

As I hurried along the crude pathway looking out for the lighthouse and other telling signs, I was surprised by Matai's aides who had come to fetch me. In an instant my state of expectancy turned to hopelessness. I could do no more than walk quietly with the two Indians to their chief's house.

Matai met me when I entered the village and escorted me to his house. I was glad to be with him again as I felt very uncomfortable in the company of his aides.

Matai's house was the largest of many spread throughout the village. It measured about forty feet by twenty-five feet and was thatched like the others with pandanus leaves. The structure's sides were partially open, but low hanging eaves and plaited screens were used to block the openings when additional shelter was needed. A low curbing of stones encircled the house, which bore the modern day purpose of a fence.

People had already gathered to watch their chief walk with me to his house.

"Enter," Matai said, directing me through one of the openings. "Sit, we shall eat soon."

The house was very bare. I observed one or two mats spread out at the far end, some weapons and clothing hanging over a rack, and a crudely made stool. The floor was simply very soft grass, and it was depressingly dark inside even though candlenuts were burning within.

Matai sat cross-legged on a mat then motioned me to sit with him. I pulled the stool towards him and sat uncertainly upon it.

I wanted desperately to wake up from this nightmare but I could do no more than force the realization upon myself that I was here to stay.

So much seemed to go through my mind while waiting for Matai to speak. First I felt quite comfortable, almost pleased with my situation, but the next moment I was panic-stricken at the thought of my exile. I had to struggle to maintain my composure as I had no doubt that the upcoming conversation with Matai would only provide further credence to my suspicions.

Matai had since summoned an aide to bring us each a cup of coconut milk. When the aide handed me a shaped coconut containing the sweet liquid I recognized him as the one who threw me to the ground earlier that afternoon, and again I felt his resentment over my presence.

"Tell me, fair one," Matai said, "where is your land?"

"I'm from England," I answered.

"Ah! You are an Englishman!" he said with excitement. "When will King George come to Tahiti?" he asked in a most sincere tone. His question stunned me but I told him King George was long dead and that a queen now ruled England. The chief was shocked over such news and said that Captain Cook had promised him King George would visit Tahiti. Again I wanted to shake myself out of this illusion, but the longer I talked with Matai the more convinced I became that I had broken the barrier of the fourth dimension.

Matai asked me how long my journey took to come here from England. This was the part I dreaded. How could I explain myself? I drank some coconut milk while debating how best to answer him. As Matai waited for my reply his other aide entered the house and said something to the chief.

"Come," Matai directed, "we shall eat outside."

A large cloth mat had been spread on the veranda and fresh plantain leaves were placed on it to serve as plates.

Distant sounds of the waves crashing against the reef carried towards us while overhead the palm leaves rustled gently in the breeze, and dozens of flickering candlenuts placed in the ground presented a quixotic air throughout the village.

Moments after Matai had motioned me to sit next to him three other men joined us. Two of them were elderly and distinguished like the chief, and the third was a young man in his twenties who was clean-shaven, and who wore his long dark hair tied on top of his head, which I later learned was a mark of the upper class.

A servant brought each of us a cup of water to wash our hands and rinse our mouths before another attendant arrived with the succulent pig and set it temptingly in front of us. Then came baked fish and vegetables carried by a third server.

Matai broke the silence while he carved the pig.

"These men, fair one, are my brothers." He pointed to the two elderly men and said their names, which I forgot as quickly as he spoke them, but the young one I remembered. "This is my grandson, Tetamoa." I looked at them and nodded. "And what are you called?" Matai inquired.

"My name is Peter."

"Pe-ter… Pe-ter…" Matai said to himself as though trying to decide whether or not he liked it. The chief then instructed us to eat. "At tama a," he grunted as he filled his mouth with a handful of food.

I asked Matai between bites how he came to speak English so well.

"I spent many moons with the Englishman, Wallis," he answered. "I sailed on his boat and showed him many lands." Samuel Wallis, I reminded myself, had discovered Tahiti.

"How *many* moons ago?" I asked, trying to identify the year in which I was now living.

"One hundred, fifty, and more," the chief answered. "But enough of my talk," he said, "tell me with whom you come to Tahiti and on what boat you come." I had decided to tell Matai the truth, hoping the old man would believe me, but it was a foolish decision because when I told him that I had flown from England he roared with laughter.

"You have been lost in the water too long, fair one!" he exclaimed still laughing, then he translated my story to his brothers and grandson who found it equally hilarious. "Show us how you fly like a bird," he said with laughter still in his eyes.

"Let me explain," I implored. "Where I come from men fly… in a machine…" I couldn't go on, it was impossible to explain, they couldn't even fathom what a machine was. Matai then turned serious and cautioned me not to tell him anymore absurd tales. I had to think quickly, should I change my story or tell him everything that happened in detail?

I decided to remain with the truth, trusting that consequences would be less severe opposed to altering my story.

I told Matai how I flew to Tahiti with Sarah and how the Hirondelle sunk in a squall, leaving me to be rescued by his fishermen. I also explained how I crossed over from the future at the time I saw the fishermen's outriggers, and I even went as far as to explain the disappearance of specific landmarks once I had traveled backwards to his time. Matai's brothers and grandson listened intently even though they couldn't understand a word I was saying.

By the time I finished my story the servants had cleared the food scraps away and refilled our cups with water for us to again wash our hands and rinse our mouths.

I was left with the impression that Matai wanted to believe me but simply found the tale too inconceivable. How could I expect otherwise when flying and machines were not to occur for more than a hundred years.

The four men stared at me and I wondered if I might be forced to leave Mahina, or worse yet be put to death as some sort of demented intruder.

"Again you insult me with these foolish tales!"

"I'm telling you the truth; I come from the future, where this life has already happened… and where my life is different…"

After a pause and looking utterly perplexed the chief said, "You are indeed a curious one. You may remain here tonight, I shall decide if you are welcome to stay in Mahina when the sun returns." Matai briefed his brothers and grandson then turned back to me and said, "Go now with Tetamoa, you will sleep in his house tonight."

I sensed a warm, friendly feeling from Tetamoa. Every so often while we walked he would give me a broad smile as if to assure me that everything was going to be alright.

Tetamoa was a tall, well-built fellow who carried himself with the royalty that was in his blood, and he wore a variety of tattoos over his bronze body, which accentuated his position in Tahitian society.

We left the main part of the village and trekked up a hill to a clearing.

I was taken by the beauty of the village when I looked down. The swaying palms and burning candlenuts, and the reef which separated the lagoon from the mighty ocean, were imposing sights.

"E haere mai 'outou!" Tetamoa called while I stood peering down at the village. I followed behind until we came upon a group of houses. Flashing another smile Tetamoa led me towards his house, which was a little smaller than his grandfather's, and like Matai's, had an opening on either side with cloth screens hanging down to cover the entranceways.

Tetamoa's wife met us when we approached. She was an elegant young woman of five feet three or four with short black hair and soft, dark eyes. Tetamoa pointed to her and said, "Heifara, vahine ha'aipoipo."

The inside of their house was no different than Matai's with large cloth mats spread over the grass to serve as a more appropriate means of carpeting; all that was missing was the stool.

Tetamoa led me to a corner of the house where he spread another mat for me to sleep on. I had no pillow but was given a blanket to cover myself.

"Te ta 'oto," he said, pointing to my bed, then he left.

I stood over my bed for a moment wondering what day it was and what time it could be, but I laughed inwardly realizing ironically that the calendar and clock would no longer have meaning to me.

I went outside with a multitude of thoughts swimming through my mind. I desperately hoped Matai would let me stay in Mahina as I would be certain to find hard times if I had to search for a new stronghold.

While sitting forlornly on the grass I felt a gentle hand on my shoulder. It was Tetamoa offering me some coconut milk. He smiled compassionately when I took it from him, then he retired for the night with Heifara. I shortly followed to my own bed as my eyes had become heavy and the air was beginning to chill my unaccustomed body.

Tears filled my eyes as I lay in this strange, dreary house. I had never felt so lost and alone in my life.

The sun had not long risen when I went outside to find Heifara and another woman in conversation. Heifara immediately fetched some fresh fruit for my breakfast when she saw me appear.

Rather than sit amongst the villagers' stares I took the fruit to where I had slept the previous afternoon. While I sat under a palm tree eating the fruit I contemplated what year it could be. If Matai said he sailed with Wallis more than one hundred and fifty moons ago, and remembering that Wallis discovered Tahiti in 1767, I estimated it was now about 1780.

When I finished my breakfast I lay back with my hands clasped behind my head wondering what Matai would decide; then, out of nowhere and with all the savagery of a wild beast, I was attacked by one of Matai's aides. Although I was taken by surprise I was able to dodge his knife and roll to my feet. As he prepared to lunge again I landed a powerful kick to his windpipe which caused him to let out a gasp and collapse at my feet. At that moment Matai's other aide burst upon me and thrust his knife deep into my breast. The pain was excruciating as I fell to my knees, and as I reeled in either direction, I watched him stare down at me. I was expecting the fatal thrust when Tetamoa leapt upon the assailant and disabled him. I was then carried to Tetamoa's house where I lay critically ill.

Besides Tetamoa I owed my life to Heifara and her young cousin, Tiare, for nursing me back to health.

When I regained consciousness I found Tiare leaning over me dabbing away the fever from my forehead. Despite making even the slightest movement I felt as though my chest would burst open.

" 'Aita, 'aita, ta 'oto," Tiare said softly as she held her hands on my shoulders to keep me still.

Tetamoa was elated when he returned to find me conscious. He talked excitedly to me although he knew I could not understand him, but I caught Matai's name once or twice, which made me believe that the chief was coming to see me.

I was able to move a little as my first day of consciousness wore on, but I was still very weak and in intense pain.

I had no sooner labored through the broth that Tiare had fed me when Matai came puffing into the house escorted by his grandson. In an instant Tiare and Heifara left the house knowing their chief's visit called for privacy.

Matai sat cross-legged next to me and said in a tone of affection, "You are fortunate to be alive, Manu, you have been on the edge of death."

"Your guards attacked me," I responded with great effort.

"I know, Tetamoa told me what happened. He was coming to fetch you when he saw your struggle. Kona is under guard; he breathes only that you may avenge his cowardly act." I looked at Tetamoa, not understanding what his grandfather meant. Seeing I did not comprehend, Tetamoa said something to Matai, after which the chief turned back to me and said pointedly, "You will take Kona's life."

I was stunned that I should be the man's executioner, but no matter how much I protested the old chief would have nothing of it.

"You will kill him when you are strong. When you have done this you may remain in Mahina."

Afraid of having to kill another human being I asked Matai if his aide's live could be spared.

" 'Aita! Kona is not worthy of life! Not only for his attack on you, but for disobeying my order that you be unharmed." Then on a lighter note, if that was possible, Matai told me I had at least saved myself the work of having to carry out two executions. When I asked him what he meant I was shocked to learn that I had killed my first assailant outright with the kick to his throat.

"Rest now, Manu, you must be strong," Matai said as he pulled himself up with the aid of Tetamoa's arm.

I was frightened by the thought of having to kill, but if I refused I knew with certainty I would be forced to leave Mahina and lose the friendship of Tetamoa, his wife and cousin, and the partiality which Matai seemed to hold for me. Though it was barbaric, I knew I had to carry out Matai's order, and as long as Kona had to die it was better it be by my hand as my welfare rested upon acceptance by the people of Mahina.

Tiare re-entered the house and immediately made sure I was comfortable. While she adjusted my blanket I wondered by what means Kona was to die. Would it be with a spear? A knife? Or an arrow shot from a bow?

"Ta'oto, Manu," my nurse whispered as she walked quietly away.

I noticed that Matai had called me *Manu* several times, and now Tiare addressed me by the same name. I learned later that it meant *Bird*, and that Matai had named me Manu because of my story of flying to Tahiti.

A full moon had come and gone before I could move about with ease.

Tiare had been spending most of her time with me while I was convalescing, and during this period it became evident that she was attracted to me.

It was on one of the many lazy afternoons I spent with Tiare that I began to take notice of her. She was a beautiful girl, probably not yet twenty years old. She stood a head taller than most of the other women and wore her soft black hair long over her shoulders. As we sat alone by the lagoon Tiare could only smile as I looked into her dark, almond eyes, for it would be many months before I would learn her language. I looked at the nipples on her young breasts, which were slightly visible through her mantle, then my eyes shifted to her long shapely legs. I said her name, questioning what it meant. I said my name and pointed to a bird flying above, then pointed to myself; I said her name again and pointed to her. Tiare smiled knowingly; she got to her feet and walked a short distance only to return a moment later holding a flower. She kissed me tenderly on the cheek after giving me her namesake.

Tiare's head was resting on my shoulder when Tetamoa came running up to us.

"Manu! Manu! Vitiviti!" he called bursting with excitement. He then took my arm and ushered me into the village while Tiare followed close behind, also puzzled over the urgency.

I was startled to look upon several hundred people waiting quietly and in an orderly fashion when we entered the village. Their eyes remained fixed on us when about fifty yards from Matai's house Tetamoa put his hand on my shoulder telling me to wait. I took hold of Tiare's hand and squeezed it nervously. A few moments later Matai appeared from his house and approached me carrying a staff to aid his feeble legs. His snow-white mantle stirred slightly in the breeze when he stopped in front of me.

"It is time for Kona to die," he said. I was taken completely off guard having forgotten all about his impending execution.

While still gripping Tiare's hand two powerfully built Indians appeared with the condemned man. Kona's hands were bound behind him and his head was forcibly bowed in shame as he walked towards Matai.

Tetamoa pulled Tiare's hand from mine and stepped back with her into the crowd.

Kona's guards stopped short of Matai and pushed the prisoner to his knees. It was at this moment that I became sickened at the contemplation of having to kill him. Even with Kona's cowardly act I could not understand why I felt bad about him having to die as he so nearly succeeded in taking my life. I concluded that in these times the chief's word had to be obeyed, therefore, Kona deserved to die, only why did *I* have to kill him? I asked myself.

A nervous perspiration took over my body. I wondered again how the prisoner was to die when one of the guards held out a long, heavy club.

"You will strike the blow to his head," Matai said. I was stunned. It did not occur to me that the weapon might be a club.

I prayed I would be able to stand up to this ordeal as Kona was dragged closer to me.

The petrified man was still moaning when one of the guards rudely held his face to the ground with his foot. Then Matai, with a raise of his staff, signaled the guard to step back. Kona looked up at me with dark, pleading eyes.

"Let him live!" I appealed to Matai.

"Manu! You will strike the blow or die *with* him!" the chief angrily responded. My situation was clear; with no further hesitation I stepped close to Kona.

The doomed Indian was on his knees with his face in the ground. The silence was gripping as I raised the club high above me then crashed it down on the man's head with all the power I could muster. There was a dull resonating thud and the most sickening squelch. Blood and brains spurted all over me as Kona's body shook itself for the last time.

I staggered away, letting the club fall from my hands and leaving the crowd to murmur amongst themselves. The sight of bits of Kona's flesh on my legs and kilt made me vomit in my tracks.

I made my way to the lagoon after recovering and lost no time cleaning myself.

A cold sweat clung to my forehead when I trudged out of the water. All I could see as I fell weakly to the ground was Kona's eyes begging for mercy and the vile aftermath of the club's impact.

I returned to the village after regaining my composure, but I was to spend many a sleepless night recounting this gruesome experience.

As I passed Matai's house the chief spotted me from his veranda and called me to him.

"Manu, you did your duty well, do not be troubled." I was tempted to ask him if he *would* have had me killed had I refused his order to execute Kona, but I decided the matter best be left alone. "I shall never understand you or the ways of your land, but you are welcome to live among my people. Tetamoa will be pleased for you to stay in his house."

I was comfortable enough with Tetamoa and Heifara but I preferred more privacy for all of us, so with this in mind and knowing that I could not return to my own time, I asked Matai if Tetamoa would help me build a house of my own.

"Excellent, Manu," the old chief said, quite pleased with the idea, "of course he will help you, I shall speak with him today."

Jack Matthews took a deep breath and peered at the ceiling from his armchair. He had been completely engrossed in Peter's manuscript but now took a long pause to reflect on what he had read.

As absorbed as he was with the document, and as anxious as he was to read on, Jack's only conclusion could be that it was a fabricated account. It was impossible; how could his son – anybody – go back in time? And how could anyone live more than one life?

As much as Jack wanted to believe this supposed record of his son's life, he knew in his highly logical mind that Peter had invented it. He suspected that Peter had actually survived the sinking of the Hirondelle – he must have if he was to have written the manuscript – but rather than come home to what he felt was an unacceptable, even an intolerable life, he opted to remain in Tahiti where he conjured through the means of a distressed yet imaginative mind, the story contained in the document.

Jack was left with a deepening feeling of emptiness when he contemplated his assessment. He covered his face with his hands in a tired and tormented way, then ran them slowly through his hair; yet no matter how much he tried he could not dismiss Peter's account of déjà vu, the sleep talking incident, and his other perceptible ties with the islands as simply coincidences. He then envisioned Peter being transported two centuries into the past by a mysterious aura. He found this impossible to believe, yet when he re-examined the weathered and deteriorated condition of the manuscript and realized how aged the pages appeared, he felt he could not discard even the remotest possibility of their origin; even time travel.

The name *Werner* came to mind. Jack became excited when he remembered Peter's references to the German psychiatrist. He felt if he could only talk to Dr. Werner and let him read the manuscript he might somehow be able to shed some light on a very complicated issue, and possibly even unravel some shattering truths that would seem to come right out of the world of H. G. Wells.

Jack was connected to Directory Assistance in Vancouver. The operator then gave him the telephone number of Dr. Heinrich Werner's residence.

When Werner answered the phone Jack introduced himself and began testing the doctor's memory with a battery of questions regarding the squall and Peter's sudden disappearance. A receptive Werner found he had to calm Jack down, and when he better understood the impassioned attorney's questions, Werner agreed to read a copy of the manuscript.

Heinrich Werner confirmed the existence of the aura just prior to Peter's disappearance, and he also mentioned to Jack how surprised he was when Peter so unexpectedly drowned just moments after he had shouted that canoes were approaching, which Werner admitted he could not see.

Jack then told Werner he would make a copy of the manuscript and expedite it to him, putting them both in a better position to discuss the subject of Peter's strange disappearance.

Feeling in some measure relieved after his conversation with Dr. Werner, Jack returned to the manuscript and continued to read of his son's new life in eighteenth century Tahiti.

CHAPTER 4

Matai kept his word and spoke to Tetamoa about the construction of my house.

The chief's grandson had recruited several villagers and it took just three days before trees were felled, shaped, and put into place to form the main supporting structures. My new home would measure about thirty feet by twenty and it was situated fifty yards from Tetamoa and Heifara's house.

The principle timbers used in the construction were cut from the coconut and rosewood trees. Tetamoa's workers planted ten-inch square side posts four feet apart and three feet deep. A groove was cut into each post that measured six inches deep and two inches wide, and a strong, thick board was secured to the grooved posts to form the walls. The rafters, measuring four inches in diameter, were next to go on. As soon as they were cut from the hibiscus, the bark was stripped off and used to make cordage, which was further required to lash the wood together. Before the rafters were placed they were left in water for two days to extract the juices – a necessary process as the juices attracted insects, which quickly destroyed the wood.

No matter how busy I remained working on the house I still suffered terribly from numbing bouts of depression. I would awaken each morning expecting to find the life I missed so much, and adding to the difficulty of my adjustment was the frustration of not being able to converse with anyone but Matai, although having Tiare frequently at my side was of great comfort. Very often when my mood changed for the worse I would just sit and stare or walk for hours on end. Poor Tiare couldn't understand my behavior at all, but she nevertheless manifested a great deal of compassion when I needed her with me, and would leave me to myself when she sensed I wanted to be alone.

While the house was in its framework Tetamoa and I decided to spend a day hunting. I hoped the adventure would at least for the time being lift me out of my depression.

We equipped ourselves with spears and bows and arrows and set off on our hunt shortly after sunrise.

The spear we each carried was seven feet long and two inches in diameter at its thickest point. Barbs of fishbone were affixed at the head of the spear, which served to tear the flesh when entering the prey, and the weapon's handle was covered with resinous gum from the breadfruit tree to give the hunter a controlled grip for throwing.

It was late morning and there was still no sign of game. Eventually we climbed to a ridge, which was one of the highest points of the island. I was perspiring and panting when we reached the top and my legs ached miserably from the climb.

We rested on the overhanging ridge and watched the surf crash against the reef as birds coming and going from their fishing excursions circled the slopes.

As usual Tetamoa and I could only exchange smiles as my Tahitian vocabulary was still extremely limited.

After hacking off the tops of two coconuts and taking a drink, Tetamoa disappeared into the foliage. I was very hungry by this time and thought how good some roast pork would taste when my friend returned carrying a long bamboo pole. I watched him carefully secure the pole into the ground, all the time smiling as he observed my curiosity. Next he walked over to a breadfruit tree and extracted the gum that was used to resin the handle of the spears and applied it to the top of the pole. He then ushered me away from the pole where we both sat very still and watched. I had no idea what he was doing, but soon noticed more and more birds circling us and guessed that the pole was a means of catching one.

In time a plump sea bird landed on it. It was immediately trapped by the gum and frantically tried to fly off, but the sticky substance held the bird's feet and the pole would not move from the ground. Tetamoa let out a shout and raced over to his catch, then with a quick jerk broke the bird's neck and pulled it from the pole. I later learned that when the Indians went on egg gathering expeditions in the high grounds they used this method to catch birds for food, although other than fowl, birds were not a common sustenance among the natives; birds were hunted primarily for their feathers.

Tetamoa had collected some twigs and set up a small spit on which to cook the bird. A few energetic rubs with a pair of dried sticks got a fire started, and before long we were watching the gull brown over the flame.

Shortly after eating we left the ridge with Tetamoa leading the way back down. Just as we reached the flat ground Tetamoa abruptly stopped.

"Tia'I!" he warned, having heard some rustling in the brush. We readied our spears and waited; then, sensing danger, a young boar came running out of the brush. I chased it in a circling route then raised my spear and threw it as hard as I could. Its flight was true, entering deep into the beast's shoulders. This time it was my turn to shout in triumph as the barbs ripped the animal's flesh with its every frantic move. I ended its life with several thrusts of my knife, which I had pulled from my sharkskin belt. Tetamoa congratulated me on my kill as we secured the animal by its feet to a strong timber and carried it with a great deal of labor back to the village.

Tetamoa again stopped suddenly soon after we set off with our prize. He had spotted a piglet. With amazing speed he dropped his end of the pole and fitted an arrow to his bow, drew back and released, grazing the animal's back. The pig was more frightened than injured when it stumbled to the ground squealing in terror, but it got to its feet quickly and began to run in confused circles. I had already fitted an arrow to my bow, aimed and released while Tetamoa was aiming his next shot. My weapon again found its mark; the young pig fell dead as the arrow sped through its neck. Tetamoa was amazed at my skill as I had certainly outdone him this day. Again he sportingly congratulated me, but we could not add to our already heavy load so we were forced to leave the piglet behind for the scavengers.

We labored with our kill for a long time and I was sweating and panting, but Tetamoa was not troubled being in far superior condition.

As we walked homeward with the sun sinking deeper into the sky I contemplated how well I handled my weapons. I had never before touched a spear or bow, yet I knew exactly how to use them, it was as though their use was second nature to me. It began to occur to me that my previous life must have ingrained in me the skills of a hunter, as I felt so natural on the hunt. I knew precisely what to do, yet I had never hunted before.

The sun had already set when we entered Mahina. I was both hungry and exhausted and didn't know what to do first, eat or sleep. I chose to take a refreshing bath in the stream, and when I returned Heifara had set out some food.

After Tetamoa and I had eaten, Heifara and Tiare joined us. I was able to pick up bits of their conversation while we sat in the evening's gentle breeze; they wanted to roast the boar the following evening and have Matai and his brothers dine with us.

"Maita'I! Tunu 'ananahi ia' po tatou," I fumbled when I grasped what they were saying, and they in response laughed and clapped their hands appreciating my ever increasing knowledge of their language.

The following sunset saw Matai and his two brothers dine with us as planned. The evening had become cool and overcast so the meal was held in Tetamoa's dining room, which was actually a thatched hut about twenty-five yards from his house. Heifara and Tiare did not eat with us because Tahitian formality prohibited women from dining with the men. As much as I disliked this custom I had no choice but to adapt to it.

The flickering shadows cast by the candlenuts still presented something of a doleful atmosphere, but it was simply a matter of time before such little things would cease to disturb me. The sides of the dining hut had no walls but were closed off by hanging bark cloth while a large mat covered the sandy floor, and the usual plantain leaves served as place mats.

"Tetamoa tells me you hunt with great skill, Manu, and that we can thank you for our food tonight," Matai said. I smiled at his compliment but suggested it was more luck than skill, to which he laughed and disagreed.

The aroma of roasting pork reached us from the cookhouse, and as I savored it I recalled that the last time I ate with these men I was afraid for my life; and now, just a few weeks later, I was a respected member of their village.

Matai was always patient enough to act as interpreter for me although he and his brothers were quite impressed at the amount of Tahitian I had learned. Each time I stumbled through a few words of their language they laughed and nodded with approval.

My attention turned inquisitively to one of Matai's brothers who talked with Tetamoa for some time while occasionally throwing a glance at me. Tetamoa then turned to his grandfather and spoke to the chief while nodding towards me. I was obviously the topic of discussion so I listened carefully, trying to pick up pieces of what they were saying. Matai then turned to me and said, "Manu, we have decided that your body should be marked like ours."

"You mean tattooed?" I flinched after realizing what the chief was saying.

"Yes, that is how you call it, you will have tattoos." I flatly refused, afraid that the primitive method of application would cause an infection; but after some urging I reluctantly consented as I did not want to take the risk of offending the elders.

"Alright, but something small… just on my arm," I said like a frightened schoolboy, not wanting to have myself marked from head to foot like Matai and his brothers.

The workers arrived to begin thatching the roof of my house when I finished my morning swim. These craftsmen had gathered pandanus leaves a few days earlier and left them to soak in a stream, and now they had selected the best leaves for the thatch. I watched them stretch each leaf on a stick, which they fixed in the ground. I was intrigued by the way they performed the thatching and wanted to learn their skill, but before I could try my hand Tetamoa had come for me. The young warrior wanted me to go with him so he led me down the hill and along the soft winding beach to an isolated house at the far end of the village.

We entered the structure and found an old withered man with a long straggly-thin beard waiting for us. It was then Tetamoa conveyed that the old man was going to tattoo me.

"Oh no!" I protested, making a move to leave; but Tetamoa, highly amused at my reluctance, took me firmly by the shoulders and sat me down at the tattoo master's feet. I wasn't angry at Tetamoa because I could see that behind his forcefulness was a great deal of fondness for me. When I motioned to get up, Tetamoa, with mischief in his eyes, pointed a finger at me and said something with the connotation that I would pay dearly if I attempted to withdraw; so there I sat, afraid, but smiling while Tetamoa stood with folded arms blocking my retreat.

The tattooist sat cross-legged opposite me with his materials at his side. The tool which applied the tattoo was a bone blade cut into sharp teeth and it was attached to a long wooden handle. At the tattooist's side was a cup of black liquid, which was derived from the ash of candlenuts. The artist ran his hand over my chest before picking up the blade and dipping it into the murky liquid. I sprung backwards and raised my hands protectively, remembering that I said nothing about having a tattoo applied to my chest, but before I could protest further the old man had the blade resting against my skin and had hit the blade handle with a weighted, hammer-like implement. I flinched and let out a yelp as a small amount of blood appeared. The old man struck another blow and again I groaned at the blade's penetration. For every stroke he would carefully dab the drops of blood and inky liquid from my chest before again dipping the blade into the cup. I knew I was in for a long, arduous time as the artist patiently went about his work. I grimaced at every bloodletting stroke and again became concerned over the possibility of infection setting into my unadapted twenty-first century body.

At last, long after Tetamoa had left me alone with the tattooist, and after hours of pain, the old man had finished. The result was my namesake – a bird – in full flight. I struggled to my feet and moaned over the soreness of my chest, but was able to thank the tattoo master for his artistry.

"Maururu, 'O Purotu," I managed. The old man laughed and nodded his head, then patted me on the shoulder as I left. I was painfully sore and ever regretted consenting to such treatment, but when I looked again at that noble marking on my body, I walked proudly, showing it off.

My house was finally completed after three more days of work, and I was infinitely grateful to the men who built it.

The durability of any house depended upon the thatching. If there was too much space between the reeds it would quickly decay, so the reeds had to be placed close together to ensure the house would last a good five years without letting in rain.

Heifara gave me cloth and mats for my bedding and floor covering. I spread as much matting as I could over the floor as there was always an abundance of insects in every house.

The item I really lacked was a chair, so I set about making one. I even went a step further and made myself a rocking chair, which Matai liked so much he insisted I make one for him. I can recall with affection the times I passed by his house and saw the aging chief rocking contentedly on his veranda.

Tiare and I often spent the evenings with Tetamoa and Heifara, and it was one such evening that will always remain special. Tiare was living with her parents when I went to call for her, and as usual I was warmly received by her mother and father. Her father was one of the fishermen who rescued me the day the Hirondelle sunk, and Tiare's mother was a beautiful woman, just as tall and elegant as her daughter.

I was again taken by Tiare's beauty when she appeared. She looked like a princess with her snow white mantle folded immaculately around her, and her hair flowing innocently over her shoulders. Tiare's dark brown complexion and Asian-like features fashioned her exquisite beauty. She kissed her parents on the cheeks before leaving with me for another lazy evening.

Tiare and Heifara spent their time chatting while Tetamoa and I enjoyed a swim. There were many streams about Mahina, all made more beautiful by the tall trees and grassy banks.

We rejoined Tiare and Heifara after our swim and the four of us whiled away the rest of the evening together. I sensed something was in the air when the two women coyly looked at me and giggled.

With a long yawn and a stretch of his powerful limbs Tetamoa said he was ready for sleep. He said goodnight with a wink and *Orua ta'o 'oto*, which meant that it was time Tiare and I were sleeping with each other. Heifara then kissed us both on the cheek before retiring with her husband.

As Tetamoa snuffed out the candlenuts Tiare took my hand and led me towards the lagoon. There was an element of modesty about her when she glanced sidelong at me.

We reached a spot by the lagoon and sat under what had become my favorite tree. Hand in hand we gazed into the moonlit water. I leaned towards her and while caressing her flowing hair, kissed her tenderly on the lips. She sunk into my arms returning my embrace, and then she lay back. I sat beside her and removed her mantle, then her skirt. The sweet fragrance of her perfume was inviting as I held my hand on her breasts, feeling her nipples harden at my touch. Then I felt her ecstasy. As I gently stroked Tiare's hair from her eyes I told her in Tahitian that I loved her.

CHAPTER 5

Several months passed since my first intimate evening with Tiare, and since then she had moved into my house. We loved each other deeply, and to the joy of Tiare's parents, and Matai – who had assumed the role of my adopted father – we made arrangements to be married.

I was now speaking fluent Tahitian, and if it weren't for my fair hair and blue eyes I would have passed for a full-blooded Indian.

My depressive moods had passed and I seldom thought of Sarah and my life in England, and when I did, they were just passing thoughts.

I was very happy in my new world and had adjusted to all forms of life as I knew them; I was no longer afraid of believing that I had once journeyed to a previous life as a Tahitian warrior. Nor did I experience more sensations related to my soul's past; but I did feel that one day something of dynamic proportion was going to happen in which I would play a prominent part, and this, I believed, would reveal the reason for my venture back to this time.

I had managed to explore all of Tahiti during the one year I'd been here, and at no time had the island seen any visitors. I wondered how soon it would be until a foreign vessel dropped anchor, as history was no doubt about to play out all over again.

While strolling alone one afternoon my attention was drawn to some excitement on the beach. I walked closer to the activity, watching the crowd grow. When I rounded a bend and was able to look into the open sea I observed a dozen boats approaching the lagoon. By now several hundred people had assembled on the beach, and I saw Matai and Tetamoa make their way to the front through an aisle politely formed by their subjects. I was fast to join them, running down a lush knoll and finding the same respect from the crowd as they moved aside to let me through.

The first boat breached followed by a stately double-hulled canoe of some seventy-five feet in length. This large vessel, with its upturned bow and stern, had a sail fitted in each of its hulls and bore a canopy to shelter its passengers.

Several Indians had already jumped from the first two boats while the other vessels were still finding their way into the lagoon.

A majestic figure of a man soon stepped carefully from the double-hulled vessel. He was regally attired, wearing a pure white mantle and a long feathered cape. He also wore numerous shell necklaces and a large headdress.

"You have grown old, Matai," the dignitary said when he grasped our chief's arm.

"And you have grown fat!" Matai comically returned,

adding, "it has been a long time, Moana; too long to have kept such accord between us at a distance."

Meanwhile, the other boats had breached and the travelers were unloading their supplies and gifts to carry into the village.

I asked Tetamoa who these people were.

"Moana is an old friend of my grandfather's," he explained. "He is the chief of Tetiaroa. His people and my grandfather's people united many moons before my birth and fought invaders from Rarotonga. I expect he comes to show his goodwill."

I learned that such hospitality exchanges were quite common amongst neighboring islands, with feasts and games being held during these visits.

While the visitors from Tetiaroa settled into the village guesthouse, which was capable of sleeping more than a hundred people, Moana moved his belongings into Matai's house.

A warrior in his early twenties had since joined Matai and Moana.

"You remember my son, Kuana," the Tetiaroan chief said proudly. "He is no longer the boy you once knew." Matai took Kuana's arm and welcomed him to his house. Like Tetamoa and now me, Kuana wore his long hair tied on top of his head in the upper class fashion.

The evening saw Matai host a fine feast to welcome Moana. We seated ourselves around a large dining cloth, which had been graced with suckling pig, fish, and fowl. Several other place mats had also been set, which provided mounds of food for the higher-ranking members of Moana's party and the prominent men of Mahina. Scurrying amidst the flickering candlenuts were male servants fetching more food and drink and doing their best to assure their superiors' satisfaction.

During the feasting Tetamoa remarked that Kuana appeared troubled or withdrawn, and I, too, saw he carried something of a grim demeanor about him.

When the feasting was over the nightly ritual of singing and dancing began. Village drummers struck up their instruments and a group of young girls began to perform a very wanton dance. The Timorodee consisted of extremely suggestive body movements and it was rendered by girls who had not yet formed a relationship.

I suddenly recalled my recognition of the Timorodee in my other world with Sarah and the Werners at the hotel. It was indeed the same fertility dance, only this time I was seeing it performed in its true form. Amid the drumbeats and occasional sounds from a flute, the girls would open their skirts and make the most sexually enticing movements.

After the Timorodee some of the younger girls stripped off their skirts and covered themselves with just a loose piece of cloth, and at certain periods of their dance they threw open the cloth and danced naked. This act of nakedness was custom, not lewdness, however, as the girls who danced in public were generally quite shy by nature.

The longer the evening went on the drunker many of the men became, and as drunk as any was Kuana.

The means of intoxicating oneself was by drinking kava, a derivative made from the root of the pepper shrub. It took me some time before I became accustomed to kava as this beverage was made by chewing the roots of the shrub, then spitting into a wooden bowl. The servants, who performed this task, added coconut milk and crushed leaves of the pepper plant before mixing the contents and removing the root fibers and leaves with a strainer. Most everyone on the island drank kava, but overindulging resulted in befuddlement and eventually passing out.

Perhaps it was the effects of the kava but Kuana was so taken by Tiare that he kept forcing his affections on her, even though he knew she and I were to be married. I paid only slight attention to Kuana's behavior, realizing that his drunkenness could be well handled by Tiare; also, I knew if I forcibly removed him from our company trouble with Moana would likely ensue. In any event, I had no doubt that it was just a matter of time until he would pass out.

Tiare simply laughed at his advances and pushed him aside only to have him come back and try again.

"Manu, why do you allow this?" an angry Tetamoa asked.

"He doesn't mean any harm," I said, "besides, if I step in you know there'll be trouble with Moana. You'll see, he won't remember a thing tomorrow."

Soon enough Kuana passed out, but not before shouting obscenities and becoming violent. Tetamoa and I wrestled him to the ground but this powerful young man broke free and swung a blow to Tetamoa's face before slumping to the earth. My friend wiped the blood from his broken lip while I dragged Kuana to a tree where he would spend the night. Meanwhile, Tiare and Heifara laughed heartily as the hapless Tetamoa bemoaned his plight and swore revenge.

"Leave it alone, I'm sure he'll be quite agreeable tomorrow," I taunted.

The evening drew to a close with men and women falling asleep in the open, many of them through the effects of the kava. One or two candlenuts made a final attempt to stay alight as Tiare and I strolled back to our house amidst some isolated giggles from the couples lying together in the grass.

After breakfast I left with Tetamoa for the boathouses where men from Mahina and Tetiaroa were waiting to set out on the fishing excursion that had been arranged the previous day. There were probably a hundred men milling about, with many of them nursing sore heads from the festivities of the night before.

Kuana showed no ill effects from the kava when he appeared. After greeting us he looked at Tetamoa's swollen lip and asked him how he came by it. While I found it amusing, Tetamoa moved angrily towards him.

"Come on, Tetamoa," I said, stepping between them. "You know he didn't mean any harm."

"You mean *I* did this? Kuana asked in all innocence. "I remember little of last night, except for the beautiful Tiare."

Canoes outfitted with sails were waiting in the lagoon while a larger double-hulled vessel was being made ready for Matai and Moana, who had no intentions of missing the sport regardless of their years. With five men to each canoe Tetamoa and I found ourselves sharing one with Kuana and two other men from Tetiaroa.

It was exceedingly hot and having little breeze behind us it took some hard rowing to travel those few miles beyond the reef in our search for albacore.

In time we stowed our oars and drifted in the calm waters. There was a flock of seabirds just ahead of the lead canoe – a sign that we were near a shoal. We sensed a catch was at hand as we bobbed closer to the birds. Then the man in the lead canoe shouted, "Va ta'I te manu!" – *The birds are crying!* was his signal. Hearing this we threw bits of crayfish into the water as bait. Then the albacore appeared. "A tu'u!" the man ordered. At this command we threw baited hooks overboard.

Moments later our line straightened with a snap and ran through Kuana's unready hands. An albacore of what must have been some two hundred pounds showed itself, twisting frantically to get away. It took two of us to contain it and bring it alongside the canoe where it continued to struggle before ultimately succumbing to the strength behind our hook and line.

Members of the other canoes were hauling in their own catches with many of them matching the weight of our prize.

Once again our line straightened, but this time the albacore escaped; however, it swam away with such force that the sudden tightening of the line, which stopped the fish in full flight, caused its jaws to be ripped away.

"Kuana! You let him get away!" Nihauiti, one of Kuana's fellow islanders barked, showing his anger at the chief's son.

"Not with his jaws on our line!" Tetamoa laughed. "He's probably already dead; come on, row after him!"

We took up oars and quickly came upon this two-hundred pounder, who was now turning on its side, remarkably still alive.

"Come, help me lift him," Nihauiti said. Tetamoa and I and the other Tetiaroan helped Nihauiti pull the albacore to the side of the canoe, preparing to raise the fish into the boat, but Kuana just sat still, pouting. "Kuana, help us; it'll take all of us to lift this monster up," the keen Nihauiti directed.

"How *dare* you talk to your chief's son like this!" an angry Kuana rebuked. "Do you not know who I am?"

"You are one of *us*, now stop your sulking and help us!" came the young Nihauiti's response.

"Come on, Kuana, we need your help, this fellow's going

to sink," I coaxed, as the albacore, finally dead, was about to go to the bottom.

Reluctantly Kuana moved to the side of the boat to help us, causing the vessel to uncomfortably tilt, but with our full effort we lifted the jawless creature onto the boat, in time to see our canoe adjust itself to its former safe and full upright position.

We rowed back to shore with prize catches, as did many of the others, who shouted their success from their following canoes.

The albacore would be placed in the storehouses once the canoes breached, where they were to be kept as cold as possible until the upcoming feasts.

Rested and refreshed from the day's fishing, I joined Tiare, Tetamoa, and Heifara for the evening's festivities, which were once more complemented with large amounts of kava, and as expected many heads were again spinning before the night was over.

Wrestling matches had been arranged between the men of the two islands that evening, and the intensity between the spectators was so strong when the contests got under way that separate fights periodically broke out amongst them.

Moana's men had become so incensed during one particular bout when their wrestler had his arm broken by his opponent forcing it backwards at the elbow, that upon the loud crack at the break and the chilling scream of the combatant, they instantly began hurling stones at Matai's champion. This in turn led the men of Mahina into retaliation and in a matter of seconds fierce fighting had erupted. Tetamoa was quick to join in the melee while I watched from a distance, wanting no part of the affair, but my involvement quickly became necessary when I saw Tetamoa struck from behind by a Tetiaroan packing a broad staff. I disabled his assailant and dragged my unconscious friend away from the fracas. By this time Matai and Moana had called a halt to the fighting, each realizing that neither side would come out the winner. Men were strewn on the ground groaning while others limped about nursing their wounds, and there were some who were worse off with gashed heads and even crushed skulls.

Matai and Moana had taken a sadistic pleasure in watching this battle, but once they decided it had gone on long enough they had the severely injured removed and ordered the wrestling contests to continue.

Tetamoa regained consciousness after a few minutes and labored to his feet.

"What happened?" he asked.

"What do you *think* happened? You got just what you deserved – one of our guests struck you with his staff. I let him knock some sense into you before convincing him to stop," I chided. Tetamoa didn't say anything, he just groaned, held his head with both hands, and slumped back down.

I left Tetamoa to his bruises and wounded pride and went for a stroll along the beach. While sauntering along I spotted Tiare and Kuana so I changed direction towards them.

"Manu, sweetheart!" Tiare called. "Kuana has invited me to Tetiaroa," she said when I reached them. "I said you and I would come together, after we're married."

"Of course, you will both be my guests," Kuana assured us before excusing himself with a hint of bitterness over our upcoming marriage.

The following morning when Tiare and I were returning from our customary swim in the neighboring stream we heard a commotion near Matai's house. When we arrived at our chief's residence we saw Nihauiti being taken away by two of his fellow islanders under the orders of Tetiaroa's chief. Nihauiti, with his hands bound behind his back, protested vehemently while struggling to get free.

"What's happening?" I asked Tetamoa, who was looking on in both surprise and anger.

"Kuana told his father about Nihauiti being disrespectful to him when we were fishing... when we were hauling in the one that slipped out of Kuana's grasp and had his jaws ripped out."

"So? Why is he being taken away?" I asked.

"They say he shouldn't have talked to the chief's son in such a rude manner," Tetamoa answered. "Now he is going to be put under guard until they return to Tetiaroa, then Moana will have him executed."

"*What?* Just for talking to Kuana like that? That's ridiculous!" I responded

"The *poor man*," Tiare said.

"Can you believe that *arrogant, insufferable...*" Tetamoa then said, referring to Kuana.

"His father is no different," I added. "To murder Nihauiti for no reason? It should be *Kuana*."

"Shh... be careful, Manu," Tiare cautioned, "someone may hear you."

"I don't care who hears me; this is outrageous, a good man like Nihauiti..."

"Manu – please," Tiare warned again.

There was nothing any of us could do seeing this was the chief's decision, a chief of an island far away and unrelated to Tahiti. We could only be sorry for the young Nihauiti and leave him to the brutality of Kuana and his father.

When the time came for Moana and his party to return

to Tetiaroa another grand feast was held the night before their departure. It was customary for the host to grant a visiting dignitary a gift of his choosing, and it was on this last evening when Matai asked Moana what would please him. Tetamoa and I listened curiously to Moana's request.

"For myself I desire nothing," he said, "but Kuana wishes to take the young Tiare to Tetiaroa with him to be his wife." There was a stunned silence. Then I jumped to my feet.

"No!" I shouted. "Never! Tiare and I are going to be married!"

"Manu, be still!" Matai ordered.

"You *can't* let Kuana take her!"

"Manu, you will hold your tongue! *I* shall decide what will or will not be done!" Matai responded angrily.

All this time Kuana sat calmly, confident that his father would be granted his request.

"Grandfather, you cannot allow this," Tetamoa stepped in. "Tiare cannot be given away like this, she belongs with Manu, it is known."

"I will hear no more of this!" Matai snapped with his patience taxed. "Moana's request will be honored!" I looked fiercely at Kuana and his father, then leapt to my feet and stormed away.

Tetamoa found me standing at the lagoon peering out to sea. He put his hand on my shoulder.

"Manu, we'll talk to my grandfather, he will not permit this once he's thought on it."

"I won't let it happen, I'll *kill* Kuana first," I said.

When I told Tiare what had developed she burst into tears.

"I won't go!" she cried. "They can kill me, I won't go! I don't want to live if I can't be with you, Manu!"

Neither of us spoke for a long time, we just held each other close for what we feared would be the last time.

I wiped the tears from her eyes and told her to stay with Heifara.

"I'll be back; Tetamoa and I are going to talk to Matai and try to make him see reason."

I found Tetamoa talking heatedly to Kuana when I returned to the main part of the village. I burst upon the intruder only to have Tetamoa keep me from assaulting him.

"Why are you doing this, Kuana?" I said. "*Why?* Tiare doesn't want to be with you, why must you destroy two lives?" Kuana said nothing; he simply stared at me then walked away.

"It's no use, Manu," Tetamoa said, "I've tried to reason with the pig."

Tetamoa and I entered Matai's house and seated ourselves on the cloth mat. The candlenuts flickered somberly as Matai spoke.

"Manu, I know why you are here. Tiare must go with Kuana when the sun rises."

"But *why*, Matai? You can stop it," I said, dreading I was going to lose the most precious thing in my life. The chief sat thoughtfully before responding.

"Manu, you are still unfamiliar with many of our ways. It is my duty to grant an eminent guest a gift before his departure, and to deny his pleasure is to commit a grave insult. It saddens me to do this, Manu, I know you and Tiare share a great affection for each other, but it must be done."

"And what if Moana asked to take *your* woman with him to Tetiaroa – if she still lived – would you hand her to him so willingly?" I challenged.

"Do not be impertinent with me, Manu!" the chief warned. "It is done."

"Matai…" I pleaded, but the chief raised his hand.

"Go now, both of you."

I had thoughts of killing Kuana and his father and said this to Tetamoa, but we knew they would both be too well protected. Tetamoa then suggested that Tiare and I escape to Tahiti-Iti. Realizing it was our only hope, Tetamoa arranged to meet us with a boat when the village was asleep.

I was impatient to return to Tiare and have her wait in the hills until nightfall lest Matai put her under guard, so we picked up our pace while going over our escape plan. But more misfortune had struck; when we reached my house we found Tiare confined within and several sentries posted outside.

"What do we do now?" I despaired.

"We'll have to take them tonight when everyone's asleep," Tetamoa said.

"Just the two of us? That's impossible, even with Tiare's father. And what about you? Your grandfather will have you suffer the same fate as Kona, remember…" I reminded him. Tetamoa frowned.

"I'll try one other thing," he said, although his heart did not seem to be in it for lack of hope. "My grandfather weighs his brothers' council very carefully; I shall speak with them right away."

"Do what you can," I said, "I have to go to Tiare." When I moved towards the entrance one of the guards thrust his spear at my chest.

"Let him pass," another guard spoke, "Matai said it was alright." I went in and saw Tiare sitting quietly with her mother. Once again I considered our chances of overpowering the guards, but when I saw as many as eight of them spread around the house I knew it was out of the question.

Tiare's mother left us when I entered. We were too overcome to talk, we could only spend our last night together lying in each other's arms.

Shortly before sunrise I took Tiare's hand and crept to the entrance of the house and looked out. It was very still. As we took a step outside the guards immediately challenged us. With this last hope gone Tiare cried and said, "Give me your knife, Manu, I'll die *now*!"

"No! You'll do no such thing!" I said as I held her tight. "That isn't the answer. Go with Kuana, I'll come for you, I promise; Tetamoa and your father will help me." I then gently wiped the tears from her eyes.

"Oh, Manu, I love you so much, please don't let them take me…" Nothing more was said; we just lay beside each other and waited.

The sun was bright when I awoke from an unexpected sleep. Tiare still lay beside me with her eyes closed. Without disturbing her I got to my feet and pried outside. There was no one to be seen, not even a sentry. I walked suspiciously down the hill to the heart of the village. I expected the sentries to have come for Tiare by now to escort her to Kuana's boat, but instead I was met by a jubilant Tetamoa.

"Manu!" he beamed, "my uncles did it! They made my grandfather see reason!"

"You mean Tiare does *not* have to go?" I asked in disbelief.

"That's right. I spoke with my grandfather just now and he confessed to being victim of a most stilted custom. He was troubled by the likelihood of a hostile response from Moana if he refused the request."

"And what *was* Moana's response?"

"He does not yet know," Tetamoa smiled cunningly.

I could no longer control my elation and let out a loud whoop and punched the air in triumph before throwing my arms around Tetamoa.

I went to Matai's house with Tetamoa intending to thank the chief for his compassion, but when we arrived we heard strong and loud words being exchanged between Moana and Matai. Matai was explaining why he was wrong to have approved the request for Tiare's hand. We heard him ask Moana and Kuana to accept the love that Tiare and I had for each other, and heard him additionally ask them to understand why it was necessary for him to now undo what he had unfortunately done. But the chief and his son remained incensed and swore revenge for the gross insult.

"Matai, I spit on you!" Moana snarled. "I will return to destroy your village and hang the heads of your family in my marae!" These words made Tetamoa move angrily towards the house but I stopped him from entering. I, too, was enraged over what I heard and would not have been sorry to see Moana and his son cut down where they stood, but Matai was more tolerant and ordered Moana to take his party and leave Mahina at once.

A crowd had gathered outside Matai's house when word spread of the fiery exchange between the two chiefs, and when Moana and his men moved hurriedly to their boats the people of Mahina hurled rocks at them and dared them to ever return.

"Remember my promise, Matai!" Moana shouted. "Remember what I say!"

CHAPTER 6

Tiare and I were married a few days after Moana and his people were chased out of Mahina.

The marriage was a very serious affair that was held at the marae of Tiare's family. This sacred ground was enclosed by large stones and shaded by tall trees.

With Tiare's family proudly witnessing the event, I was represented by Matai and his family.

The ceremony included a rite in which the women of both families gashed their heads with sharks' teeth and let their blood flow onto a sheet. The mixing of the women's blood symbolized the joining of the two families. At this stage Tiare and I stood on the reddened cloth and took our vows.

Although the ensuing days remained peaceful, I was still troubled over the prospect of Moana returning with the invasion force he threatened.

"He will not dare to show his face here again," the impetuous Tetamoa growled.

"I wish I could be as certain," I said; "we have to be ready for the possibility."

I returned to the village late one night after spending the day fishing with Tiare's father, Midori, and after unloading our catch we walked home.

I pulled the cloth aside that was covering the entrance to my house and anticipated Tiare's greeting. I stepped over to the bed but saw nothing in the darkness.

"Tiare," I whispered. "Tiare?" I saw she wasn't there as my eyes focused on the bed. My immediate impulse was to go to her parent's house where I suspected she would be, but when I turned to leave I heard a muffled scream and what appeared to be scuffling outside. I ran from the house and saw two men dragging Tiare down the hill and towards a boat waiting in the lagoon. Terror shot through me when I saw my wife struggling helplessly, but my fear was beset by rage and I raced towards her abductors.

Suddenly I was felled by a crashing blow to my head. When I tried to get to my feet a second blow struck and I reeled backwards. I looked up through glassy eyes, unable to move, then I recognized Kuana standing over me. Before turning to join his accomplices he spat on me with bestial pleasure and damned me to hell.

I lay stunned for a long time, desperate to find help, but was unable to move or cry out.

When the pounding in my head lessened I moved slowly to my feet, but immediately slumped back to the ground and passed out.

I came to with Midori cradling my head trying to get me to take some water.

"Manu, what happened?" he asked.

"Tiare, they took her… Kuana…" I struggled.

Midori took me back to his house where his wife tended my wounds and saw that I rested.

After awakening from a long sleep I was visited by Matai and Tetamoa. They listened angrily as I recounted the events of the previous night.

"We'll go after them – right away! I'll cut Kuana's wretched head from his body!" Tetamoa reacted.

"You are being impulsive," Matai rebuked. "We must consider our course carefully. There is nothing we can do now, Kuana is a full day across the water. Manu, you rest now, we shall talk again when the sun leaves us and decide then what is to be done."

Sleep was impossible for me; all I could think of was Tiare being so cruelly taken away.

I was able to move about after a few more hours, but I still had a terrible throbbing in my head and a constant feeling of nausea.

The council took place in Matai's house at sunset. People watched solemnly as Matai's two brothers led the way to the chief's quarters followed by Tetamoa, myself, and other high-ranking citizens of Mahina. An unnatural silence gripped the air suggesting only too well that war was imminent.

Matai opened the assembly by advising that we join forces with other villages and mass an army large enough to overcome Moana's people, and also be capable of turning aside other villages of Tetiaroa should there be outside retaliation.

"What about Tiare?" I reminded Matai. "We can't overlook her safety."

"Manu is right," her father was quick to agree. "As soon

as Moana's people see our boats her life will be in danger."

"This is true," Matai pondered, "we must find a way to fetch her to safety." Tetamoa then suggested dispatching a boat with myself and three or four other warriors a day before the invading force departed, the plan being to swim ashore at nightfall, find Tiare and take her to the safety of the waiting boat. Matai favored the idea and agreed that I and three other men be sent ahead to carry out the rescue.

Rather than combine the resources of several chiefs, Matai decided it would be better for Tetamoa to sail to Tahiti-Iti and summon the help of just one chief, the great Vehiatua. This famous man was the leader of Tahiti-Iti and ruled over villages inhabited by more than two thousand warriors. By combining forces with the renowned Vehiatua we would strike Tetiaroa with a compliment of over three thousand men.

It would be ten days before Vehiatua's forces could reach Matavai Bay, which was time enough for Matai's people to prepare their vessels for the journey to Tetiaroa.

Tetamoa left for Tahiti-Iti the following morning while the men and women of Mahina prepared for war.

The threat of war would always bring about an immediate increase in boat construction, but Matai was fortunate to already have enough seaworthy vessels in the boathouses.

Matai had twenty large boats at hand, each able to carry fifty men. Each va'a, or war canoe, measured seventy-five feet in length and was built of two dugout bottoms that were fitted together. The front of the va'a was narrower than the rear, and it had a long flat bow piece and a high upward curving stern, which gave the vessel a look of demonic swiftness. The va'a was propelled by two sails, one in each of its hulls, and its steering was engineered by stout paddle-shaped rudders. For overnight voyages, such as the three day journey to Tetiaroa, the va'a was fitted with special features which included a board across the gunwales forming a platform on which the warriors could sit, sleep, or cook; and when the va'a was outfitted for war additional platforms were placed over the bows to accommodate more fighting men.

While Mahina was busy preparing for battle Matai was approached by the high priest. The holy man reminded him that for Oro to look favorably upon the enterprise it was necessary to offer a sacrifice to the red god. After consulting with the priest, Matai arranged for the pre-battle ceremonies to take place once Vehiatua arrived from Tahiti-Iti.

Word soon spread that Matai was to find someone for the sacrifice and this caused a great deal of unrest among the lower class villagers.

The following day, accompanied by the priest and his aides, Matai approached a group of men loading weapons onto one of the boats. As the workers respectfully bore their shoulders to their chief, Matai pointed to one of them and calmly said, "Him." There was a moment's silence, then realizing what had just happened, the man screamed in terror, "No! No! Not me! Let me fight in Tetiaroa! Please! Not me!" He was taken away flaying his arms and legs and confined until the ceremony would begin.

The days passed quickly since Tetamoa's departure. The va'as had been outfitted with weapons that included spears, bows and arrows, clubs, rasps, stones, and battle-axes; and supply boats stored with food and water had also been readied for the journey.

A marae boat had additionally been prepared for the crossing; this special vessel carried sacred items from the district's burial grounds. A battle of this measure called for the floating marae to protect the warriors or ensure they would join their ancestors should they fall in combat.

While awaiting the arrival of Vehiatua and his warriors, Matai directed his men to prepare themselves physically for battle. Boxing and wrestling matches were held along with spear and stone throwing exercises.

Finally Vehiatua's boats were sighted off Matavai Bay. The citizens of Mahina lined the beach to watch the approach, and when Vehiatua's stately canoe entered the lagoon, Matai, in full regalia, stood ready to welcome the celebrated chief.

The sight of fifty of the stoutest vessels being ushered into the lagoon was an inspiring show. When Vehiatua's boat breached, the great chief and Tetamoa both stepped ashore. The other boats breached in quick succession and all two thousand warriors from Tahiti-Iti were jubilantly welcomed by the fighting force of Mahina.

Matai escorted Vehiatua to his house where he apprised him of the events that led to the decision to go to war.

While the chiefs and their advisors talked over battle strategies the warriors of Mahina and Tahiti-Iti spent their time in further training to sharpen their combat skills.

Mahina's high priest again addressed the matter of the pre-battle ceremony. He reminded Matai that the ceremony would require *three* sacrifices to capture the favor of Oro. The first sacrifice was to awaken the god and ask for his assistance; the second represented a public declaration of war, and the third served to break the treaty, which presently bound Tahiti and Tetiaroa as allies. Matai promptly ordered the priest to find two more men for the service, not minding whether they were from Mahina or Vehiatua's villages; neither chief was concerned over such incidentals when it came to the favor of their god.

A few moments later a hysterical scream shot through the village, then another rang out; two men had been seized by the priest's aides and placed under guard. The mere presence of the priest made the people nervous, and when a man was taken away by his aides they knew only too well what fate awaited him.

When the echoes of the screams faded Matai suggested the strategy meeting be concluded.

"Let us rest tonight," he said to Vehiatua. "We shall make our peace with Oro when the sun returns."

Touched by a gentle breeze in a cloudless sky, the birds sang in the new day. It seemed somehow unimaginable that in a land such as this where nature manifested herself so beautifully, three human beings were to be brutally slaughtered, offered in a sacrificial rite.

As the condemned men were dragged towards the altar, watched silently by the fighting men of Mahina and Tahiti-Iti, I contemplated the wickedness and savagery of such a faith; but when I found myself embraced by Matai, Vehiatua, and others of the upper realm, my contempt wavered. It was as though I accepted the intent of the order. I felt perhaps my apparent agreement with the society's laws was drawn out through the subconscious recollections of my previous life – when I was familiar with such customs and believed in their purpose.

When the men were brought to the altar, still wriggling and moaning in a last futile effort for salvation, the priest raised his hands to the sky and prayed to the almighty Oro. The sacrifices were carried out quickly and in the same manner in which I had executed Matai's aide, Kona – the priest crashed his club to the earth, smashing the victims' heads in a bloody mess.

With time drawing near for my departure to Tetiaroa, a nervous excitement came over me when I thought of being reunited with Tiare, but I soberly faced the possibility that she might already be dead or that the rescue attempt could fail, ending in my own death.

A twenty-five foot, single-hulled canoe with outrigger lay ready for my journey. Accompanying me were three warriors who were familiar with the crossing to Tetiaroa. They waited for me beside the boat while I exchanged final words with Matai and Vehiatua. The chiefs reminded me they would set out the following morning, giving me almost a full day start and enough time to find Tiare and get ourselves to safety before the fleet arrived.

While taking those lonely steps to the boat I glanced back at the two great chiefs. Though growing old, Vehiatua was still feared and respected for his battle exploits. He was very much like Matai with tattoos etched over most of his body, and he, too, wore a neatly trimmed beard, which complimented his proud, gray features.

We rowed smoothly from the lagoon towards an opening in the reef. Once in the open sea the crescent wind set us on course.

There was little to do during the crossing other than again go over the plan. Our navigator, Maetua, had plotted the location where the two other men and I would leave the boat and swim to an isolated part of the island; from there we would make our way into Moana's village.

On the second night I lay back in the bobbing vessel thinking of our forces following behind. I looked up at the ebony sail puffing in the breeze.

"Manu, eat something," Nako said, stirring my restless mind as he handed me some dried pork. Nako was just a boy of no more than seventeen, who for a short time had lived in Moana's village before returning to his family in Mahina. It was Nako we were relying on to find the safest route into the village that held Tiare.

On the third day, with the sun edging onto the horizon in a bright orange ball, Tetiaroa's hills became visible. This grandiose sight assured us that our approach would be concealed by darkness.

Night had fallen when we sided up to the reef. Maetua was careful to maneuver the vessel to a place that was hidden by a large rock. The only light that hinted our presence came from the moon, but then the shadows from the hills cancelled the telling reflection that was initially thrown onto the boat.

Nako, the masterful Teura-Kanokoa, and I secured our knives and prepared to slip into the lagoon and swim ashore. Maetua reminded us in a whispering voice that he would set back out to sea if we did not return by dawn, and with no more words spoken we climbed over the reef and swam as quietly as we knew how towards shore.

After resting for a moment at the base of the hill we set off cautiously towards the village with Nako leading the way. As the young warrior did not know Kuana's house, our plans required the taking of a hostage.

We continued to walk, always alert for a possible encounter with Moana's sentries. Suddenly Nako stopped.

"We enter the village where the path forks," he whispered, pointing ahead.

We were at the edge of the village within a few moments. It was deathly still and dark except for the occasional candlenut flickering under the stars. We moved on, creeping behind some houses.

"Who is there!" a voice snapped, breaking the silence.

We stopped dead and looked at each other, questioning our next move. Then Teura-Kanokoa staggered towards the enquiring sentry and said with a slur, "Help me find my house, I've had too much kava." Before the sentry could react I moved behind him and threw a hand over his mouth while locking his arm against his shoulder blade with my other hand.

"Where is Kuana?" Teura-Kanokoa snarled as he held the tip of his knife against the man's throat, causing some blood to appear.

"Take us to him or you'll die!" I said pushing harder on his arm and making him drop to his knees.

"Don't kill me, I'll take you!" he pleaded. Nako then tore off a piece of the sentry's kilt and stuffed it into his mouth to ensure his silence. With his arm still locked against his shoulder blade he led us towards Kuana's house.

It was not long before the sentry stopped and made a muffled sound. I let his arm go, and after favoring his weakened limb he pointed to a house standing alone near the base of the hill. Teura-Kanokoa moved forward cautiously followed by Nako and myself with the hostage. The stillness was tense as we stood hidden behind the house. I let Nako hold the sentry at bay with his own spear. Not a word was said. Teura-Kanokoa pointed to himself, then to me, and then to the house. I nodded. We drew our knives and crept to the entrance, which was covered by a hanging cloth. We had to move smartly as the entrance was in full view of the starlit village. I pulled the cloth aside cautiously and edged in; and there, sleeping softly in a dim light was Tiare! But Kuana was not to be seen. I crept up to Tiare and put my hand gently on her shoulder. She awoke with a start but I touched my finger to my lips telling her to remain quiet. She sprung to her feet and flung her arms around me then quickly followed Teura-Kanokoa and me outside to where Nako stood waiting with his prisoner.

Once we had retreated to a safer distance Teura-Kanokoa stopped; with intensity lining his face he pointed at our captive. Without saying a word it was clear what had to be done. Teura-Kanokoa moved behind the trembling sentry and with a motion almost too quick to see thrust his knife into the man's back. The sentry jerked violently before slumping to the ground with his face twisted in pain. After ceremoniously wiping the blade on his victim's kilt and sliding the knife back into its sheath, Teura-Kanokoa pulled the dead man into the brush making sure he was well hidden. We then sped from the village and found the path that would take us back to where Maetua lay waiting.

Nako was the first to scamper down the hill to shore.

"He's there!" he called softly as we trailed after him. We slid into the water and swam towards the reef and the waiting boat.

Nako climbed on board and stood panting with his hands on his hips while I followed with Tiare and Teura-Kanokoa. Suddenly I froze, stunned along with the others. Maetua was lying on his back with a knife thrust in his chest.

Teura-Kanokoa's coolness saw to it that we rowed with smooth, smart strokes.

"Tiare, please steer, the rest of us… we pull till our backs break." Nako and I then took up oars along with Teura-Kanokoa and we rowed for our lives.

We watched the sun rise as we drew further out, but our fears were met when several canoes appeared in vigorous pursuit two or three miles behind us. There were probably

twenty warriors in each canoe, which clearly meant we would
be caught; but fortune again smiled upon us as we sighted
our fleet before the pursuers had gained much distance. Tiare
and I fell into each other's arms when we saw our vessels
bravely approaching Tetiaroa.

It was not long before the hunters realized they had
become the hunted, and seeing this they turned their boats
around and hastened to the safety of their shores.

Tiare maintained the helm while Teura-Kanokoa,
Nako, and I rested our exhausted bodies. We sat back and
savored our success while waiting to join up with Matai and
Vehiatua.

Reflecting on the events just completed, I turned to
Tiare.

"Where was Kuana?" I asked her, thinking his absence
from the house was strange, although it made the rescue a
great deal easier.

"Kuana has many women," Tiare said as I motioned
Nako to take the helm from her. "I prayed he would never
return to me each time he went away, but he always came
back. I tried to escape after the first few days but got no
further than pulling the puho's out of the shed when I was
stopped. Kuana beat me when he found out and kept me
confined. I could not leave his house for days, and when he
returned at night he would be drunk and attack me." Her
voice broke as she continued, "I just wanted to die; I was
going to end my life but I could only think of you, Manu,
and pray you would come. I knew you would come..." she
burst into tears, unable to go on. I sat in a cold silence while
holding her in my arms. All I could think of now was to find
Kuana and kill him.

Matai had directed his helmsman to maneuver alongside

us, and when our boats touched I climbed aboard the chief's vessel. Matai welcomed me as though I were his own son.

"I am delighted, Manu," he said as he took my shoulders firmly. When I told him of Maetua's death he offered a hard look but said nothing. He then appointed two of his men to board my boat and take Tiare and Maetua's body back to Mahina, as Nako, Teura-Kanokoa, and I were intent on facing the enemy.

I re-boarded my boat and took Tiare into my arms.

"Come back to me, Manu," she whispered. I desperately wanted to return home with her but death had to be challenged once again if we were to forever rid the threat of Moana and his son.

Our fleet of seventy vessels closed in on Tetiaroa's shores as Tiare's boat pulled further away.

Many of the warriors had fitted themselves with a form of armor consisting of a network of sennit cord wound around their body and limbs. This covering served to lessen the blows from clubs and stones. Also, many of the fighters superstitiously wore prized possessions. One such item of battle dress was the taumi – a wickerwork breast shield decorated with shell, shark's teeth, and feathers. Other valued possessions the men attached to themselves ranged from simple good luck charms to sacred items from their maraes.

Before winding a strip of bark cloth around my temple I untied my long hair from the top of my head and let it hang down; had I not done this I would be taken as a leader or a man of importance that would invite special attention from the enemy.

Moana's fleet was sighted just beyond the reef waiting to intercept us. We were fortunate that Tetiaroa's chief had not had time to recruit warriors from his outer villages as it became alarmingly apparent to us that even with Vehiatua's army we might yet be outnumbered.

Moana had formed his boats in three rows with a warrior standing in the bow of each front row canoe waiting to lash the opposing vessels together to open the way for hand-to-hand combat.

As we neared Moana's line of defense I told Vehiatua that a volley of arrows should be fired down onto the enemy canoes. This surprised the chief as the only time the bow and arrow was used in the islands was for hunting, never warfare, so the fact that I urged this weaponry be brought along for use was of an intrigue to both Vehiatua and Matai. This unconventional mode of attack took Moana's warriors completely off guard and they fell in masses having no defense against the raining arrows.

Warriors of both sides furiously rushed each other the moment the boats touched.

Although Matai and Vehiatua kept their vessel in the rear to assume a safer position, spears and stones still whistled passed their boat.

Screams rang out as stone blades tore into the flesh of men of both sides during the vicious hand-to-hand fighting.

The effect of the raining arrows had markedly weakened the enemy and Moana's demoralized men could not stop our advancing army. Those who weren't cut down managed to retreat to shore and join their land forces, while the men who could not escape our assault were shown no mercy.

Matai and Vehiatua watched with confidence as their men raced towards Moana's village. I had stayed away from the fighting until this point, but now I leapt from the chiefs' canoe and made my way to shore. I ran towards the village with the same passion as my comrades, only the driving force behind me was Kuana. I had to find him.

A volley of spears and stones suddenly met our rush, then another, causing the attack to break down. Then came more close-in fighting as Moana's warriors counterattacked.

I soon made my first kill, thrusting my spear through the body of an onrushing warrior.

I detoured from the battlefield and again made for the village. It was unlikely I would find Kuana there but I could think of no other place to begin my search for him.

There was no sign of my adversary when I entered the village, only women and children and some men who were too old to fight cowering helplessly in a withdrawn section of the compound.

"Where is Kuana?" I shouted at them. "Where *is* he?"

"We don't know," an affirmed old man pleaded while shielding some children from me.

Moments after I turned from the frightened group, our warriors came charging into the village led on by the trumpeting of conch shells. Some of the men carried torches and began setting fire to the houses while others overran the remainder of Moana's forces.

I sighted a group of men watching the onslaught from a hill and guessed that Kuana might be among them. At that moment a spear flew inches passed me. When I spun around with my knife drawn I saw Teura-Kanokoa club my attacker, then lunge on top of him and scrape one of the cruelest weapons ever contrived across the man's body. The Indian let out a harrowing scream as the rasp — made from the serrated backbone of the stingray — tore into his flesh and laid open his entrails. Teura-Kanokoa then ran with me to the base of the hill, leaving his victim writhing in mortal agony.

Teura-Kanokoa was a tall, frightening warrior whose

savage appearance and overpowering frame was likely to turn any opponent aside through mental submission. His image was further exposed by the gripping tattoo of a wild boar he carried across his chest.

"That will be where Kuana and Moana are holding out," he said, pointing to the men standing at the top of the hill, supporting my own suspicions.

When we climbed over the ridge we were met with triumphant shouts from our own warriors who had since taken control of the area.

"Where are their chiefs?" I called out, afraid that Kuana might already be dead.

"We have them," one of the men answered as he ushered me to where a group of captives sat bound together. I was relieved to see Kuana among them. When I saw the defiance still in his eyes I crashed a blow to his face that brought blood from his mouth and sent him flying backwards.

"I do *not* want this one killed," I ordered, turning away.

I walked on with Teura-Kanokoa inspecting the devastation around us. Down below the houses' wooden frames crackled while black smoke continued to rise carrying the stench of death towards us.

"Let's find Matai," I said to Teura-Kanokoa. We marched down the hill and headed back to shore. We found Matai and Vehiatua on the beach and told them that Kuana had been taken, then I enquired of Moana. Matai pointed to one of the breached boats. Tetiaroa's chief was tied to the mast with a spear thrust in his body.

Anxious to celebrate our victory with Tetamoa, I asked Matai where I would find his grandson. The chief did not respond for a long time, he seemed to be looking through me.

"Tetamoa is dead," he finally whispered.

By evening the men had caught and roasted some wild pigs. Kuana, who was tied to a tree nearby, nervously watched the activities. He began to squirm when I walked towards him fitting an arrow to my bow. The crowd fell silent, curious at what I was about. Fear bit into Kuana.

"No!" he shouted when I took aim. "Please! Don't!"

"Kill the pig!" a voice shouted out.

"Kill him!" "Kill him!" others sounded, but I lowered the bow. I wanted him to suffer for all the suffering he had caused Tiare. Kuana relaxed his body when I turned away. But a short while later I again approached him. The crowd once more fell quiet as the prisoner wriggled in apprehension.

"This time I shoot, Kuana," I scowled, "only you will not die, not yet; you will die slowly for what you have caused. Look around you!" I shouted; "this is *your* doing!" He whimpered like a frightened child as I took aim, and cried loudly when the shaft bit into his stomach.

The morning had brought fresh winds and a clear sky to carry us homeward. It was while waiting for the supplies to be stored on the vessels that Tetamoa's death began to affect me. It had made me feel bitter and empty and left me wanting to inflict all the suffering I could on the prisoners. Then I thought of the grief that would come over Heifara when she learned of her husband's death.

"Manu! The pig still breathes!" a voice called to me. An eager young warrior was pointing to Kuana.

"Kill him," I said calmly.

It was not long before I became tormented over the death and destruction we had left behind, and I thought of all the injured and terrified people we discarded to rebuild their homes and mend their shattered lives. I relived the moment I shot Kuana, ensuring that he would have a slow and painful death. Then I became afraid of a divine punishment for my cold-blooded act. I asked myself what gave me the right to kill an unarmed man, especially in such a cruel way, no matter what he had done. Then I rationalized… in this time and place there were no laws that Peter Matthews had once known and had to follow. Killing was a way of life here, more a means of survival. Peter did not kill for the pleasure; it was Manu who killed of necessity.

CHAPTER 7

An uncertain quiet hung in the air as our approach into Matavai Bay was watched tensely by those who had remained behind.

Three hundred men had been killed between Matai's and Vehiatua's forces, and it was likely that Tetiaroa had lost five times as many.

I had again become tormented with terrible guilt when I reflected on so much devastation. It was Vehiatua who finally lifted the cloud from my conscience.

"Listen to me, Manu," the chief said, "they would have set upon Mahina had we not touched their shores first." I contemplated his words but said nothing. "You wonder about Tiare... you have much to learn, Manu, you are too soft; Tiare is your woman – it was your duty to bring her back and our duty to support you; what followed could never have been prevented. Now go to your wife and enjoy the fruits of victory."

Mahina saw a great deal of mourning during the days that followed. The bereaved families openly wept for their champions who lay dead on the shores of Tetiaroa.

Tetamoa had been brought back from the battlefield to be buried with his ancestors. The news of his death had left Heifara in a frightening state; after a hysterical reaction she fell into a silent and motionless condition, which required Tiare to constantly watch over her.

Tiare was eventually able to break through Heifara's shell. I watched sympathetically as my wife pleaded with her to turn away from her death-inducing behavior.

"Heifara, please, Tetamoa would not have you this way. Do you think for a moment he will rest knowing you invite death upon yourself by grieving so?"

Slowly Heifara's eyes moved in our direction.

"I know," she whispered at last. "It is foolish, but I want him so much!" she cried. It was a heartrending sight, but it was also a sign she was releasing herself from her severe state of depression.

While Tiare comforted her cousin I wondered if Heifara might hold Tiare and me responsible for Tetamoa's death. It was a possibility I feared, but then I felt nothing could ever break the bond that held these two young women so close to each other.

"Leave me now," she said, "I'll be alright, I promise, I just want to sleep." Tiare and I glanced at each other uncertainly.

"You'd better look in on her later," I said when we stepped outside.

We could not have been gone more than a few minutes when we heard a chilling scream come from Heifara's house.

We ran back pushing our way passed the crowd that had quickly gathered. When we entered the house we found Heifara's mother cradling her daughter in her arms. Heifara had plunged a knife through her broken heart.

The demise of persons of social importance was always followed by a wake, so it was arranged that Tetamoa and Heifara lie in state before they would be buried side by side. It was during this period that they were bathed and oiled to minimize the rapidly developing odor of decay, and after this cleansing they were dressed the whitest mantles and kilts.

There was a belief in the islands that hostile spirits would consume the departing soul if food offerings were not set beside the body, so during the period of the wake servants fetched fresh fruit and meat to where Tetamoa and Heifara lay.

The loss of my two friends hit me very hard. Apart from Matai they were the first to show me kindness upon my arrival, and I was afraid that the closeness Tetamoa and I shared with each other could never be replaced. I had lost a brother and a friend in one blow.

Tiare and I both participated in the mourning ceremonies. One of the many rituals saw the family members of the deceased gash their heads and breasts with a shark's tooth and catch their blood on a piece of bark cloth and give the stained material to the deceased's nearest living relative. The purpose of this rite was to strengthen the psychic bond with the souls of the deceased's ancestors. This practice left me cold, but I was compelled to share a large mat with Tiare and along with her scrape the pointed tooth across my forehead and breast and let the blood flow onto the cloth. The pain was sharp and the wounds left conspicuous scars that would take some time to go away. What distressed me more, though, was seeing Tiare inflict these wounds upon herself, and in addition, while sobbing continually she hacked at her beautiful long hair in yet another display of grief.

The Otahaa was another ritual that was staged by an appointed group of mourners. These mourners performed behaviors that consisted of the most frantic expressions of grief; and they acted as though they had lost control of their senses. They were comprised mostly of women who wailed in loud tones, ripped out clumps of their hair, and cut themselves with shark's teeth until blood flowed profusely from their wounds. Their agonized wailing and hideously distorted faces, compounded by their blood-soaked bodies, gave them an almost inhuman appearance.

At the culmination of the Otahaa still another ritual was observed. The Tyehaa was a demonstration of mourning even more grisly. I was becoming afraid that these dark customs were going to destroy my love for the islands.

Seeing Tiare in a constant state of sobbing with her gashed forehead and breasts, and her hair chopped unevenly above the shoulders, threw me into a state of depression. For the first time in what was now two years I asked myself why was I here? I wanted to know again *why* I had been sent back in time, and I wondered once again if Peter Matthews was *really* reincarnated and whisked back to his soul's previous homeland. I felt alone all over again and wanted to end this adventure by waking up as Peter Matthews in the modern world he had left behind. Even my despair over Tetamoa and Heifara was being prematurely lifted by my constant exposure to these pagan grieving rituals, and I felt I could not even relate to Tiare during these times.

The Tyehaa was a ceremony that could last any number of days. It was a ritual attended by masked mourners where each mourner armed himself with a paaeho – a staff edged with shark's teeth. This liturgy was madness of the highest order.

As I stood in the background that afternoon watching the servants again bathe and oil Tetamoa's and Heifara's bodies to further stall the decaying process, my attention was drawn to the twenty-five or so mourners who were readying themselves for the Tyehaa. They were blackening their faces and bodies with charcoal and spotting themselves with a reddish clay. The mourners then adorned themselves with masks of bright pearl shell, a petticoat made from pandanus leaves, a waist girdle, and headgear consisting of cloth and red-tipped feathers. Suspended over their chests from each mask was a bright crescent-shaped board about a foot long that was covered with a network of chips of mother-of-pearl. These chips were threaded through the smallest perforations at each end, and they were bordered with black feathers from the man-of-war bird. Their frightening appearance was complete when each mourner further armed himself with a hunting spear or club.

I watched with a curious uneasiness to see what would happen next. The mourners began with the familiar wailing, then they went into gruesome body contortions; then they began running… running like crazed animals through the village. I absorbed the true horror of the affair when one of the servants who was attending to Tetamoa and Heifara moved into the path of the oncoming mourners; the devil-clad madmen battered him to death with a flurry of blows from their clubs amidst their chilling wails and screams. As the mourners continued rampaging through the village I heard distant shouts of "Run! The Nayneuvas are coming!" These masked mourners were looked upon as lunatics who were driven mad with grief and were consequently held blameless if they maimed or killed anyone who got in their way.

The Nayneuvas terrified the entire community. When *anyone* saw them approach they flew from their path, usually to the nearest marae where the lamenters were forbidden during their period of mourning.

The Tyehaa continued for three more days with all the savagery of which it began. There were more slayings and many beatings of people who happened in the path of the Nayneuvas. I, too, was surprised by them; while returning home on the second day of mourning I found myself face-to-face with two of the mourners. Their lamenting turned into screams when I crossed their path. They charged me flaying their clubs and had every intention of pummeling me into the ground, but my reaction was quick, I felled both of them with blows to the head and escaped quickly to the safety of my house. It was likely these two Nayneuvas knew who I was and knew of my social standing, yet had I not got the better of them they would have guiltlessly battered me to death.

I remained in the seclusion of my house until the Tyehaa ended, as did most everyone, and during this period I reflected upon the behavior of the people of this island. It was astounding to me how their characters would change so radically as certain rituals dictated. I recalled the night Heifara took her life – when Tiare was finally able to reach her grieving cousin and tell her that such a death-inducing state would benefit no one – yet when the wake for Tetamoa and Heifara began Tiare herself was struck with a grief so intense that she was to thoroughly contradict her words to Heifara. It was as though Tiare and all the people who participated in the mourning were programmed to behave in such a strange and frightening way.

When the mourning was over Tetamoa and Heifara were wrapped in sweet-scented tapa cloth and placed in coffins carved from tree trunks. They were then removed to rest in a mountain cave in Matai's marae.

The wake had lasted fifteen days, and at its conclusion the people of Mahina went back to their routines knowing they would no longer have to contend with the threat of the Nayneuvas; indeed, even the Nayneuvas themselves had returned to their normal activities, seemingly unaware of their earlier behavior.

The night of the burial Tiare and I lay together with a candlenut flickering in the darkness of our house. She now carried a scar on her forehead where she had ritually scraped the shark's tooth. I was terribly upset over her wounds and felt further distressed when I ran my hand through her short, uneven hair.

"Do not be troubled, Manu," she said softly, "it is the way things are in Tahiti." She then kissed me on the cheek and rested her head on my chest.

Immediately after the burial a thanksgiving service had been held to commemorate the victory over Moana. This service saw the high priest dismiss the spirits of war and recall the spirits of peace. The holy assembly was concluded when Matai placed Moana's dismembered limbs on his marae as a sign that the enemy had been vanquished and peace had once again returned to the land.

In the weeks that followed the wake Tiare and I developed a close friendship with my battlefield comrade, Teura-Kanokoa, and his wife, Rina, which did well to lessen the grief we felt over the loss of Tetamoa and Heifara. Matai had taken me closer still to his heart during this period, and soon the void created by Tetamoa's death had been filled.

The turmoil of the wake had left me despondent for a long time, although the transformation of Tiare to her former elegant and passionate self brought a great relief to me. The delirium of the funeral rites, however, had affected me to the point where I thought often about the life I had left and I once again attempted to calculate the year in which I was presently living.

On one of my many walks along the beach I thought about the incredible likelihood of me being able to watch history repeat itself, and I wondered if it was possible for me – whether I was conscious of it at the time or not – to cause or alter events which could actually change the course of recorded history. My inner beliefs, or rationalizations as it were, told me that history could not be *directly* altered – although I was in a position to attempt such a thing, but being in this position I felt that I might actually *cause* events to occur that could *indirectly* alter history. My thoughts became vague and confused through pondering over such staggering possibilities, but I was sure I would have the answers in time – as I witnessed the growth and development of Tahiti, and when I could actually see things happen again as I had learned of them in my other world. Then, and only then would I know just how much power and control I might have.

CHAPTER 8

The ensuing months passed happily and with little incident. The only visitors Mahina saw were wayfarers from Raiatea who called at Matavai Bay seeking provisions for their ongoing journey.

I spent a great deal of time during this period hunting and fishing with Teura-Kanokoa. I particularly enjoyed these expeditions away from the village, but I always looked forward to Tiare's welcome after a day or two at sea.

Tiare was growing bigger every day with our child, and she looked just as lovely as the day I first took notice of her with her hair once again falling gracefully over the shoulders and her deep brown skin as soft and beautiful as it ever was.

With Tiare in the latter stages of her pregnancy, her mother and attendants went about preparing the birth-houses for the upcoming event.

Matai had given permission for Tiare to have use of the

birth-houses, which were restricted to immediate members of royalty; but then it was commonly known that the old chief looked upon me as he would his own son and was likely to afford me special privileges.

The birth-houses consisted of three separate constructions on a sacred piece of ground adjacent to Matai's marae. The fare-rau-maire, or house of sweet fern, was where our child would be delivered; the fare-hua, known as the house of the weak, was where Tiare and the baby would be taken to convalesce; and the fare-noa was a special house in which the attendants and closest relatives would stay during the days preceding and following the birth.

I stayed close to the house of sweet fern when Tiare went into labor, but with Teura-Kanokoa and other sporting friends teasing me about my state of nerves, I chose to remain in their company and lose myself over several drinks of kava. While Tiare's family chanted prayers for a safe delivery my friends and I filled ourselves with the alcoholic beverage.

The following morning, with spinning head and churning stomach, I trudged to the fare-noa where I found Tiare's father and other anxious family members.

"How is she?" I asked, propping myself against a supporting beam.

"She still cries with pain," Midori answered. This news made me worry over Tiare's prolonged labor, and I was also concerned over the coarse methods of delivery, although the women of the islands indeed seemed to take childbirth quite casually.

The effects of the kava had wreaked havoc with me, forcing me to lie down in the fare-noa and sleep off an old-fashioned hangover, but I was soon awakened by the cry of "Ua muhuta mai nei te atua!" I jumped to my feet and fell into a throng of well-wishers congratulating me on the birth of my son.

I longed to enter the house of sweet fern when I heard his cries, but Tahitian custom forbade the father from doing this until the mother and child's final day in the house of the weak.

Being familiar with certain stages of childbirth, I recalled the procedure in which the chief attendant let the infant cry for a long time and breathe strongly before severing the umbilical cord; the intent of this was to let the child receive full life from its mother. After the attendant cut the cord with a razor-sharp bamboo stick the child was anointed with sandalwood oil and wrapped warmly in soft tapa cloth.

A day after the birth of our son Tiare and the infant were taken to the house of the weak where they remained for the customary five days. It was incredibly frustrating being unable to see Tiare and the baby. The days passed slowly no matter what I did to keep busy. I would hunt with Teura-Kanokoa; reinforce the roof of my house although it did not yet need it, and I would end each day in the company of Teura-Kanokoa and Rina, or Tiare's parents.

On the last day of Tiare's convalescence the priest permitted me to enter the house of the weak. When I went inside I saw Tiare resting on a bed of fine mats with our son sleeping in her arms.

"Look, Manu," she whispered, "he is so handsome, just like his father." She looked on proudly as I leaned over to take him from her. He was a beautiful, exotic child, with Tiare's dark almond eyes and my fairer complexion.

The months went by and I enjoyed each day to the fullest with my family.

We spent many happy hours swimming and picnicking

at a favorite inlet by the Tuauru River, often with Teura-Kanokoa and Rina and their two young children. Our boy, Taomi, whom I had fittingly nicknamed 'Tommy', was a delight to watch when he splashed about in the stream under the guiding hands of his mother.

I often repaired to the Tuauru's shaded estuary where I could enjoy nature's enchanting show while debating what the future in this world might hold for me.

I set out to this peaceful spot one morning just as the sun began to peek over the horizon. It was exhilarating to swim for long stretches in these cool secluded waters. While resting on the bank shaded by tall, arching trees, I would listen to the birds sing in the new day, and I would watch the water flow lazily into the boundless sea.

I often wondered what I might find on the other side of that vast ocean. The thought of going out on the first foreign vessel that dropped anchor in Matavai Bay *had* occurred to me, but I was afraid of what I might find on the other side, and I felt I might even be tempting the provinces of time if I attempted to leave Tahiti. I didn't know *what* I would do when a ship arrived; I wouldn't know until it happened.

Tiare caught me by surprise that morning while I lay by the water gazing into a blue sky.

"I always know where to find you, Manu," she said affectionately.

"Tiare, come and sit with me," I said, patting my hand on the grass beside me.

"Where's Tommy?" I asked.

"He's with my mother. It's terrible how she spoils him so." After a lazy silence Tiare staggered me with a question I had never expected to hear.

"Manu, you will not leave Tommy and me when the big

boat returns, will you?" The impact of her question left me speechless. "Promise me you won't leave us," she added with emotion breaking in her voice.

"What boat?" I asked.

"They said they would come back. Promise me you won't go away with them, Manu." I couldn't get any more information from her as she simply didn't know anymore; all she knew was they came from across the ocean. I could only guess that the *big boat* was the last foreign vessel to call at Matavai Bay, probably and English or a French ship. Once again my situation was like a fantasy… a disturbing fantasy. Tiare had evidently sensed my feelings over the past days and was visibly upset at the thought of me leaving Tahiti. As much as I was tempted to venture out I still did not know if I could cope with what was on the other side. Besides, I loved Tiare too much to ponder it any further. If I didn't have her and Tommy it would be altogether different.

"Darling," I assured her, "you and Tommy are everything to me; I could never leave you." She gave me a big hug and lay back at peace with the world when she heard these words.

"Come on, you imp!" I said playfully, "let's have a swim." Always ready for some sport she sprung to her feet and removed her mantle, baring her breasts in an unassuming mien, and slipped into the cool water. We swam up and downstream, sometimes drifting on our backs watching the birds fly from tree top to tree top.

I heard some laughter nearby while resting on the bank after our swim.

"I wonder who that is," I said inquisitively.

"Oh, probably some children playing," Tiare suggested.

As the laughter grew louder two young girls appeared from amongst the trees.

"Hello!" one of them said when they saw us.

"Well, hello," Tiare obliged.

"I'm Maimiti, this is my friend, Tana," the outgoing one answered. "We're exploring."

"Oh, yes? We explore here all the time," Tiare cheerfully played along.

"It's so pretty here," little Maimiti offered. Then in an instant they shouted good-bye while running off in the same adventurous spirit in which they had appeared. They were stunning little girls, ten or eleven years old, and both dressed in the customary cloth kilts that fitted quaintly around their tiny waists.

"Aren't they adorable?" Tiare remarked.

"Hmm," I acknowledged while in deep thought.

Tiare's conversation was far away to me during our walk home, and upon realizing this she questioned my preoccupied mood.

"What's the matter, Manu? You're so pensive."

"I don't know," I shrugged. "There's something about that little girl…"

CHAPTER 9

The following five years saw the passing of Matai and his brothers, which saddened an otherwise very happy period of my life.

I grieved a great deal over Matai's death as he had treated me like his own son, and if it wasn't for him my sudden and strange presence in Mahina might not have been accepted. Not only did he afford me special privileges over the years, it was through him that I held a high political and social position in the district.

For a long time Mahina was the center of terrible mourning over the successive deaths of Matai's brothers and eventually the old chief himself, and as in the case of Tetamoa and Heifara, a wake was held for each of them, and every time the death-watch concluded with the Nayneuvas rampaging through the villages maiming and killing anyone who happened in their way.

The chieftaincy of Mahina was inherited by Hitihiti, a relative of Matai. Hitihiti was a tall, jovial man likely somewhere in his fifties. He could also be termed portly, or even fat, depending upon how polite the observer might be. I did not know him terribly well before Matai's death, but shortly after he became chief I spent more time with him in provocative conversation. Surprisingly this man spoke a few words of English, which he told me he learned when Captain Cook came to Tahiti.

My family had also grown during this period with Tiare giving birth to our daughter, Neolani, who like her brother was a beautiful child with the most compelling Indian and Caucasian features. Tommy, meanwhile, had grown into a handsome boy, and like all the children of the islands he loved the water and had become an excellent swimmer.

With Tommy now in his seventh year and Neolani starting to walk, Teura-Kanokoa helped me build an extension to our house so that we could have private sleeping sections for the children and ourselves.

He also helped me re-thatch the roof, as it had probably been five years since I did any work on it, and it would just be a matter of time before the rain seeped through.

During these renovations Tiare had weaved enough cloth to spread new mats over the grass floor, and she also provided new bedding while I took time to fell a tree and shape the trunk into a settee. I carved out the top half of the trunk and filled it with feathers and other padding, and then I covered it with the cloth that Tiare had left over; and Tiare had sewn three sides of measured cloth together and stuffed mounds of feathers into it, then sewn the fourth side closed so that we enjoyed the comfort of pillows at the back of the settee. Despite its irregular proportions, my unusual handiwork was remarkably comfortable and was a novel topic amongst our visitors as the only furniture still to complement any other house was at most a simple stool.

The nights remained romantically mysterious to me. The trade winds blew a cool, inviting breeze, and the coconut palms rustled gently in the background.

One particular night while feeling unusually restless I took a walk down to the lagoon and reflected on the past few years. I had been immensely happy with Tiare and in watching my children grow, but now I began to wonder what was on the other side of that mighty ocean. I wondered if I ventured out whether I would be caught in another time warp and returned to the period from which I came. Then I wondered if I might find myself flung into yet another time zone should I reach one of the continents, and still I wondered if I would remain in the present no matter where I went.

Such intense contemplation inevitably led me to the question of why I had not yet seen the landing of a foreign vessel in all the years I had been here.

Once again I tried to gauge the year in which I was living. I remembered Matai telling me when I had first appeared so mysteriously that he had sailed for a while with Samuel Wallis more than one hundred and fifty moons before my arrival, and knowing that the Englishman had anchored in 1767, I calculated the year now to be around 1787, which accounted for my nine or ten years in Tahiti.

I eventually abandoned my efforts to pinpoint the present year and continued to peer into the ocean as though waiting for it to provide me with the answers.

My thoughts shifted once again to the theories of reincarnation. I mentally traveled back to the vacationing days I spent in Tahiti with Sarah just prior to being flung into my present world. I vividly recalled how the déjà vu sensation and sleep-talking incident had so greatly alarmed me, and again debated whether I had experienced a life before Peter Matthews existed. I could only reach one conclusion – my familiarity with the islands was simply too strong... and there *had* to be a reason why I was brought back to this era.

Darkness had come as I continued to ponder my fate. Sensing deep within me that each soul has a previous life and progresses to a higher level of learning at some point after the death of its body, I wondered why – as with me – a person could not recall key elements of his or her previous existence. I quickly realized the answer when I remembered how terrified I was upon believing that I had conceivably had a previous life – I was on the verge of a mental collapse. I affirmed to my own satisfaction that no person at man's present level of intellectual or psychic development could cope with the trauma of recalling experiences of their own previous incarnations. Perhaps in centuries to come would the mind be developed to the degree where it would be ready to handle such a phenomenon.

I took a great deal of pleasure in my hunting trips with Teura-Kanokoa, and it was while returning from one of our hunts that the most incredible event was to begin. Teura-Kanokoa and I spotted a crowd lining the bay; many of them were waving excitedly. A nervous shiver went through me when I focused my eyes on the faint figure of a ship bearing masts and full rigging. The day had finally come. I felt a combination of emotions... curiosity, excitement, and awe; but most of all I felt fear.

"Well, Manu," Teura-Kanokoa said quite calmly, "our friends have returned; it has been a long time."

"Who are they?" I asked. "Where do they come from?"

"They come from a land beyond the great water," he answered, not meaning to be vague. I asked him what he thought the purpose of their visit might be, hoping to learn more about them, but again Teura-Kanokoa could not produce their identity or purpose.

"They speak in a strange tongue, as you once did, Manu," he said.

I left Teura-Kanokoa and scurried down the hill, paying little attention to the tricky terrain. I stopped and called back to Teura-Kanokoa.

"How long until it reaches the bay?" He waited to catch up to me before answering.

"When the sun returns, I would think."

I lay awake that night wondering what flag the ship was flying. Tiare had sensed my uneasiness even before the vessel was sighted, but she refrained from questioning me, evidently feeling that the time would come when I needed her confidence and comfort.

It was not yet dawn when I lifted myself from my bed and went outside. The air brushed coolly against my body as I walked with apprehension to the edge of the hill and looked out on the sea.

Even with the fishermen's torches lining the beach, the darkness still concealed the ship. I remained at my vantage point anxious for the first hint of light. I found myself hoping that the night had carried the vessel away to distant waters; it seemed a logical posture as I was safe and happy here and did not want to jeopardize my position with the arrival of a foreign vessel. A hand on my shoulder momentarily startled me. Tiare had awakened and followed me to where I sat.

"What is it, Manu?" she asked. "Have they come to fetch

you?" I looked at her faint, innocent outline and cupped her face in my hands. I could no longer contain myself; I broke down and cried. I didn't know why, I just knew I was on the brink of something momentous.

"Manu, it's alright," Tiare consoled, holding me close to her. "You don't have to go away with them… do you?" she suddenly trembled. There was a long silence.

"No, my darling, I don't have to go," I whispered.

I remained on the hill through the night and watched the birth of another day.

The green hills and alluring coastline welcomed the visitors who were approaching the passage between the westerly point of the reef before Point Venus and a large, partially submerged rock which was often used as a landmark.

Dozens of canoes had set out to escort the vessel to her place of anchorage long before she had neared the opening in the reef.

I studied the ship closely. She looked to be about a hundred feet in length, and her heavy hull and short masts gave her the appearance of a whaling vessel. I watched her edge closer, wondering when she would drop anchor; then with a sudden impulse I turned and ran towards Teura-Kanokoa's house.

Rina met me when I arrived and told me that her husband had gone to see the 'big boat'. I immediately turned and ran down the hill to the beach, falling part of the way and scraping patches of skin in my haste. I decided to row out and look at the ship. I had to know who these people were – *now*.

Hundreds of villagers were still lining the beach bursting with excitement as they watched the broad vessel draw closer to the bay. I spotted Teura-Kanokoa among them.

"Teura-Kanokoa!" I called, "come with me! I want to look at the boat!"

"Manu! I came for you at sunrise! Where were you?" he shouted back.

"Never mind," I answered when I reached him, "let's find a canoe."

We took a four-passenger canoe with a fitted sail, which was one of many breached around us.

I heard shouts of *British* when we drew close to the transport. Then I saw the Union Jack flying proudly from her mast. Many of the canoes that had set out earlier were bobbing about empty as the Indians had exuberantly climbed aboard the vessel. I was gripped by the strange and scruffy appearance of the sailors as Teura-Kanokoa maneuvered the canoe to the ship's starboard.

The commotion was overwhelming with endless shouting and laughter. The excitement in me had now risen to breaking point; I was actually nauseous with anticipation.

The vessel's cannons, which were mounted on swiveling blocks, captivated me; and I took particular notice of the ship's stern as we rounded her. While examining the ecclesiastical-like windows, I caught sight of something that staggered me beyond all proportion of definition. I sat paralyzed. Below the windows in the center of the ship's stern was a sign painted in striking bold letters, which read BOUNTY.

It took Teura-Kanokoa a few moments to bring me out of my state of shock. The man could not understand my behavior; while he was ready to climb on board I wanted desperately to return to shore.

"Teura-Kanokoa! I've got to get back! Now!" I shouted at him. Then I started rowing furiously. Teura-Kanokoa's expression was a cross between annoyance and confusion, but rather than sit idle or row towards the *Bounty* he pulled *with* me. We moved past the bobbing canoes that had now engulfed the ship and rode the waves back to shore.

When we reached the sands I left Teura-Kanokoa and ran. I ran for miles. I had to get away from this madness.

I found myself alone in the high ground, far away from sight or sound of life except for the birds or animals nearby in the bush. I was too dazed to think rationally, and I was emotionally and physically exhausted, I had to sleep.

I examined my historical knowledge after waking. I recalled with a jolt that after the mutiny, the *Bounty* returned to Tahiti for supplies before sailing on to her final anchorage at Pitcairn's Island. I also recalled that the *Pandora* took those who remained behind on Tahiti back to England in irons some two years later. It came back to me how the *Pandora*, under Captain Edwards, was commissioned by the Admiralty to bring the mutineers back to England to stand trial. I decided there was only one thing I could do to protect myself – no one of the ship's company could be made aware of my identity; no matter what, I was a native of the island and had never known any other way of life, nor had I ever spoken another language. To explain my fair hair and Caucasian features I would say I was the son of an English seaman, although I was aware of the possibility that my age might raise a question of doubt as it was only about twenty years earlier when the first white man was known to have set foot on Tahiti. But as long as I contemplated my situation this seemed the only safe and feasible explanation for my presence.

I felt somewhat easier once I had decided how to deal with this event. But how in God's name could this be happening? How could life be lived again by these men?

They were long dead before Peter Matthews was born! In an effort to lift the mental strain I considered myself fortunate to be able to witness history in the making, but I was afraid of being involved and wondered if I might inadvertently do something to alter history. I was convinced I had to remain in the background and not attempt to tamper with the course of events – but no one could change what had already happened. Or could one?

I remained in seclusion for several hours, afraid to go back to the village, but I knew sooner or later I had to face the situation, so I started on my way home.

It was already dusk when I focused my eyes on the candlenuts lighting the village. I followed their glow to the hill where my house stood overlooking the ocean.

My sudden appearance startled some of the people as word of my strange flight had quickly spread. Tiare met me when I approached the house.

"Manu! Where have you been? Teura-Kanokoa said you ran off as though you were crazed."

"Tiare, please don't ask me any questions," I responded in a quiet but deliberate voice, "just go and get Teura-Kanokoa and Rina."

"Manu…" she insisted.

"Tiare, *please*, just do it."

I went into the house while Tiare fetched our friends.

The three of them came inside with curiosity lining their faces.

"Manu, why did you run away like that?" Teura-Kanokoa asked.

"Not one man from the English boat must know where I come from. Please don't ask me any questions, just do as I ask and keep my identity from them. As far as they are to know I am from Tahiti; they are to know I was born here and have always lived here, and I have never spoken in another language. Do you understand?" They sensed the urgency of my instructions although they would never know the reasons for my fears.

"How will you explain your fair hair and your other white man's features?" Teura-Kanokoa inquired – a question I anticipated.

"They are to be told I'm the son of an English seaman, but *only* if they ask about me."

"What is all this about, Manu?" Tiare sighed.

"If I could tell you I would, but I cannot explain where it will make any sense to you, so please just do as I ask and trust me, my life may depend upon it."

Tiare, Teura-Kanokoa, and Rina, were understandably baffled over not having an explanation, but being afraid for my safety, they assured me of their cooperation.

I sat outside with Teura-Kanokoa listening to the laughter below where the sailors were letting out their frustrations brought about by so many months at sea. Tiare and Rina, meanwhile, quietly talked in the house trying to determine the connection between the ship and myself.

Before going about my routines the next morning, I made a point of telling Hitihiti and the others who knew me well not to reveal my background to any of the *Bounty's* crew.

The chief had already taken a member of the ship's company into his household, a young midshipman named Peter Heywood, who had been commissioned to write a dictionary of the Tahitian language. I encountered Heywood when I left Hitihiti's house that morning. He seemed to look through me when I walked passed him; perhaps it was due to my native tan and variety of tattoos because I was certain he would pull back at my fair hair and blue eyes. I took in the young man during that brief moment; he was attired in cut-off trousers, or breeches, and wore a dirty white waistcoat and a midshipman's coat complete with tails.

Once I had finished my talk with Hitihiti I kept a distance from the *Bounty's* crew as I could not afford to divulge my knowledge of the English language. Also, I was afraid of being stared at or questioned about the color of my hair and eyes, and other contradicting traits.

I was still overwhelmed at seeing the actual landing of this famous vessel. It was a feeling of awe and apprehension that would not soon leave me.

I found it impossible to completely avoid contact with the Englishmen. When I returned home from my fishing trips or while hunting game I would come across some of the sailors strolling hand in hand with their new mistresses, or they would be gathering the breadfruit plants for their intended transportation to the West Indies.

I thought about what lay ahead for those forty or so men of the Bounty. If they could only know that their journey to the West Indies would never be completed because of the mutinous act of one Fletcher Christian, and if they could only know how that impulsive act by the master's mate would so dramatically affect their lives.

I had not yet looked upon the celebrated Christian, nor had I encountered the ship's captain, Lieutenant William Bligh, whom many historians claimed brought about the famous mutiny himself through cruelty and intimidation. I refrained from any potential meeting with them simply out of fear; I literally trembled at the thought of seeing these men in the flesh. The time came, though, when I realized that I could not prevent the inevitable; but in truth my curiosity was beginning to take the upper hand – I *had* to look upon these two men.

I made a point of attending the next feast that Hitihiti hosted for his visitors. The dining room was the same thatched building in which I spent many pleasant mealtimes with Matai. There were already many of Mahina's more eminent men seated in the house when Teura-Kanokoa and I arrived. While the aroma of roast pork and baked fish teased our palates three uniformed men walked smartly towards us.

"Bligh!" Hitihiti called. "Come! Eat! We have plenty pig!" he said in his broken English.

As the three guests settled down for the meal I recognized Peter Heywood standing outside trying to make himself understood to Vehiatua's niece who was visiting from Tahiti-Iti. My eyes remained fixed on the Englishmen as the servants set the food in front of us. I studied Bligh carefully. He was a stocky man of medium height. His penetrating eyes and firm mouth set a strict countenance. He wore a blue and white-trimmed coat with tails over an ornate waistcoat, and his breeches and stockings were of fine white material. My eyes shifted to one of the men at his side. This kindly looking officer was John Fryer, the ship's Master. His older years seemed to give him something of a drawn appearance. Then I turned to Fletcher Christian. He was a young man in his twenties whose confidence flowed from his handsome but brooding features. Each man, including young Heywood who had since joined the others, had his hair combed all the way to the back of his head and had it neatly tied at the neck with a small ribbon.

In the three weeks since the *Bounty* had dropped anchor no one of the ship's company, including the linguistically talented Heywood, had learned enough words to hold even the slightest conversation with any of the natives. This disadvantage naturally kept them dependent upon Hitihiti's limited English.

"How does your work come, Bligh?" the chief asked.

"Extremely well, thank you; we have found plenty of healthy plants and have many of them potted," Bligh answered very properly.

"Good, Bligh, good," Hitihiti grunted between bites.

The chief's generosity did not come without repayment, however. In exchange for the breadfruit the *Bounty* had brought with her countless tools and trinkets for the people of Mahina.

"I don't know about you, Mr. Fryer, but I think I could remain here forever." Had any of the officers been observant they would have seen me turn knowingly at Fletcher Christian's words.

"Aye, Fletcher, it is a beautiful land," Fryer responded; "heaven knows the men can do with some time to enjoy it."

I learned during the evening that the white man was always welcomed in Tahiti and was looked up to by the Indians. This made me wonder why I was not immediately accepted when I appeared so long ago; I could only speculate that it was because of my unbelievable tale describing my means of travel. I also learned that it was the custom of the natives to take one man as a special friend, or tiao, as Hitihiti had done with Peter Heywood by welcoming him into his home. Yet another interesting discovery was that the Tahitian women adored the white man and willingly gave themselves to him no matter how ugly his features might be. Suddenly I shuddered at what I heard come from Fletcher Christian's lips.

"Look at that fellow over there, opposite," he said, addressing himself to the three other officers. "I'd swear he was an Englishman with that fair hair." I was careful not to react to his comment. I calmly struck up a conversation with Teura-Kanokoa in an attempt to divert any further probing of my background.

"I'd say so," Heywood spoke. "I've passed him by a time or two; do you know his eyes are as blue as the water."

"Curious," I heard Bligh remark, "I've seen Indians with mixed blood before but never quite like him." Fortunately the subject changed when a servant set down a dessert of fresh fruit for the Englishmen to round out their meal.

The four men thanked their host when the evening drew to a close and walked leisurely into the night.

I left the dining room a few minutes later and stood outside thinking over what I had just witnessed. I was relieved at having finally seen these men in person.

I watched from a secure distance as Bligh and Fryer said goodnight to the two younger officers and stepped into the *Bounty's* launch that was waiting to take them back to the ship for the night. As Christian and Heywood turned from their superiors I saw Hitihiti's niece, Maimiti, meet them and take Fletcher Christian's hand. I thought nothing of it at first and watched them walk away, but then it hit me like a thunderbolt… Maimiti was that same little girl whom Tiare and I had met five years earlier at the Tuauru River! That name, I knew I was familiar with it when I first encountered her; she was to become Fletcher Christian's lover! I should have associated her with the eventual arrival of the *Bounty*!

The mental strain brought about by the evening's events left me tired so I started for home. On my way I encountered some of the ship's crew relaxing on the grass with their women while others talked idly amongst themselves.

I perceived the common seamen to be an unclean and unrefined lot. Their attire consisted simply of tattered trousers, a shirt, perhaps a scarf or a cap, and some wore ragged buckled shoes or were barefoot either by choice or chance, and they were all unshaven with an unwashed appearance. My attention suddenly turned to two burly men arguing across the way.

"Damn your blood, Mills! I'll feed your liver to the sharks if you even *look* at my woman!" This man Mills dared the other on then crashed a blow to his jaw that would have laid most men to their rest, but the sailor found his feet and set about evening the score. Within moments several of their shipmates had come rushing over to enjoy the brawl, with many of them quick to make wagers on the outcome. Blood from the combatants' smashed noses and battered mouths stained the grass, and their faces bulged from the brutal fight. The noise from the clash quickly reached Christian and Heywood who came rushing towards them.

"Break it up you bloody half-wits!" the Master's Mate shouted. When they finally pulled them apart Christian barked an order to the men looking on, "Get these damn fools out of here and clean them up!"

CHAPTER 10

Thoughts of the approaching mutiny frequently played on my mind, and although the event was still what I estimated to be three months away, I wondered what might happen if I attempted something to prevent its occurrence. Of course I had no right to attempt such a thing, even though I had the forehand knowledge of both the suffering and anguish that was to come upon the ship's crew and to many of the Tahitian men and women.

If I succeeded in preventing the mutiny I would have actually changed history. It could be done... a knife in Fletcher Christian's back, or in Bligh's, or even both, leaving the ship's command in the capable hands of John Fryer. I even thought of revealing myself to Christian and telling him to refrain from any mutinous acts no matter what the provocation, but if I did this I would be jeopardizing my own safety.

I fought with my dilemma for days. Should I do something or leave the situation alone?

Although I had a feeling of unmatched power, I knew that I had no right to tamper with history. If I managed to prevent the mutiny and the *Bounty* returned to England by way of Jamaica, Fletcher Christian and the mutineers would not have remained with their women and sired their children and their future generations would not be born. I further justified my decision not to interfere with a rather dramatic rationalization… If I prevented the mutiny and caused the *Bounty* to return safely to England, I believed it to be within the realm of possibility that anyone of the would-be mutineers – after his return – might father a child who could one day have a calamitous effect on future lives, whereas if I saw to it that history stayed on course, that theoretical child would never be born.

Perhaps it was true after all that no one could change history. Alter the course of events that lead to the end result – *maybe*, but not change the end result itself. Under no circumstances, then, was I going to attempt any interference. I would just be a spectator.

Two weeks before the *Bounty* set sail on her short-lived voyage to the West Indies an incident occurred which appeared to substantiate my theory that history could not be changed, and for the first time I truly felt there was a purpose behind my journey to this place in time. Three members of the ship's crew had deserted some weeks earlier and when they were finally apprehended, Mr. Bligh set about administering punishment. The ship's company had been assembled on deck to witness the floggings, and having cause to be on board at the time, I saw just how cruel and inhuman this particular punishment was. After Bligh read from the Articles of War with a solemn dignity, each deserter was stripped to the waist and lashed to an upright grating. The sudden overcast sky typified the mood of the moment as the boatswain's mate laid on the cat of nine tails with a determined will. The first blow alone raised a large ugly welt, which seeped blood and left the victim gasping with pain. After each blow the boatswain's mate would run the cat through his fingers to separate the inter-locked strands, and then he would lightly shake the steel-plated strips to further ensure they hung free from each other. I did not recall the number of blows inflicted, but when the sailor was cut down in an unconscious state his back resembled a slab of raw meat and the spot where he was flogged was red with blood and knots of flesh. When the third man was cut down the ship's surgeon came forward and ordered the victims taken below to have their wounds treated.

There was to be an additional punishment of a midshipman named Thomas Hayward who had been on watch the night the three men made their escape. It was young Hayward whom Bligh held responsible for the men's flight, and on account of his perceived inattentiveness to duty, the captain had ordered Hayward to be whipped over a gunwale. Now it was at this time when history was moments away from taking an altogether different course. Hayward's Indian tiao, or friend, was so incensed over the upcoming punishment he managed to steal on board with a concealed pistol. When Hayward was brought trembling before Bligh, thinking he was to be flogged like the common seaman, the midshipman's friend, standing unnoticed behind the ship's company, pulled out the pistol and aimed it at Bligh. As he was about to fire I lunged at him and pushed him to the edge of the deck where the weapon flew from his hands and dropped harmlessly overboard.

Incredibly nobody had seen the Indian come so close to killing the captain.

Bligh was visibly put out by the scuffling and growled at the ship's master.

"Get those scum off of my ship, Mr. Fryer!" The Indian and I were then quickly ushered over the side where we climbed into our canoes and rowed to shore.

I cannot with conviction say if my spontaneous intervention proved that history could not be changed, but it certainly showed that without my presence on the *Bounty* that day Bligh would most likely have been shot and possibly killed and history would have run a completely different course. Simply, Bligh's death or even wounding would have meant no mutiny. Perhaps this was the reason for my journey to this time… to keep history *on* course… to keep the end result from being changed.

I felt it had to be providence that sent me to the home of my soul's previous entity, as I would be naturally adaptable to an already familiar way of life, and would therefore be in a better position to deal with any subtle forces that might inhibit the necessary course of events.

After almost six months on the island it was now two days before the *Bounty* was to set sail, and as a token of friendship many of the natives sent gifts to the ship for their tiaos.

That afternoon while in the company of Hitihiti and Peter Heywood I gained some insight of the mood on board when Heywood remarked that Bligh was confiscating all gifts for the ship's stores and the Crown. This caused a great deal of resentment amongst the crew, especially since it was suspected that the captain was keeping a good supply of food and other items for himself.

"Why doesn't he let the men keep what's been given to them?" I asked Heywood.

"Captain Bligh has an exceptional knowledge of the sea; he is a master of navigation, but his sentiment toward his fellow man leaves something to be desired," the midshipman replied in very good Tahitian.

With the aft section of the ship laden with hundreds of potted breadfruit plants, Bligh sent word that the *Bounty* would set sail the next day and ordered all officers and men to return to the ship my nightfall.

It was touching to see the sadness in Maimiti's eyes as she clung to her lover. The little girl whom Tiare and I met long ago at the Tuauru River had grown into a beautiful young woman. Christian himself had a worn look about him, likely the result of his despondency over leaving Maimiti and the thought of having to endure several more months at sea under Bligh's biting command.

Hundreds lined the beach the following morning to watch the *Bounty* set her sails and stand ready to enter the Pacific.

It was a quiet farewell with many feeling empty now that the Englishmen were on their way, but if I was correct it would be just a few weeks until His Majesty's Ship returned to these same shores… only with Fletcher Christian in command.

I was bursting to share my knowledge of the *Bounty's* eventual return and tell the story of the mutiny that was to shortly occur, so after some deliberation I decided it was safe to tell Tiare, Teura-Kanokoa, and Rina that the ship was going to come back, only without Bligh and those loyal to him – who would be set adrift in the ship's launch. As I expected, they wanted to know how I had knowledge of this.

"Please don't ask me," I said, "I told you when the ship arrived that I could never explain things in a way you would understand. Just believe me, the ship will come back. And remember, this is never to be told to anyone, not even Hitihiti."

Tiare questioned me again as we lay in bed that night.

"Manu, how can you know they will return? How can you tell the future?" Still not wanting to attempt what would be a fruitless explanation I touched my finger to her lips and kissed her. From that moment the subject was dropped.

As I professed, the *Bounty* returned to Matavai Bay five or six weeks later. Though they had been told with my fullest conviction, Tiare, Teura-Kanokoa, and Rina were nevertheless amazed at seeing my words come true.

A story was quickly spread that Bligh had joined Captain Cook at Aitutaki where he found it necessary to send Christian back to Tahiti for more supplies. My only conclusion for this fable was that because the Indians were firm believers in discipline, the Englishmen were afraid they would be denied the provisions they needed if the Indians knew that Christian and his men had overthrown their captain.

Once the supplies were on board Christian set off in search of an island that was isolated enough and where chance of capture would be extremely remote.

Tiare and Rina were no longer curious about my forehand knowledge of the *Bounty's* activities, but it was not so with Teura-Kanokoa.

"If you say Christian took the ship and set Bligh adrift in the launch," he said, "why did Christian say that Bligh and his men stay in Aitutaki?" I told him the real reason behind Christian's story, and also told him that the *Bounty* would return to Tahiti yet one more time through being unable to find a suitable island on which to settle.

"Some of the Englishmen will remain here," I said, "and others will sail on with their women and some of the men of our village." Teura-Kanokoa stared at me for a long time.

"Who are you, Manu?" he finally said. "Where do you come from?" I smiled at his dramatic questions and put my arm around his broad shoulders.

"Never mind that," I said, "just remember, my friend, this is between us and nobody else, alright?" He gave me a disconcerted look upon my polite rebuff. It was beyond him how I could see into the future with such pinpoint accuracy, but being the true friend he was, he never pushed me for further explanations, nor did he ever break his pledge to keep my confidence.

I kept busy during the following months by building a sturdy double-hulled canoe with Teura-Kanokoa. Hunting was especially enjoyable for me in this period now that Tommy was old enough to come along. Although he was only eight years old he loved the adventure of the hunt and was becoming a fine shot with his diminutive bow and arrows.

It had been at least three months since the second departure of the *Bounty*. I kept a watchful eye for the ship, as I believed it could be any day when we would again see her re-enter the bay. After such a long absence Teura-Kanokoa teased me about the vessel failing to return, but the *Bounty* was sighted exactly a day after his sporting remarks.

Just as I had told Teura-Kanokoa, a few of the English-men set up homes in Tahiti. Peter Heywood was one of them; he had returned to live in Hitihiti's house. I knew from my historical readings that Heywood was not involved with the mutiny but was forced to remain with the *Bounty* for lack of room in the ship's launch.

I did not know which of the other men took part in the seizure of the *Bounty*, but I did know that about a year after their return to the island, all of these men would be apprehended by the frigate, *Pandora*, and be transported back to England in irons to stand trial for mutiny.

I thought of what could happen to me when the *Pandora* arrived. I became alarmed at the possibility of being arrested as a mutinous member of the *Bounty's* crew. Although I was a deep brown and bore several tattoos, it was not impossible to tell that I was a full-blooded white man.

I theorized that if past events could not be changed – or rather the final outcome itself could not be changed – my presence on the island could not impede the scripted events, meaning I would be left alone by the *Pandora's* men. But then I realized the obvious… *the course of events leading to the end result could be altered*, therefore, it *was* possible for me to be arrested and taken back to England in irons – all without any of my involvement affecting the end result of the *Pandora's* mission.

I pondered the matter for days. I took long walks and thought deeply over what I should do when the *Pandora* landed.

There was no doubt in my mind that it was possible for me to be taken by the *Pandora*. My arrest would not alter the end result of the frigate's mission, but it *could* end in my death at sea – when the *Pandora* sunk near the Endeavour Straits, as history told it; or if I reached England with the survivors of the shipwreck there was no telling what fate might be in store for a mutineer, as no doubt I would be labeled such. It was clear what had to be done. I had to leave

Tahiti before the *Pandora* arrived and return after she left with her prisoners. I could not risk being on the island while the pursuit ship was here.

The following weeks saw the Englishmen build their homes and take a great deal of pride in cultivating their gardens. After coming to know Heywood quite well during this period I wanted to warn him of the *Pandora's* eventual arrival, but I knew I should not attempt to directly interfere. Spontaneous or unplanned involvement was entirely a different matter, however, as with my intervention in the assassination attempt on Bligh; but in the case of Heywood and his shipmates, I had to let history stay its course.

I was not surprised when Heywood eventually asked me about my background. When I kept to my story of being the son of an English seaman and a Tahitian woman he gave me a doubting look. I learned later from Hitihiti that Heywood had also asked *him* about me, but the chief honored his word and assured the midshipman that what I had told him was indeed the truth.

MICHAEL BRIAN BRUSSIN

CHAPTER 11

In the fifteen months that passed since the Englishmen returned to Tahiti, Heywood had married Vehiatua's niece and had gone to live with her in Tahiti-Iti, as his new wife, Tehani, wanted to remain close to her aged uncle. Some of the other men had also taken wives and appeared perfectly happy at the thought of spending the rest of their lives in Tahiti, and they showed no evidence of concern over the prospect of pursuit by His Majesty's Navy.

I estimated that it would be about three more months before the *Pandora's* sighting, so I began thinking about my getaway from Tahiti. I decided to find an island in the Tuamotu Archipelago, as I was certain that the *Pandora* did not call at the Tuamotus either heading to or departing from Tahiti.

I intended to stay away for as long as six months, which I knew was more than sufficient time to see the arrival and departure of the frigate.

The only person to know my destination was Teura-Kanokoa, whom I had asked to accompany me on my self-imposed exile. I was afraid if it was known to anyone else, even Tiare, it could lead to the *Pandora's* men learning of a white man who sailed to the Tuamotus just before their arrival, which in turn could result in them giving me chase.

As I expected, Tiare could not accept my decision to leave her and the children for such a long time, at least not without a logical explanation, so I reminded her of the *Pandora* coming to take the *Bounty's* men back to England, and because I, too, was white, they would try to take me with them. She accepted this reasoning, but returned to her previous annoyed curiosity over how I had prior knowledge of these events.

Although I had told Tiare before we were married that I came to Tahiti from the future, much as I had told Matai, and even though she said she believed me, I knew she never even remotely understood the context of my other world; but with my strange predictions of the *Bounty's* activities coming true she became more supportive over the necessity of my leaving, however, her frustrations flared further when I refused to tell her *where* I was going.

The day before my departure for the Tuamotus I decided to take Tommy on a wild boar hunt as it was going to be a long time before I would see my son again. Teura-Kanokoa and I armed ourselves with a spear while Tommy walked proudly alongside sporting his own special bow and quiver of arrows.

It wasn't long before we heard some rustling in the brush. Teura-Kanokoa and I raised our weapons, and Tommy seeing us stand ready lifted an arrow from his quiver. Moments later a boar emerged from the bushes. Teura-Kanokoa was quick to heave his spear into the animal's shoulders. The boar bellowed long and loud as it shook its body in a frantic effort to rid itself of the barbed projectile. Seeing the plight of the beast and sensing his first kill, Tommy approached with his bow fitted with an arrow. I watched helplessly as the wounded animal charged at Tommy just as he let fly his arrow.

"Tommy! Get out of the way!" I shouted, and ran towards my son only to see him fall in his haste to get away. To my horror I watched the animal tear savagely into Tommy's leg leaving the little warrior screaming in pain.

Oblivious to the danger, I charged the boar and repeatedly thrust my spear into it until it fell dead.

I was cradling my unconscious son when Teura-Kanokoa reached me.

"Get him home quickly, Manu; his wound is bad," Teura-Kanokoa said. A mound of flesh had been ripped out of Tommy's thigh, and the deep blood-soaked cavity told me that my son's life was in the balance.

Still in a state of shock, I ran with Tommy back to the village. Startled onlookers whispered amongst themselves at what they saw, and Tiare threw her hands over her face and sobbed when she saw me approach with her son draped over my arms. This was the only display of emotion I saw from Tiare. From that moment she calmly nursed Tommy day and night, and she said little other than whisper prayers and soft words of encouragement to her motionless child. Even our little daughter, Neolani, stood over her brother sensing he was gravely ill.

Another day went by as I watched Tiare tenderly dab the fever from Tommy's forehead.

"He grows weaker, Manu." Her voice was muted. I had never felt so helpless in my life. There was my son dying before me and I was powerless to prevent it.

Sympathizing villagers offered prayers for Tommy's recovery, but it was at this time I found myself wishing for the technology of twenty-first century medicine to save his life.

"There must be *something* we can do to save him," I said to Tiare. She showed no expression at my imploring words but touched her hand to my cheek and left.

Tiare returned to the house with a strange woman. The woman was very thin and very old; she had stringy gray hair dangling below her shoulders, and she carried with her a variety of herbs wrapped in tapa cloth.

"You must do something for him or he will be dead before the sun returns," Tiare said to her. The woman lifted the bandage from the wound and muttered some unintelligible words, and then she carefully warmed the bag of herbs over a small fire, which she had asked me to build. When the herbs were sufficiently warmed she placed the bag in the cavity where the flesh had been ripped from the thigh.

"Leave the bag on his leg tonight," she instructed. She then gave Tiare a second piece of cloth containing more herbs and told her to warm them in the morning and replace the first bag with the new one. The mysterious old woman then prayed over our son and shuffled from the house.

I awoke at sunrise to the smell of the herbs interacting with the infection in Tommy's leg.

"How is he?" I asked Tiare, who had not moved from our boy's side.

"The wound is closing," she answered, again with no expression, but this time with a suggestion of hope in her voice. I raised the bag and saw she was right; it was as though the finest layer of skin – membrane-like – was forming over the once gaping bloodstained hole.

Another day went by and the thigh, from the build up of infection, had taken on an immense shape. It was at this stage that the old woman was summoned back. She immediately knew what to do; she took a knife from me and after heating it over a flame, lanced the infected area and let the pus flow from the leg.

It was obvious to me that the wound had to be stitched if Tommy was to avoid a gross deformity, indeed if his leg or even his life could still be saved. While the old woman cleaned the area I meticulously stripped the thinnest pieces of thread from excess tapa cloth and prepared to stitch the gaping cavity with it. Tiare and the old woman watched in amazement as I pierced the sagging skin with a needle I made from fine but sturdy fish bone and painstakingly closed the wound.

Tiare and I were watching over our son during the critical hours that followed when Teura-Kanokoa came bursting into the house.

"Manu! Come quickly! The big boat has returned! The Englishmen are here!" I charged outside with Teura-Kanokoa and stood at the edge of the hill squinting into the morning sun. I set my eyes on a ship with full sails approaching Matavai Bay. It was the *Pandora*! Tommy's injury had caused me to lose all concept of time and forget about the pursuit ship's impending arrival.

I had no time to lose. The ship was fast approaching the westerly point of the reef where she would enter the bay. In disbelief I continued to watch history once again unfold before me.

"They've come for the Englishmen," I said to Teura-Kanokoa. "We've got to leave before they come ashore or they'll take me back with them."

Teura-Kanokoa and I immediately ran for the boathouses and hastily began loading food and water onto the double-hulled canoe that we had built. We worked fast, storing the necessary supplies while anxiously watching the ship draw nearer.

When we were finished I found Hitihiti and asked that he not mention me to the crew of the *Pandora*. Although he did not know the reason, the curious chief gave his word not to divulge my existence to the foreigners.

Then came the moment I had to say farewell to Tiare, Neolani, and Tommy… whom I had to leave not knowing whether he would live or die. It was a bitter ordeal as I held my son in my arms possibly for the last time. Tiare looked at me with tears in her eyes. She knew I'd be in danger if I remained on the island, but would still never understand why.

Teura-Kanokoa and I left the stillness of the lagoon and rolled over the waves. We passed the frigate just as she began her approach into the bay. My appearance to the English sailors from the distance between our two vessels could not reveal even a hint of my race, but I still watched tensely, partially concealed, as the *Pandora* inched closer to shore. I had made my escape, but just barely.

CHAPTER 12

My decision to escape to the Tuamotu Archipelago, a succession of atolls and islets some five hundred miles east of Tahiti, was supported by the assumption that if I held out within the Society Islands I would be dangerously close to the outer boundaries of the *Pandora's* search.

I had originally reasoned that if the *Pandora* went around the treacherous Horn it would be unlikely that she would come close enough to the Tuamotus to warrant stopping at one of the islands, and if she went around the Cape of Good Hope I would be completely safe from capture, as the hunters would not even pass the Tuamotus. These calculations obviously meant nothing now that the frigate had already arrived; still, my holdout on one of the Tuamotu islands was sure to keep me well hidden from the *Pandora* during her pursuit of the mutineers, and in the course of her journey homeward if she tested the waters of Cape Horn.

Our twenty-five foot vessel consisted of a pair of hulls joined together to form the double canoe. Each end of the boat supported a sturdy mast and sail, and a ladder was lashed to each mast for use in adjusting the rigging. The depth amidship was four feet, and the canopy fixed above afforded us good shelter.

Fair winds and a calm sea carried us to the first island in the Tuamotu chain at the end of the second week. Mehetia was a large, well-populated island with soft white beaches and lofty mountains. I initially thought this would be an adequate sanctuary, but soon felt uncomfortably close to Tahiti when I sensed it just possible that the *Pandora* might come this far in her search for the mutineers, or might even stop here for reasons unknown on her return journey. I could not take any chances so I told Teura-Kanokoa that we had to set off deeper into the network of islands.

The next five days took us deep into the Tuamotus where we finally settled on a small island called Aki Aki, which was no more than five miles in circumference.

The inhabitants of this tiny island made us very welcome when we breached our canoe. We told them we wanted to remain for three full moons, which was more than enough time to see the *Pandora* several hundred miles out of Tahiti before we set our return course for Matavai Bay.

The people of Aki Aki allowed us all the timber we needed to build a hut for our stay. The custom of some of the men saw them offer us their wives for our pleasure. While I declined this extension of their hospitality, Teura-Kanokoa was only too pleased to accept.

I counted the days by carving notches on a tree near the hut. The thought of waiting almost ninety days before starting homeward gave me cause to consider staying for only half the time, but again I had to let logic dictate my actions, not emotions, so I resolved to remain the full term in case we found the *Pandora* still anchored if we returned sooner. Even my anxiety over Tommy could not let me risk leaving the island prematurely.

I spent the early days fishing with the men of Aki Aki, and also took time to sail to some of the close-in islands, but no matter what I did the days passed slowly. My thoughts were constantly on Tiare and the children, and I agonized over Tommy, not knowing if he was even alive. The only other thoughts to go through my mind were of the *Pandora's* pursuit of the *Bounty* mutineers. Although I had seen history in the making, indeed repeat itself, I never ceased to be amazed at the unfolding of these events. Even as I lay dozing under the distant Tuamotu skies, I envisioned the *Pandora* anchored in Matavai Bay with the mutineers held in irons in the ship's damp and fetid brig. Without a doubt I resolved that I would have been among them had I not left.

During our stay on Aki Aki I saw little of Teura-Kanokoa. While he had settled with a sensuous young woman, I fell into a state of idleness, spending more of my time each day at the hut wrapped in thought.

"Manu! We have to leave! *Today!*" an animated Teura-Kanokoa surprised me early one morning.

"Why? What's wrong?"

"It's my woman, she expects to become my wife!" he responded, sounding extremely put out and amazed at the whole thing. I burst out laughing at hearing this.

"We can't leave for another ten days, you'll just have to marry her," I said looking very serious.

"Manu, this is no time for jokes! She's an important person; she'll have her family after me!"

"You *are* serious, aren't you? What did you tell her to make her think she's going to be your wife?"

"I thought she had a husband and none of this would matter, but she is unattached and has the impression that we will be married... don't ask me how – let's just get the boat loaded and go home!"

Confident that the *Pandora* was now a safe distance from Tahiti although the full three months had not quite elapsed, Teura-Kanokoa and I stored enough supplies on the boat to take us back to Mehetia, and with nothing said to the people of Aki Aki, we set off on our westerly course.

Teura-Kanokoa and I added to our supplies on Mehetia, and after an overnight stay we set our final course for home.

Excitement filled me when we sighted Tahiti's familiar peaks. Thoughts of being reunited with my family danced through my mind. I visualized Tommy and Neolani leaping into my arms, and I could see Tiare's loving smile welcoming me home.

I was suddenly jolted from my daydream by an unusual change in the boat's movement. When I looked up I was astonished to see a strange, glowing aura shimmering on the water... and it was pulling us into it at an alarming speed. I immediately recognized it as the portal that had sent me tumbling back to the eighteenth century ten years earlier.

"Manu! What *is* that?" Teura-Kanokoa said. I didn't answer him, I just sat mesmerized. "Manu! It's pulling us!" I found myself now having to make the most important decision of my life... whether to return to Tiare and my children or let our boat enter the portal and tempt the fate of time.

"Manu! Help me!" Teura-Kanokoa shouted as he desperately rowed against the aura's pull. I was greatly tempted to let the boat enter the turbulent waters inside the aura, but I couldn't be sure if the portal would return me to the period when the Hirondelle sunk – or if the mysterious colors would carry me to yet another pocket of time.

Teura-Kanokoa was still rowing hard against the force of the aura and cursing me at the same time for not pulling with him.

My instinctive desire to let the boat cross the aura's perimeter in the hope that it would return me to Peter Matthews' time was quickly constrained when I realized that it meant losing Tiare, my children, and the life I had grown to love. I was also quick to realize the possibility that I could even be thrown into an unfamiliar period if I entered this doorway.

"Manu! If you don't row we're done for!" Teura-Kanokoa shouted. But it was too late – when I took up my oar the boat was already at the edge of the shimmering circle.

"Take the rudder!" I shouted over the noise of the thrashing waves within the aura. Teura-Kanokoa dropped his oar and gave the rudder a full turn. It was too late – we were pulled across the colored rings. "It's no good! Let the rudder go and help me row!" While we were thrown about by the raging waters within the aura, the sea outside remained eerily calm. "Pull!" I shouted. "For God sake, *pull!*" Teura-Kanokoa struggled to reach his oar, then in an agonizing moment when the boat reeled sharply, his foot became entangled in the ladder that was lashed to the mast, and as the vessel rocked again Teura-Kanokoa lost his balance and was flung overboard. "Teura-Kanokoa!" I screamed. "Hold on! I'll get you! I'll get you!" But it was no use, he was gone. My closest friend was swept to his death.

The waves continued to batter the boat until I found myself at the edge of the aura. I seized this opportunity to break through the rim and row to a safe distance. I circled the aura still hoping to find Teura-Kanokoa, then the rings began to fade and the waters within them became calm, so I rowed to the heart of the area that had consumed my battle-field comrade but there was no sign of him.

There was nothing more I could do but sail the last few miles to shore. The loss of Teura-Kanokoa had left me devastated, but then I thought it possible he could make his way to shore as he was the strongest of swimmers; although I knew better, no one could have survived those violent waters.

I continued to ponder the possibilities as I sat with my hand on the tiller. It then occurred to me that Teura-Kanokoa could have been thrown somewhere into another time by the aura, just as I had been. If he were, at least he would have a chance of survival in another world; but as Tahiti's shoreline became visible I snapped myself upright, alarmed at what suddenly went through my mind… Teura-Kanokoa and I were *both* in the aura when he went overboard. It was at that moment I realized and dreaded it may have been *me* who was flung somewhere into time.

I was gripped with anticipation as the boat glided over the final wave and breached itself on a desolate and unfamiliar shore. I leapt out of the vessel and ran directly towards the rise. The turmoil of the aura had caused an error in my navigation as I had obviously missed Matavai Bay, but I knew with equal certainty that I had reached Tahiti. As I scaled the hill I wondered if I was still Manu or was once again Peter Matthews.

The hill's incline and piercing foliage had left me drained and badly scratched by the time I reached the top. Perspiration dripped from my forehead as I crouched panting with my hands on my knees. After a brief rest I set off in the direction of some houses I had spotted. I scanned the area for a paved road, this time hoping not to find one. Suddenly there was a hand on my shoulder and I froze, afraid to turn around.

CHAPTER 13

I let out a huge sigh of relief when our eyes met.

"*Manu*, where did *you* come from?" Tiare's father said, greeting me with a firm two-handed grip on my shoulders.

A feeling of profound disappointment came over Jack Matthews when he read that the hand on Manu's shoulder belonged to Tiare's father. Jack had hoped, even expected that the aura had returned his son to the present.

Jack had been so engrossed in the manuscript that he found himself believing Peter's story without reservation. When he realized this he sifted through the pages and shook his head in a show of admonition for letting himself even consider for a moment the possibilities of the manuscript's contents being authentic.

"Time travel. The *Bounty*. Reincarnation. It's bloody

ridiculous," he said to himself. But the discoloration and brittleness of the manuscript again stood out, and he once more found himself open to the prospect that it *could* be over two hundred years old.

To ease his torment and remove any element of doubt over the age of the document Jack decided to have one of its frayed pages dated. After making some inquiries he located a company in London that was equipped to do the analysis.

Jack left the page with a member of the laboratory's staff then stopped for a beer before driving home.

He found a pub filled with businessmen enjoying their after work drinks and politely pushed his way to the bar. Jack was anxious to talk to Heinrich Werner once the psychiatrist had read the manuscript, but he had yet to send him a copy. Jack drank his pint thoughtfully while scanning some travel posters on the pub's walls. When he focused his eyes on a framed print advertising Canada he thumped his fist on the bar as though he had just found the solution to a puzzle. He then emptied his glass and strode out.

Heinrich Werner muttered under his breath when the telephone woke him.

"Hallo," he mumbled.

"Dr. Werner, this is Jack Matthews, I talked to you yesterday about my son, Peter."

"Who?"

"Jack Matthews, I'm calling from England… about my son – he drowned in Tahiti…"

"Ah, yes, Peter… his diary, I remember. I am sorry, it is two o'clock in the morning here…"

"Oh, my goodness, please forgive me, I didn't think," Jack apologized. "Dr. Werner, I'm booked on a flight to Vancouver tomorrow; I'd like to meet you and talk to you about my son's disappearance, can you meet with me?"

"Yes, or course," Werner agreed; "just call me when you get in and we can make the arrangements."

"Splendid; I'll look forward to it… and I'm terribly sorry for waking you."

After retrieving his passport and packing a suitcase Jack settled back to read more of Peter's manuscript…

"Midori! Thank heaven it's you! How is Tommy? Is he…"

"Your son is alive, Manu," he smiled, "but he carries a great scar and limps badly. He has spirit, though, and he will get stronger." I was momentarily overcome by the news and wiped the tears filling my eyes.

I followed Midori still not knowing where I was.

"Where is Teura-Kanokoa?" he asked, sadly reminding me of his loss.

"We encountered sudden turbulent waters a few miles from shore; Teura-Kanokoa was thrown overboard." Midori was stunned over the loss of one of Mahina's most important citizens and questioned me at length on the incident.

"He will be painfully missed, especially with the Pomare situation growing worse."

"Midori, where are we? Why are they looking at us like that?" I asked when we passed a group of men who appeared to be watching us with a great deal of caution.

"You don't know where we are? How did you get here?"

"I lost my bearing in that strange storm," I explained.

"This is Pare; you should be familiar with it."

"*Pare, of course,*" I realized after looking around more deliberately.

We presently stopped at an isolated house that was being guarded by two men with spears. I recognized the warriors as our own men of Mahina and wondered why they were guarding a house in another province.

"What's going on here? What are you doing so far from Mahina?" Midori moved between the two sentries and stood at the entrance of the house.

"Come inside," he said, pulling the hanging cloth aside. The mystery began to unfold when I followed him into the house. Sitting cross-legged before me was Hitihiti.

My unexpected appearance was warmly received by the chief. I learned from him and Midori that during the months I was away, Mahina had become embroiled in a growing power struggle with its neighboring province, Pare, the stake being political dominance of Tahiti.

The Pomares, who controlled the district of Pare, were growing rapidly in strength and it had become evident that this powerful family was forcing Tahiti's political control away from Mahina.

The elder Pomare, after retiring to Moorea, appointed his brother, Vaetua, chief of the heavily populated district of Ha'apaino'o, which was another indication of their increasing strength, and he also made Vaetua guardian of his son, Otoo, who resided in Pare.

"What are you doing in Pare if there is such friction between us and the Pomares?" I asked Hitihiti.

"We called for this meeting with Vaetua when Pomare appointed him chief of Ha'apaino'o. We want his word that he will not attempt to expand the holdings of the Pomares. Vaetua may have been appointed chief of Ha'apaino'o but the people still oppose him. We do not want Pomare-backed armies imposing their rule on other districts," the chief summarized.

"How has the meeting gone?" I asked.

"Not good," Midori responded. "He told us we have no right to intrude in his political affairs. He said it was a matter of time before *all* of Tahiti would come under Pomare rule, and he went as far as to warn us that it would be better for Mahina to acquiesce *now* to their order." I was troubled over what I had heard and asked if there was to be another meeting with Vaetua.

"It would serve no purpose," Hitihiti said. "We will return to Mahina shortly. All we can do is keep ourselves strong and maintain a constant watch on Vaetua's movements."

I left with Hitihiti and his party for the bay and the chief's waiting vessel. We walked amid distrusting stares from the people of Pare. They were well aware of the increasing tension between Vaetua and Hitihiti, and they sensed the ever-present danger of a conflict between their province and Mahina.

"My daughter has been watching for your boat since the last full moon, Manu," Midori said when we set sail. I smiled at his words and mentally urged the men at the oars to pull harder when I thought of holding Tiare in my arms once more.

"You were right, Manu, the English boat came and the men took their white brothers away with them," Midori told me. "*Would* they have taken you had you not left?"

"I'm certain of it," I said, watching the coastline parallel our course.

"How did you know they would come for these men?"

"Let's just say I'm a prophet," I joked.

"I don't suppose I'll ever understand you, Manu," Midori then said shaking his head with a smile.

"That's just what Teura-Kanokoa would say," I answered, remembering my lost friend.

Hitihiti's vessel was instantly recognized when it entered Matavai Bay and was escorted to shore by several canoes. Word quickly spread that I had returned with the chief and I was given a hearty welcome upon landing.

News of my return had also reached Tiare, and while I stood on the beach talking with those who had met me I saw her approaching with Tommy and Neolani at her side. My heart beat faster when I pushed through the crowd. Tommy favored his injured leg as he limped alongside Tiare, and little Neolani had to occasionally go into a trot to keep up with her mother. Tiare's hair flowed behind her when she ran up to me, and within a few moments my life was again complete when we stood in a long embrace.

The flickering candlenuts shed a romantic light on Tiare as we sat cozily in our house that evening. She raised her head from my shoulder when Tommy and Neolani came in.

"Metua tane, when can we hunt again?" Tommy asked.

"Soon," I said, putting my arm around his shoulders. "How's that leg? Is it strong enough yet?"

"*Oh yes,*" my son assured me, "I can even run now."

"Manu, I don't want him hunting again," an alarmed Tiare reacted. "You have been back not even one day and you already want to take him on another hunt; have you forgotten how close to death he came last time?" I ran my hand over Tommy's recessed, scarred thigh.

"If our son doesn't face another stalking boar he will grow up weak. When a warrior is wounded he recovers and fights another day. If he will not go into battle again he becomes a jellyfish, not a warrior. We cannot shelter our son from life; we must *prepare* him for life."

"I know," Tiare conceded, "but at least let him get stronger before you take him again."

"Of course I will, I'm not going to take him *tomorrow*," I emphasized with a patronizing smile. "And you, my little soldier, keep exercising that leg," I instructed with a fatherly pat on his behind.

It was just a few days after Hitihiti's discouraging meeting with Vaetua that grim news was received by Mahina's leaders. Pomare had defiantly proclaimed his son, Otoo, as supreme sovereign of the islands of Huahine and Raiatea, and Vaetua, acting on behalf of Pomare, had ordered Hitihiti to accept Otoo as ruler of all Tahiti as Mahina was now the only province remaining that openly opposed the Pomare regime.

Hitihiti called a meeting with Mahina's elders directly after a messenger from the Pare camp delivered Vaetua's demands. The majority of the council members strongly opposed submission to the Pomare family, but there were those who did not want to risk a war with the stronger district of Pare or any other Pomare-backed province and voted to accept the powerful family as rulers of all Tahiti.

If Hitihiti capitulated it would be likely that Vaetua himself would govern Mahina until Pomare's twelve year old son, Otoo, became mature enough to take control of Tahiti and the outer islands.

"Have you all gone soft?" an angry Midori said, turning to the three or four elders who elected to bow to Vaetua. "Do you want this Pomare puppet to come here – to Mahina – and swallow up our freedom? Do you want to see him force Hitihiti from our core and decimate our lives?" Our chief looked gravely at Midori and the opposing elders.

"What chance do we have if we defy him?" one of the

dissenters said, "Vaetua will combine an army from the other provinces and wipe us out. We won't know what hit us. Even the great Vehiatua who fought with us on the shores of Tetiaroa has laid down Tahiti-Iti to Pomare."

Resenting the invasion of our right to self-rule I opposed Vaetua's ultimatum.

"We may have a fight on our hands if we resist Vaetua, but if we don't take a stand against this tyranny we can be certain of a life of oppression."

"He will walk all over us, Manu!" another of the elders stressed.

"Not if we walk over him first," Midori interjected.

"What do you mean?" Hitihiti asked, already sensing the answer.

Midori got to his feet and addressed the group, which was seated attentively on the matted floor of Hitihiti's house.

"I say we attack Pare," he proposed in a soft but deliberate voice. "We can strike before the sun rises when they are sleeping and unprepared. If we disable Vaetua it will take Pomare a long time before he can again be in a position to challenge for total control of Tahiti. If anything, it will give us the opportunity to force Pomare to the bargaining table where we can demand a divided government."

"What right do we have to attack another district?" one of the opposing council members argued.

"*What right?*" A furious Midori reacted. "*What right!* If we agree to Vaetua's demands we lose our autonomy, and if we send his messenger back with a rejection he will attack us! We're backed into a corner and you ask what right we have to attack? The only way out is to fight our way out!"

"Manu?" a troubled Hitihiti said turning to me.

"I don't want a war, but if we don't do something now

to weaken Vaetua's hold on Tahiti, or rather Pomare's, we will all share a painful future. It's not as though we would be the aggressor if we strike Pare; Vaetua has in reality declared war on us by delivering this ultimatum. Remember, we do have something in our favor… we're strong enough to inflict a great deal of damage on Pare and Vaetua by using the element of surprise."

"I wish we could hear Teura-Kanokoa's words," Hitihiti remarked.

"I know what he would say," I responded.

"How long will it take to prepare for the march on Pare?" Hitihiti then asked.

"We can be ready in two days," I answered, with Midori nodding in agreement.

"No!" one of the dissenters exclaimed getting to his feet. "We've had enough war! Let's live in peace, even if it means under Pomare!"

Suddenly there was a commotion outside. When I went to investigate I saw our warriors beating Vaetua's messenger.

"Stop! What are you doing?" I shouted.

"They ambushed us, Manu!" one of the warriors answered.

"Who?"

"Vaetua's people – they killed two of our men – they ambushed us while we were hunting – inside our own borders!"

"Let him up!" I ordered as I separated the enraged men from the bloodied courier; "he's of no use to us dead!"

The disturbance had caused the council members to follow me outside.

"Vaetua's men killed two of our hunters… within Mahina's borders," I repeated to Hitihiti.

"Keep him confined until we decide what to do with him," the chief directed, motioning to the messenger. "It is time to plan our strategy," he said, resigning himself to the necessity of a campaign.

Murmurs passed between the council members when they filed back into the house.

"So it shall be. Manu and Midori – see to it our warriors are prepared to march in two days," Hitihiti ordered.

"What about the messenger?" one of the elders asked.

"Kill him!" Midori barked in retaliation for the murder of our two hunters.

"No, wait," I intervened, "we can use him to our advantage. Send him back to Vaetua with word that we want to talk. Let him tell Vaetua that Hitihiti will come to Pare to negotiate terms."

"What will that accomplish?" one of the dissenters asked.

"It will give Vaetua a false sense of security," I said; "he'll believe we're willing to accept Otoo as ruler – he'll *never* suspect an attack." There was some deliberation over the idea before Hitihiti gave his approval.

"It is a good plan, Manu," the chief said, "but we must be sure the messenger does not discover our motives."

Hitihiti himself told the messenger that he would arrive in Pare in three days to meet with Vaetua, and with this welcome information the courier set off on the four hour run back to his province.

The distribution of arms was efficiently carried out in the darkness in case Vaetua had spies watching our movements. Midori and I were to spearhead the attack, which called for our army to rush Pare's villages before sunrise.

Five hundred men armed with spears, knives, and

torches set out for Pare before midnight. The sight of this legion marching quietly in the darkness created a foreboding atmosphere.

When we neared Pare's border I dispatched a party to run ahead and disable the outlying sentries.

Intermittent sounds of a night bird carried towards us. It was the signal from the frontrunners telling us that they had overpowered the guards. I then motioned the warriors to encircle the first village, using two flanks to close the circle.

It was certain that those who were not sleeping would see the light from our torches flickering closer to their homes, or would hear the rustling of leaves under our feet as we closed in.

People began to stir, sensing that something was wrong, but before they could react I gave the order to charge. Savage screams and war whoops rang out as the warriors swarmed through the unprepared village, putting their torches to the houses and mercilessly cutting down everyone in their wake.

The people of Pare were so defenseless we were able to run through the villages burning and killing at will.

The sad cruelty of war had left people cremated in their homes as they slept, and it saw them – men, women, and children – brutally beaten as they tried desperately to run for safety.

After leading the initial thrust I left the battle area and watched the onslaught with Midori from a nearby sector.

An uneasiness came over me as our army moved deeper into the province, leaving behind more death and destruction. I sensed that Pare's outer villages would be able to assemble a force strong enough to counterattack when they saw the rising smoke and heard the cries.

"We've done enough, Midori! Now let's get out of here!" I said. "Get word to circle back and run for home!" My command took Midori by surprise.

"Why? We have them! We can destroy them!" he exclaimed.

"No we can't! We've wiped out half of Pare, but there are villages ahead of us that are untouched; they'll be ready to fight before we get much further. We've got to turn around *now*!" Midori weighed the possibilities before finally conceding.

"You're right," he agreed; then he called for runners to spread the order to return to Mahina with all speed.

There was no indication of a counterattack developing as we sped homeward surveying the trail of bloodshed and ruin, but when we reached the safety of Mahina the district was put on full alert in the event of an assault by Vaetua's forces.

Late the following afternoon, with our army lining Mahina's borders, a group of men carrying a symbol of truce were escorted into our province. The men were from Pare, and with them was Vaetua himself. I approached the party and stopped directly in front of Vaetua.

"What is your business?" I said to Pomare's brother.

"Let me speak with Hitihiti," Vaetua responded with equal disdain. The group was held where they stood while I went to fetch the chief.

A conference with Vaetua ensued when I returned with Hitihiti. The outcome of the meeting was a peace settlement. Pare had suffered such extensive losses in the raid, Vaetua, speaking with Pomare's approval, had decided that it would be in their best interests to cease hostilities and end the expansion of Pomare's holdings.

Life returned to normal once the conflict was formally ended, but it was nevertheless an uneasy peace as there remained a great deal of distrust between the two sides.

CHAPTER 14

Not long after the treaty with Pare, two more English ships entered Matavai Bay. As I lay beside Tiare the night of their approach, I recalled how afraid I was during the landing of the *Bounty*, but now the sight of a ship did not disturb me, as I believed from an historical relevance I would no longer be in danger.

Sunrise saw the vessels already at anchor, but no one had yet come ashore. There were probably a hundred canoes drifting about the ships when Tommy and I rowed out for a close look.

HMS *Providence* and HMS *Assistant* were the vessels commissioned by His Majesty's Navy. We drifted alongside the two giants for some time before a longboat was lowered from each ship. Moments later a party of officers and men climbed into the boats for the short pull to shore.

"For God sake!" I let out, of all things in English, which

turned more than one head from the longboats. It was Bligh! He had come back! I couldn't believe my eyes but there he was, proud as you please.

"What is it, father?" Tommy asked with concern in his eyes. "They *are* our friends, aren't they?"

Once again I tested my historical knowledge while following the longboats to shore. I recalled that Bligh did indeed return to Tahiti, on a second mission to secure breadfruit plants for transportation to the West Indies.

The crews were enthusiastically received, and again Hitihiti entertained Bligh and his officers with a lavish feast.

My sudden outburst upon seeing Bligh climb into the longboat was fortunately forgotten by those who had heard it, and I continued to move about inconspicuously, except of course for some initial looks that came my way on account of my Caucasian features.

As the days passed I sensed the captain was no less harsh with his crew than when he commanded the *Bounty*. The men spent long hours gathering and cultivating the breadfruit plants, and they were allowed little time to enjoy the pleasures that the island had to offer.

There was a distinct uneasiness amongst the people of Mahina during Bligh's stay. Even though we were at peace with Pare and the Pomares, it was felt that renewed fighting would break out once the Englishmen left.

Other than Pomare, Hitihiti was the next most influential man in the Society Islands, and being so troubled over the continuing growth of the Pomare followers, and the likelihood of defeat if fighting broke out again, Hitihiti confided in me that he intended to ask Bligh to take word back to King George petitioning on his behalf that Tahiti be made part of the British Empire. The chief's intention stunned me; I could not accept the fact that he was willing to relinquish Tahiti to a foreign power.

"Are you mad!" I exclaimed, forgetting for a moment to whom I was speaking.

"We have to be realistic, Manu," Hitihiti said, "we will never withstand the combined forces of Pomare's followers. He is eventually going to put together an army that will wipe us out if we don't accept Otoo as absolute ruler, and if we *do* accept him life will be insufferable for all of us in Mahina; at least we will be protected with the British here."

"Surely it's better to have total freedom," I argued, "freedom from the Pomares *and* the British. Do you *really* think we will be free under the British? Once you submit to anyone – especially a foreign power – you will never be free; we will be better off fighting the Pomares. And besides, before the British can get here in any measure we may have to fight them anyway."

I was deeply troubled over Hitihiti's design for British rule, and my frustration and anger remained evident. How I knew that Bligh, or any other officer of the king's navy for that matter, would leap at the very opportunity of carrying such news back to the Admiralty.

As the days passed with more breadfruit plants being potted and loaded onto the *Providence* and *Assistant*, and with time drawing nearer for the ships' departure, I asked Hitihiti if he had yet spoken to Captain Bligh on the issue of British occupation.

"I shall do so before he sails," he said with impatience in his voice, still well aware of my opposition. Clearly not wanting another debate, the chief strode away leaving me to watch the sailors carefully picking and potting the plants.

I went after him nevertheless, visualizing a British flotilla arriving to raise the Union Jack over Tahiti and her sister islands.

"Hitihiti, have you considered it just possible that Pomare will *not* take control of Mahina? Why bring the British here?" I appealed when I caught up to him. Hitihiti stopped dead and gave me a long, provoked look.

"Manu, you know well enough that Pomare will eventually control Mahina and *all* of Tahiti; the British will be our only protection from that man's tyranny, now leave me and do not take up the matter with me again." I had stretched the chief to the limit of his tolerance and found myself with no choice but to mind his warning.

Just prior to Hitihiti speaking with Bligh, an incident occurred which gave the captain cause to gather the ship's company on shore to witness punishment of two men who had made the indiscretion of napping under the midday sun instead of gathering breadfruit plants. It was at this time I again witnessed the brutality of flogging. I glanced at Hitihiti as he watched the boatswain's mate strip each man to the waist then tie his wrists and wrap his arms around a tree, and I studied him when the cat of nine tails tore into the first man's back and ripped away bits of bloodied flesh.

"Look well at the Englishman's punishment, Hitihiti," I said as the first sailor gasped in pain and cursed Bligh under his breath.

"I think a dozen more, Mr. Morrison," Bligh said to the boatswain's mate; "by heaven, I will not be cursed by *any* man!"

The chief looked soberly into my eyes before walking away. He was clearly disturbed by what he saw.

The sight of the white man's punishment coupled with

my earlier warnings led Hitihiti to more carefully weigh the potential effects of his decision, and this ultimately convinced him of the dangers of inviting British occupation.

I believed that my success in dissuading Hitihiti was crucial in maintaining Tahiti's political and cultural development, which would ensure eventual French possession in the early nineteen hundreds. Here, then, was a second example of me keeping history on course since having prevented Bligh's assassination when he commanded the *Bounty*.

The day came when *Providence* and *Assistant* raised anchor. After watching the vessels sail from Matavai Bay I reflected upon the fifteen years I had been a part of this society. Our recent success in the conflict with Pare led to what I believed would be the beginning of a long period of peace. I looked back upon the day I awoke in my new world, so frightened and confused. I recalled the traumatic execution I carried out on my would-be assassin all those years ago; I remembered my growing love for Tiare, and our wedding; the war with Tetiaroa; and I fondly thought of the births of Tommy and Neolani. I relived the arrival of the *Bounty* and my escape to the Tuamotus, and I again brooded over the loss of Teura-Kanokoa.

With all my memories there were two events that played on my mind... the assassination attempt on Bligh, and of course the most recent incident of near-British colonization. I marveled again at how, in preventing the killing of Bligh, I had kept history on course by assuring the mutiny took place, which in turn assured that the future generations of the English sailors and their Indian women would be born.

My actions which prevented Hitihiti from yielding Tahiti to the British also made me examine the effect of my involvement. I was certain I had kept Tahiti and her outer islands from becoming British possessions, which would have gone completely against the course of history.

The mental impact of knowing what I had done made me think all the more of *why* I was thrown back to this period. The question was not difficult for me to answer… I believed it was to do exactly those two things. I also saw in retrospect that Peter Matthews was a reincarnate of a Tahitian warrior, which I further believed was a necessary link to my preordained journey back in time. These realizations, and the recollections of so many other events over the years, found me wanting to document my life from the day I awoke as a stranger in Mahina.

I thought how I might get hold of the materials necessary for this autobiography. The only source seemed to be from the officers of a foreign vessel, from whom I could bargain paper, quills, and ink. I had no choice but to wait for this opportunity, whether it took a month, a year, or several years. I could not recall which vessel would next arrive or the year it would come, and there were no means at my disposal to undertake the project except perhaps the possible use of liquids from the burned candlenuts which could provide the ink, and feathers from the man-of-war bird which might be used as quills. But I had no access to paper and no matter how hard I thought there was nothing I could use that was comparable.

Frustrated over the inability to record my story, I chose to spend frequent periods with Tiare's father catching fish and game for Mahina's storehouses. After another day at sea with our pahi laden with fish, Midori and I steered for home. As we turned the canoe towards the familiar opening in the reef a bright shimmering light appeared just before the opening and about ten boat lengths from us; and to my astonishment, within the glowing rings were three men being carried towards the reef. It was the aura… still bearing the same brilliant colors.

"Manu, what *is* that?" Midori said as the turbulence inside the rings carried the men closer to the reef.

"It's the aura!" I answered; "remember – you pulled me from it when *I* appeared!" Midori quickly recalled the event and became instantly afraid of its power, while *my* impulse was to try to rescue the men. But Midori wanted nothing to do with it or any attempt in rescuing the strangers, and remembering the fury of this phenomenon on my return from the Tuamotus with the doomed Teura-Kanokoa, I elected to put up my oar with Midori and watch the men ride the swirling waters to the reef. But as the glowing band touched the reef the men and the aura went rapidly faint, then all three disappeared from sight and the water that had been encircled by the rings just as quickly became calm.

"What happened, Manu?" Midori gasped, "where did they go?" I sat in awe with my arms resting on my legs, wondering who those men were, where they were from, and where they went.

"I don't know," I finally answered. "I don't know."

I told Tiare about the aura returning and of the men inside it. She still didn't really understand the implications of the aura, even though it had brought me into her world and her life, and also had taken Teura-Kanokoa from his. Midori, too, talked to others about the aura's appearance, and this time about people being inside it, but surprisingly it did not raise a level of interest and the subject was as soon forgotten.

As the days passed I could not get the aura out of my mind, especially after seeing three men inside it. Who *were* those men? What *happened* to them? I was unable to put it behind me; even with the woman I loved and the children I cherished, my emotions rose from within… I had to encounter the aura once more and find my way back to the twenty-first century; or, if a ship bound for England or the European continent should first appear, then Peter Matthews had to take passage in search of the aura and his destiny.

"How can you leave me, Manu? And Tommy and Neolani? How *can* you?" Tiare pleaded when I told her of my need and decision to go out in search of the world from which I came. I tried my best to explain that after again seeing the aura I had a rising obsession for my own time… Peter Matthews' time.

"Then take me and the children with you, Manu, *please!*"

"Tiare, *my love*, it's just not possible. First of all, I don't know when or where I'll see the aura again, or if I ever *will*, and I don't know when another ship will come; maybe I'll be too old to leave the next time another ship comes." Tiare begged, still not understanding. "Tiare, it won't work, you'll never settle in my world, you won't understand it, you'll be lost; alone."

"Not if we are with you, Manu!"

"Tiare, it's no use," I said, moving to put my arms around her, but she stepped away, too hurt and with a growing anger. I went outside, leaving her to herself and me to my own questioning thoughts.

I peered into the sunset, watching the reflection on the water. I wondered if tomorrow would truly carry me to the life I believed I wanted back.

"Hello, daddy," Neolani greeted me, taking hold of my hand in the fading light. I looked into her loving, dependent eyes and smiled. I stroked her flowing hair and walked with her into the house.

"Did you tell your children?" Tiare said as she lit the candlenuts.

"No, I will…"

"Tell us what, daddy?" my daughter said. She was so much like her mother; soft and beautiful, with that touch of innocence.

"Where's Tommy?" I asked. Neither knew, so I said that I would tell them tomorrow, together. But Neolani insisted, sensing something was wrong. At that moment my son came into the house.

"*Now* you can tell them," Tiare said.

"Tell us *what?*" Neolani again insisted.

I sat them down and explained my intention of venturing out, doing my best to let them understand my need, more so for the elder Tommy to accept what I had to do.

After thinking over all I had said Tommy placed his hand on my shoulder. But Tiare's and Neolani's heartache was evident, especially Neolani's; she could not handle the thought of her father going away and never coming back. Unlike Tiare, she could not be angry or resentful, she could only cry and seek comfort from her mother. Tommy, on the other hand understood, knowing my background was not native but was indeed mysterious.

In supporting my decision to leave, Tommy asked me to take him along when the time came. As much as I wanted to have him with me I couldn't take him away from his mother and sister, even though he was approaching adulthood.

Weeks passed with me constantly watching for the aura. Finally, after two full moons and still no sighting, I took stock of myself. I contemplated the years I had been on the island, my family, my social standing, and the forty-two years I had lived. Not that I considered myself old by any means, I questioned whether it might be too late for me to undertake what could become a long and dangerous search for my twenty-first century comforts.

With the lack of results, the strain between Tiare and I went away. We didn't think or speak of the aura, or of my possible passage on a calling vessel; we had unassumingly slipped back into our tender and happy ways.

Just as I had decided to undo my foolhardy plan, HMS *Assistant* unexpectedly returned to Matavai Bay. There was now no question that I would take this opportunity to sail to England and hope to encounter the aura on the way.

After making myself known to some of the crew I learned that most of the breadfruit plants the vessel was carrying were destroyed by a sailor who had gone berserk, and under Captain Bligh, commanding from the *Providence*, *Assistant* was ordered back to gather more plants before following her sister ship to the West Indies.

" 'e went complete aht of 'is mind 'e did," one of the scruffy sailors told me. "Near tossed the lot overboard; went barmy 'e did. 'e'll spend the rest of '*is* time in irons till we gets back 'ome 'e will." A second sailor kept staring at me while his mate explained the ship's return.

" 'ere, 'oo are you?" the other asked.

"It was a wreck – a long time ago." I kept my explanation short and simple; the sailor sensed I was not in the mood to take any questions and thought better than to probe further. "How long will you be here?" I asked.

"That's up to the cap'n," the first one answered, "but 'e's told us it 'as to be quick like." By 'quick' I guessed it would be just as long as it would take to gather and pot as many plants necessary to replace the lost ones, probably with the crew laboring from sunrise to sunset.

Soon after leaving the two seamen I encountered the ship's master, and after introducing myself I was told he expected the captain to raise anchor within seventy-two hours. I fielded some questions about myself then told him I wanted to earn passage back to England.

"I can't say we don't need extra hands, Matthews, but that's not up to me."

"Then who *is* it up to?"

"Cap'n Forsythe."

"Can you take me to him?" The officer thought about it for a moment.

"The cap'n'll be on shore this evening; you can meet him then."

"Thank you, Mr…"

"Sims, John Sims."

The *Assistant's* officers rowed ashore late that afternoon where they would dine with Hitihiti. I found Mr. Sims and motioned him to me. I asked him if he knew yet when the ship would sail. He still believed within seventy-two hours.

"Can you introduce me to Captain Forsythe now?"

"Alright; come with me."

The voice of Peter Matthews asked Captain Forsythe for permission to sign on and earn passage as a member of the crew. His initial surprise upon hearing my fluent English beneath a brown skin and a measure of tattoos left him with enough uncertainty to refuse me status, believing I might be a fugitive or rogue rather than an innocent shipwreck survivor of years before. But with the need for additional hands he overlooked his doubts.

"Come aboard before nightfall tomorrow and see Mr.

Sims; sign your name and we shall bind the bargain," he said, appearing to see me in a more favorable light.

After watching the captain's longboat sail back to the *Assistant* that night I went home racked over leaving Tiare and the children. I tormented myself saying if I really loved Tiare I wouldn't leave, but again with resolve and rationalization – at which I was now so accomplished – I saw how necessary it was that I seek out the time and place of Peter Matthews.

Tiare and I sat under the stars. I put my arm around her and she rested her head on my shoulder.

"I know you're going to leave, Manu," she said, "I cannot stop you." I felt my emotions being twisted with the realization that I may never see her, Tommy, and Neolani again, and I wrestled once more with the gravity of my decision. But still the feelings of Peter Matthews overpowered those of Manu and I prepared to leave my family and Tahiti the following day as Able Seaman Matthews of HMS *Assistant*.

Tiare and I shared a last, loving night. We lay together refreshed by a cool breeze on our bodies.

"If I don't find the aura by the time I reach England I promise I'll come back and never leave you again, I promise, I just…"

"Manu, don't make promises you cannot keep," Tiare stopped me; "do what you must do, I try to understand you, I try…" She turned away from my embrace and began to cry.

CHAPTER 15

With a torn heart I stole away from Tiare and my children the following afternoon. The crew had just finished transporting the remainder of the breadfruit plants to the ship and left them to the gardener and his helpers for storing. The captain, meanwhile, had sent word that they would sail on the morning tide and had ordered the officers and men to be on board by nightfall. When I entered the launch that afternoon for the pull to His Majesty's transport, I was no longer Manu, but had become Peter Matthews.

The *Assistant* measured a hundred feet in length and had a beam of perhaps twenty-five feet. The captain's cabin stood aft, overwhelming two smaller ones situated on either side of the ladderway; these diminished cabins were assigned to the ship's master and master's mate.

I found Mr. Sims on the quarterdeck.

"Ah, Matthews, good; come with me, I'll show you

your berth." He then turned towards the ladderway and I followed. "For some reason Cap'n Forsythe has put you with the midshipmen. That'll please your messmates – Johnny Newcomer getting the preferential."

We passed the seamen's quarters, which was enormously cramped with wooden benches and stools and slung hammocks. The heat and smell in this dim and dismal bay was ghastly, and this was under normal conditions. I began to wonder whether I should abandon this escapade as I now questioned my ability to survive several months at sea under such conditions, and for what… the faint hope of encountering the aura, which, if found, may not even return me to the time from which I came. But I had signed my name and was now bound to His Majesty's Navy for the journey to the West Indies and onwards to England. If I had a change of mind and jumped ship would Forsythe come after me? I continued to follow Sims, thinking…

The midshipmen's quarters were merely a screened-off space on the lower deck on the portside, parallel to the main hatch. The dimensions were barely more than a hundred feet square, and myself and three midshipmen were to make this home when we weren't working. But compared to the seamen's bay it was luxurious, it was clean and fresh in comparison. I could manage it, as long as I wasn't later relegated to the other place, although I was anxious that the young midshipmen would not be resentful over having to share their already inadequate space with this 'Johnny Newcomer'.

I had brought enough material with me that I could use for bedding, and I could also make large strips into a new mantle or possibly a shirt.

After stowing the cloth Sims took me to meet the midshipmen. The captain had already told the future officers of my presence so I was politely received by the young gentlemen even though I was of seaman class; perhaps it was due to my older years or authoritative look. After the introductions Sims directed me to again follow him.

"You can meet your messmates now," he said. I stepped along smartly but with a good deal of apprehension this time as I knew the common seaman was often an uncouth and rowdy type and could be downright violent at the turn of a hat. I had to show confidence.

"Slater!" Sims barked, "Come over here!"

"Right, Mr. Sims," the scruffy bare foot sailor obeyed with a quick touch of his forelock.

"This is Matthews, he's signed on to Spithead; take care you show him the way." The ship's master then turned and left.

The boatswain's pipe called all hands just before daybreak; it was time to hoist the sails and raise anchor. The stars were still bright when I labored on deck. Captain Forsythe stood on the quarterdeck with Mr. Sims and the master's mate, Edward Clements. The captain gave Sims the order to loose the topsails. With topsails filled and the yards braced, *Assistant* lifted anchor and made way under a gentle south sea breeze. I stood by the bulwarks alongside my berth mates – Messrs. Thomas Brown, Daniel Goodwin, and Lester Bottomly. All three were likely in their mid or late teens with Brown and Goodwin the more athletic in appearance over Bottomly's studious and rather clumsy bearing.

As the sun rose in another cloudless sky I looked back at Matavai Bay and the hill that housed and protected my family. I felt choked and ever regretful over this decision to leave. What if I didn't find the aura? And what if I did? Where would it take me? My regrets and questions didn't matter; it was too late; *Assistant* set a pace like a racehorse, speeding into the open sea with her topgallants fast set.

I don't know what it was that set me apart from the other men, but by berthing with the midshipmen, and now finding myself standing by them instead of amongst the seamen, I overheard Captain Forsythe instruct Mr. Sims to see that I undertook a midshipman's duties.

"You will assign Mr. Matthews to one of the watches, and he is to keep order when the men are aloft or at the braces, and he will see that all hammocks are stowed at the start of the day."

"Captain, this man is not a midshipman, sir, we need his hands…"

"Mr. Sims, you will kindly do as I ask. I shall find some additional duties for him presently; I believe he is an educated man."

"Yes, sir," the master reluctantly obeyed, I suspect feeling resentful over my growing favor with the captain.

As I was now officially tasked with midshipmen duties my time was most spent with Brown, Goodwin, and Bottomly. I did look the odd one out, though, being about twenty-five years their senior and dressed as a common salt, largely contrasting their natty attire.

The four of us managed to swing our hammocks each night in the ten foot by ten quarters. Being of class or junior officer rank the midshipmen, fortunately including myself, were brought our mess by a young seaman named Mick Scholes. Unbeknownst to me the midshipmen had paid Scholes upon leaving England for his services, which also included the stowing of our hammocks in the mornings. Happily, the young men forgave my situation when I offered my regrets over having no money to share in their expenses.

They even appeared to welcome me all the more into their shipboard and social activities; I think again it was because of my maturity and self-assuredness.

On the morning of the second day Captain Forsythe sent young Scholes to bid me dine with him that evening. No longer having the comfort and luxury of the cool streams in which to bathe, I took care to freshen myself as best I could. I tucked my mantle into the seaman's trousers I'd bartered before coming on board, and having no shoes I wrapped some bark cloth around my feet and tied it firm with individual strips above my ankles.

Captain Forsythe's quarters were astern on the lower deck, and as dusk was settling I made my way to join the commander. I presented a sorry sight in my ugly orange and brown striped trousers and poor substitution for shoes.

I found Mr. Sims, the master's mate Mr. Clements, and Midshipman Brown already at the table with the captain.

"Come in, Matthews, sit ye down," the captain said. The table was set with salt beef and cabbage, cheese, bread, and mashed peas. There was also plenty of red wine that the captain urged us to take pointing at two open bottles. The cabin was furnished with a settee, a desk fixed to the floor, and a table also fixed to the floor, which was our dining table, and there were several shelves with books which were secured against the ship's rocking by end-to-end straps. There was also a pair of cutlasses mounted on the wall, and I counted at least a half a dozen lamps hanging overhead, of which any number could be lit to brighten the cabin.

Captain Forsythe was a seasoned officer of about forty years of age. He was tall and of slender build, and was somewhat thin-lipped which unfairly presented a perceived meanness at first glance. At least this was how I initially judged him when asking for working passage to England, but I quickly discovered otherwise and saw in him a depth of goodness. Sims, on the other hand, had a bullying way about him; I doubt he was any younger than Forsythe, and after so many years he was still unable to obtain a lieutenant's rank and seemed destined to leave the navy as a ship's master. The master's mate, Mr. Clements, in contrast to Sims was a man of about twenty-five and soft spoken, but with a confidence and strength about him that would suggest a fairly quick progression to the rank of captain.

Even knowing I were to enjoy midshipmen duties, I was nevertheless surprised at being invited to dine with the captain; something had certainly impressed him about me.

"Mr. Matthews, if you are to be a midshipman, albeit rather an old one," Captain Forsythe said with a touch of humor in his voice, "you must at least dress a little better. I know... you have no other attire," he went on, holding up his hand to stop me from explaining my lack of fashion. "Mr. Clements, please see that Mr. Matthews is better fitted with shirt, breeches, and some shoes and stockings – I trust we can find some shoes for him?"

"Yes, sir," the master's mate responded. I offered a humble 'thank you' to the captain while feeling a biting stare from Mr. Sims.

"So, Mr. Sims," the captain said while still chewing on some salt beef, "tell me about my young midshipmen, are they performing their duties as well as they did en route from Spithead?"

"Yes sir, indeed they are sir, especially this young gentleman here," Sims said, nodding at Thomas Brown sitting next to me.

"That is good; they show me fine progress in their navigation and trigonometry studies." It was usual for the captain to teach navigation and nautical astronomy, and sometimes trigonometry himself to the midshipmen if a schoolmaster was not assigned to the ship, as was the case with Captain Forsythe and my berth mates.

"I *would* say, however cap'n, that Mr. Bottomly is not quite satisfactory in *his* duties, sir," Sims added.

"Oh, and why not sir?" inquired the captain. Brown looked with concern at Sims.

"He's clumsy, sir, he can't get anything right; he's a doss-pot."

"I'm sorry to hear this, Mr. Sims," Captain Forsythe said; "he's a first class student and will one day make a first class navigator."

"Captain Forsythe," I stepped in, "Lester Bottomly is a little uncoordinated but he tries hard and wants to do well at his duties; what he needs is some encouragement and perhaps someone to work with him; his physical development and coordination will come, I'm sure."

"Well spoken, Mr. Matthews. Mr. Sims, you will work with Midshipman Bottomly. I expect him to succeed."

"Very well, sir, but I can't say it'll do much good."

"Mr. Sims," the captain responded a little impatiently this time, "if Mr. Bottomly does not succeed, *you* do not succeed, do you understand?"

"Yes sir," came Sims' acknowledgement, seemingly a little surprised by the captain's caution.

The captain finished his plate by wiping the mashed peas with a piece of bread and popping it into his mouth. He then turned to me.

"Mr. Matthews, I believe you understand that you will be assigned to Mr. Clement's watch; you will maintain order when the men are aloft or at the braces, and you will see that all hammocks are properly stowed each morning. I will also have you work with Mr. Brown, our gardener. You *have* met Mr. Brown?"

"Yes, captain."

"Good. You will do his bidding and make certain our cargo is properly cared for; we cannot afford another catastrophe that brought us back to Tahiti. I dare say Mr. Bligh would have me at the wrong end of a yardarm if something else goes awry; you wouldn't want that, would you, gentlemen? I see you giving it some thought, Mr. Sims; why I do believe you might enjoy such a spectacle," he laughed, staring at Sims' flushed face.

The following morning while Brown, Goodwin, Bottomly and I were making ourselves ready for duty, Mick Scholes came in with our beverage. He put four cups of a hot, bitter smelling coffee on one of the chests then went about stowing our hammocks. Heaven knows how he found room to move about with all of us squeezed in so tightly.

"Good morning, Scholes," Brown greeted him.

"Mornin', sir."

After a brief silence Scholes spoke with a bit of nervousness in his voice; it was as though he was afraid he might get into trouble for telling us what was on his mind.

"I 'ope you gentlemen don't mind me sayin', but that Mr. Sims don't 'alf 'ave it in for you, Mr. Bottomly, sir."

"What do you mean, Scholes?" I asked as Bottomly listened with some concern, characteristically pushing his drooping spectacles back into place with a forefinger.

"I dunno sir, I just 'eard 'im tellin' Mr. Clements that 'e was gonna make 'im – that's you, Mr. Bottomly sir – that 'e was gonna make 'im wish 'e'd never as much seen a ship afore in 'is life, sir."

"And what did Mr. Clements say?" I asked.

"Nuffin' sir; nuffin' 'cept that e'd best leave off 'im."

"Okay, Mick," I said, "you'll let us know anything else that Mr. Sims might have to say about Midshipman Bottomly, won't you?" There was a pause. "Don't worry, Mick," I added, "I'll make sure nothing happens to you."

"Right, sir, Mr. Matthews," Scholes brightened as he left us.

"*O – K?*" Goodwin quizzed. I realized the expression was new to them.

"*All right,*" I clarified.

"O – K!" Bottomly confirmed with a laugh, ending the bit of levity.

Goodwin then became angered.

"Why should Sims have it in for Lester anyway? Bottoms?" he said, turning to the scholarly youth.

"Don't look at *me*, Goodwin," he said. "Just because I can't climb aloft as quickly as the others, or bend canvas, or reef or furl a sail – *blast*, I don't know."

"Don't worry, Bottoms," Brown said, "you'll be alright; you should have heard Mr. Matthews here stand up for you at the captain's table last night when Sims had a go at you *then*."

"You mean he complained about me then as well?" Bottomly asked.

"Yes, but Mr. Matthews put him in his place, and Captain Forsythe even complemented you on your navigation and trigonometry. You don't have to climb any mastheads when you know *that*," Brown finished.

Mick Scholes found me later that morning working with the gardener, William Brown, watering the breadfruit plants. The young dark green plants had been placed in large pots and they stood thick and healthy in their racks along the port and starboard sides. Many of the plants had to be placed in the master's mate's cabin for lack of space on the ship, which necessitated Mr. Clements moving in with the ship's adverse master. There may well have been a thousand potted plants in all on the transport, making it resemble some kind of botanical garden. William Brown, I recalled as he meticulously sprinkled water on the plants, had been assigned to the *Bounty* on its fateful voyage under Captain Bligh. I was curious to ask the gardener about the events of the mutiny but chose to leave the past alone, as it were.

"'Scuse me, Mr. Matthews," Scholes said, "compliments of Mr. Clements." He then handed me some clothes, which consisted of a more presentable pair of trousers, black in color and flared at the bottom, a white frilled shirt, and luckily what looked to be a good fitting pair of shoes. Also, for appearance and comfort my wardrobe included a pair of long, pale stockings. I then excused myself to Mr. Brown and returned to the midshipmen's quarters to outfit myself.

Now handsomely dressed, with buckled shoes and all, I returned to work with Gardener Brown. But I stopped briefly and looked out into the vast Pacific. The ship swayed gently on course, cutting through a fine fresh wind. I had been so engrossed in the events at sea I had lost sight of my intent... to look out for the aura. I scanned the ocean, wishing for the phenomenon to appear. But the longer I looked the more futile I realized my endeavor; and, oh how I now wished I was home with Tiare and my children.

"Mr. Matthews!" a voice bellowed from the quarterdeck. "Do you think you are holiday-making?" The voice came from Sims. "I believe you are assigned to Mr. Brown, are you not! I'll be bound if I don't report you to the captain! Don't let me see you lounging again or I'll have the end of a rope against your backside I will!" My blood boiled at Sims' viciousness and cowardly way, but I had to take heed; all I was left to do was shoot a look of contempt at the ship's master and smartly make my way back to Mr. Brown.

Later that night while Goodwin was on watch, Brown and Bottomly were passing the time playing a card game called Ablewhackets, which was popular among midshipmen. I didn't know the rules except that if a player called a card incorrectly his opponents called out 'Watch!', whereupon the defaulting player had to extend his hand for each of the other players to whack with a sock filled with sand. If the losing player swore or cried out in pain, there was another shout of 'Watch!' and another round of hand whacking. As luck would have it poor Bottomly called the wrong card, and when Brown whacked his hand exceptionally hard Bottomly screamed, "Ow! Damn you Brown!" Then he ran outside gripping his stinging hand, but slammed straight into Sims who was walking by.

"You little twerp! What do you think you're about?"

"I'm sorry, Mr. Sims, we were just having a game of Ablewhackets and Brown…"

"I think a night on the masthead should straighten you out – keeping the ship awake all night!" Brown dared not say anything to Sims about his treatment of Bottomly but I protested, even though I, too, was of lesser rank.

"For God sake, Sims, he didn't do any harm – he was playing a lousy game!"

"Mind you don't go too far Matthews or I'll have you up there with him, don't you think I won't! You can toady all you like up to the cap'n, it won't do you no good!"

"Mr. Sims," I tried in a more reasonable tone, "it's a very cold night, he'll freeze, let me go in his place." Sims seemed to contemplate my offer when Brown jumped in.

"No, Mr. Matthews, let Bottoms go up, it's the only way he'll get the confidence." Brown was right. I stepped aside and let Sims have his way with the unfortunate lad.

Brown and I followed Sims and Bottomly to the mast. Bottomly's leg shook nervously as he placed his foot in the bottom rung of the rope ladder, and his hands shook as much when they gripped the sides.

"Go on, up with you!" Sims ordered.

"Go on, Lester," I coaxed, "you'll be alright, go on, easy does it; you'll be climbing it like a monkey before you know it." Bottomly settled down and the shaking went away. He made it halfway with Brown urging him on. Finally he reached the top, and after a triumphant shout to us he crouched down and prepared to spend a long, cold night.

Brown and I left Bottomly to his misery and Sims to his brutish satisfaction. We went directly back to our quarters and poured ourselves a generous measure of rum.

Goodwin was relieved of his watch at midnight and returned to the midshipmen's quarters. His flickering lantern woke me.

"It's a *perisher* out there, I'm afraid ol' Bottomly's going to freeze his bottom *off*," Goodwin said, setting out his hammock.

"Sims had no call to send him up," Brown said, also awakened by Goodwin's arrival.

No sooner had Goodwin snuffed out the light and climbed into his hammock when there was a blood-curdling scream that lasted several seconds, then a loud, cracking thud. The three of us charged outside along with the entire ship's company to the sight of Lester Bottomly's broken body.

Captain Forsythe pushed his way through the crowd to reach the midshipman. Sims and Clements had reached the body before anyone else; they stood stunned alongside Goodwin, Brown, and me.

"I gather Mr. Bottomly was relegated to the masthead tonight?" the captain asked. There was a silence before Sims spoke.

"I sent him up, sir. He deserved the punishment."

"And why was he being punished, Mr. Sims?" was the captain's next question. Sims became agitated.

"He was making a devil of a ruckus, sir… Ablewhackets – he was keeping the ship…"

"You sent him to the masthead for playing Ablewhackets!" Forsythe blew, not letting Sims finish his explanation. There was total silence; only the slight whistle of the wind could be heard under the stars. One could almost feel Sims' stomach turn where he stood.

"*Well!*" screamed the captain.

"Sir, he was keeping the ship awake with his pranks…" Sims struggled.

"Then why is it he did not awaken *me*?" the captain screamed yet again, now even more red-faced. "Sims, you've had it in for that young man since we left Spithead! Is it because he was so weak and helpless that you picked on him? You are a *bully*, sir, and a coward! Well, now you've *killed* him!" The captain was now out of control, shaking with rage; it was all he could do not to attack Sims.

"Captain Forsythe, sir, I didn't mean any harm to come to Mr. Bottomly… his behavior was not becoming of a junior officer and I saw it my duty…"

"Mr. Clements," Forsythe cut him off, "see to it that the

former ship's master is made comfortable in the brig. By God, Sims, you'll pay for this. This poor wretch is only the nephew of Sir Joseph Banks!"

I knew that name as well did the others; he was the president of the Royal Society, and a companion of Captain Wallis and Captain Cook. It was Sir Joseph Banks who was instrumental in commissioning many of the south sea expeditionary voyages under Captain Cook and other celebrated naval officers.

"Mr. Clements," the captain continued, "you will take over Mr. Sims' duties; Mr. Matthews, you will assume the duties of master's mate."

The new ship's master motioned to the boatswain's mate to take Sims in charge, and smartly obeying the order the boatswain's mate slapped the man next to him and both men escorted a defeated Sims to the confines of the brig.

"Poor old Bottoms," Brown said, "he didn't deserve this; he never hurt a fly. God, he didn't deserve this."

"I hope Sims gets what due him," Goodwin added.

"I think he will, gentlemen," I said, my first spoken words as *Assistant's* number three officer.

CHAPTER 16

I took on my duties as master's mate in fine style, showing a natural competence at sea and as a leader.

With Sims in the brig I moved out of the midshipmen's quarters and into Mr. Clements' cabin with the new master.

Bottomly's death left a quietness with Brown and Goodwin that lasted a long time. When they were not on duty they spent their time either being tutored by Captain Forsythe or with their heads buried in their books.

The weeks went by and I continued to watch for the aura but it never appeared; it was as though the aura was of divine power that would only materialize when *not* being sought.

While dining one evening with Captain Forsythe, Mr. Clements and I, and the ship's master-at-arms, Kenneth Baird, were reminded by the captain that *Assistant* would make way for Jamaica via Cape Horn.

"Captain Bligh will have taken *Providence* around the

Horn and we must do the same. We cannot afford to lose any more time for the comfort of Good Hope. Gentlemen, we shall stop for supplies at Namuka then make all speed for the Horn."

"Do you think we can make it around the Horn this time of year, captain?" Clements asked with some doubt in his voice.

"Yes, we can, Mr. Clements, and we shall. Mr. Matthews," the captain turned to me, "you will see that all hands put aside their lighter clothing for warmer once we leave Namuka."

We were about six weeks out of Matavai Bay when we sighted Namuka in the Friendly Archipelago.

HMS *Assistant* laid anchor about a mile from shore. With the wind being southward we had a difficult time making our position, so the ship's arrival was long known before we finally settled in about twenty fathoms. Canoes quickly surrounded the ship, with the natives shouting to come on board. The Namuka Indians, although resembling the Tahitians in color and stature, had a reputation for downright thievery and a sometimes unprovoked violent side, at least this is what Mr. Clements and I were told by Captain Forsythe. To avoid the risk of snubbing the islanders, Captain Forsythe elected to invite the chief and his aides on board.

Captain Forsythe ordered the supply parties to do their jobs as quickly as possible because of the volatile nature of the inhabitants. The captain put Thomas Brown in charge of the watering party, and he directed the ship's carpenter to take the men he needed to fell a tree and saw out sufficient wood for plank. The captain required Mr. Clements and Mr. Baird to remain on board with him and the minimal crew while assigning me the task of protecting the men on shore. I selected a dozen men and had Mr. Clements issue muskets and ammunition to all. When ready, Brown and his watering party climbed into their longboat for the pull to shore. Daniel Goodwin led the carpenter and his men in the second boat, and the sentries and I rowed in line in the ship's launch.

The two groups immediately set about their work after breaching. I assigned five men to stay by the boats, and the remaining eight, which included myself, stayed with Brown and Goodwin and their charges.

In no time scores of Indians had gathered, most of them having followed us from the ship's anchorage. They milled around us watching the carpenter and his men lay their hatchets into a tree. Others followed Brown and his group from the boats to the stream and back again with the filled barrels. We were tremendously outnumbered should the Indians want to make any mischief, but my men and I kept a keen eye and a ready trigger. I was relying on the power and 'magic' of the muskets to stop any rush and make the Indians freeze should we have to use the weapons.

The work went well. In fine fashion the carpenter – a gritty pigtailed seaman of about fifty – had felled his tree and cut away a good portion of wood, which was being carried back to the boats.

"Look smart, lads!" I shouted, seeing the last of the barrels being filled. "Let's be on our way! We've been lucky so far; let's keep it that way! Damn it Mick! Stop dancing about like a bloody monkey and pick up that wood!" I shouted at Scholes, who was too often the clown. "The quicker we get in the boats and make way the better off we'll be!" No sooner had I ushered the men onwards than an Indian snatched the hatchet from one of the carpenter's men, then another tried to wrestle the hatchet from the carpenter. The old salt held it firm and pushed the man to the ground.

"Get away from me you foul smelling savage!" he yelled.

"Come on, men, move it!" I barked, not wanting them to run but still pick up the pace. The Indians, though, came closer to us, angry over the carpenter's retaliation. Then three or four of the impudent ones pushed the carpenter when we reached the boats. Another tried to take his hatchet again.

"You'll get it in your thieving head – leave off you bastard!" he shouted.

"Muskets ready!" I ordered. "Don't fire – wait for the word!" I said as the sentries stood with their backs to the boats and with their weapons aimed. The Indians seemed to know that the muskets meant danger and they backed away.

"Alright, men, push off," I said. Within moments we were in the bay pulling our way to the ship. I drew a deep breath and let it out. We had come close to a fight. If any one of the sentries had let fly there was no telling if the Indians would have scattered or whether they would have rushed us. My instinct told me they would have rushed us.

One by one our boats were raised and the supplies off-loaded and stored.

"Good job, Mr. Matthews," both Goodwin and Brown said.

"I thought we were in for it, sir," another man added.

"It was dodgy," I responded. "Well done all round."

It was the month of April when we left the Friendly Islands. Captain Forsythe had the topgallant masts lowered and new sails bent. *Assistant* was made ready for the winds and seas that lay ahead.

The weather became markedly colder each day until we

eventually encountered consistent days and nights of misery with the wind hauling to the southwest and hails of snow biting deeper into our bodies. Both Mr. Clements and Mr. Baird openly remarked to me that we would never stand a chance of rounding Cape Horn had it been February or March.

With the icy winds and crashing sea not only was I convinced we wouldn't make it, I feared the ship would be flung over and join so many others at the bottom, but with the gale blowing at such force the captain ordered *Assistant* hove-to under its staysail, ensuring that the vessel pitched safely into the breaking sea while going nowhere.

The ship's seams opened under the Horn's onslaught causing the pumps to be manned at least every hour. When it appeared inevitable that we would have to put up helm and bear away for the Cape of Good Hope, the winds began to lighten, just slightly. Captain Forsythe instructed we wait. The winds had definitely eased, and the snow flurries stopped. Then when the fury of the sea declined the captain turned us around and in time we were able to roll through the waves. We had made it, surely following Captain Bligh's skills in piloting the *Providence* through the same tumultuous path. The crew displayed a euphoric pride in its success at crossing the South American tip, and they were not shy in showering praise on their captain for his stout leadership.

The fine weather we now enjoyed took us speedily to the Caribbean and nearer Jamaica. I once again began scanning the sea for the aura, but still saw nothing.

Five months out of Matavai Bay and just a few days after entering the Caribbean we sighted Jamaica.

Accepting the futility of my search I decided against making the onward journey to England, that was if Captain

Forsythe would release me from my obligation to Spithead. I hoped that once the cargo was delivered he would let me go. My mind was also constantly on Tiare and my children; I had to get passage back from Kingston and return to my family.

I took the opportunity in a quiet moment on the quarterdeck to make my request to the captain.

"You've served me well, Matthews," Captain Forsythe said. "I still don't know anything about you, but you make an excellent master's mate; I wish I could have you on all my commands."

"Thank you, captain," I acknowledged. I waited for Captain Forsythe to speak again while watching the sun set over Kingston Harbour.

"I *will* say I may have been a fool for taking you on and making you my number two, but… I wasn't; sometimes the greater the risk the greater the reward, would you not agree, Mr. Matthews?"

"Indeed I would, captain."

"Well, then, I shall put you in charge of the offloading; when that is done I shall wish you Godspeed."

Assistant entered the bay after nightfall. The captain intended we lay calm through the night and draw in and anchor at sunrise. I looked forward to a good night's rest, and then after finishing my remaining task in the morning I would seek out return passage to Tahiti. I realized that chances were little there would be a ship already in the harbor whose destination was Tahiti, meaning I would need some money to get by until such time. I presumed to find some kind of work after completing my obligation to Captain Forsythe, but I intended to pursue a reasonable favor with the captain – that he might see me on my way with a few pounds of officer's pay.

Captain Forsythe called all hands at full light and we made the remaining distance to our place of anchorage. The harbor was crowded with shipping, mostly merchant vessels, although there were three or four of His Majesty's ships of war at anchor. The front was surrounded by dark green hills, not unlike Tahiti's, and tall leafy palm trees were abundant except on the front itself, which was if anything a rather ordinary and bland looking town center with its standard two-level wood buildings. Before going ashore with Captain Forsythe I tasked Brown and Goodwin with ensuring the potted breadfruit plants were carried to the ship's longboats. I suggested the midshipmen split the crew into two groups, assigning each one to a longboat.

"You won't need every man," I said, "the plants are going to take up most of the room in the boats; just get them loaded and take as many men as will fit with you, and remember, there'll be no handing over until you receive the purchase papers authorizing receipt."

"Understood, Mr. Matthews," Brown confirmed.

"And one more thing, you two… wait for my word from shore before you pull out, I want to make sure the buyers have arrived."

Captain Forsythe and I were taken to the wharf in the ship's launch. The front was alive with beggars, sailors, and soldiers in their red coats with white straps crisscrossed over their torsos; and many well-dressed white well-to-do'ers passed to and fro with as many local blacks who were commonly dressed in white shirts and trousers. I lifted myself out of the launch and extended my arm to Captain Forsythe for him to follow.

I took leave of the captain to have a walk-about and

inquire into the expected arrival of the buyers of *Assistant's* cargo.

I walked along the streets of Kingston, treading the smooth but cracked roads. I found myself on King Street, which was busy with businessmen and tradesmen with their horse-drawn carts, and there were a large number of soldiers on patrol. I assumed the garrison was a constant precaution over potential invasion considering that France and Spain had joined forces in 1782 and launched an unsuccessful attack on Jamaica.

After getting a feel of the town's layout in preparation of finding work and lodgings, I returned to the wharf to be ready for the arrival of the plantation owners or their representatives.

More and more horse-drawn carts were gathering. The occupants were generally an authoritative-looking white man and a slave.

After making some inquiries and examining several paid-up purchase documents I was satisfied that these people were *Assistant's* customers.

I had gathered that the *Providence* had long since offloaded her cargo and delivered it to the first-comers.

By now the wharf was teeming with men and their carts waiting to take possession, so I moved in view of *Assistant* and waved my arms crisscross above my head, signaling Brown and Goodwin to come ashore.

It would likely take a few hours to complete the transfer, and then I would start my inquiries into passage back to Tahiti.

I stood on the wharf near the waiting carts watching the movement on *Assistant*. I was excited over my decision to return to Tahiti; I missed Tiare and the children terribly and it made no sense to hunt for something that could not be caught. I did find, though, that this journey to Jamaica was a tonic for me in that it gave me almost six months of activity and adventure and that all-important thing called 'hope'. Even though my goal was not achieved, I did at least *get it out of my system*, and now perhaps in no more than another six months I would be back with my family where I belonged.

While waiting for the longboats to reach the wharf with their first load I noticed two familiar figures coming my way. One of them was Captain Forsythe. As they came closer I saw a certain familiarity with the other. He wore the same uniform as Captain Forsythe. When they reached me Captain Forsythe gave me a nod and said my name, but I did not offer a salute or respond in kind, my eyes were fixed on the other man. Our eyes made direct contact. His were stabbing eyes. As the two men walked past I turned and watched. I suddenly shuddered within myself… it was Captain Bligh. At that moment Bligh stopped dead; waited, then turned around to see me staring at him. Captain Forsythe turned also, curious over Bligh's pause. Then came a shout from the *Bounty's* former commander.

"That man! Seize that man!" In a heartbeat I knew… Bligh remembered my face and took me for one of the *Bounty* mutineers. My only thought was to run, which I did, but before I could go ten steps I was tackled by two soldiers who were standing nearby. I struggled to free myself as Bligh approached.

"Yes…" he said slowly, looking me up and down. "One that got away; well now, by heaven, I have you, and I will have Fletcher Christian and the rest of his cowardly lot."

"You have me mistaken for someone else!" I fired back.

"I was never on the *Bounty*!"

"Did I mention His Majesty's ship?"

"No…"

"Then why did you run?"

"Captain, I was already living in Tahiti when the *Bounty* arrived. I was never *on* the *Bounty*!"

"And I say you were, sir! No less issuing muskets to the rest of your cutthroat accomplices!"

"Then what is my name?" I returned.

"I do not know the name of every jackal in my command, nor do I have the time for an exchange with you; we shall let a court-martial decide from which yardarm you will hang!" I was now frantic and pleaded with Captain Forsythe to intercede.

"Matthews, I haven't a clue what this is about," he said, then he turned to Bligh, "Captain, this man served as my master's mate from Tahiti, and a first rate job he did; what *is* this about, sir?"

"I'll tell you what it is about, Captain Forsythe; it is about you employing a wanted mutineer from His Majesty's Ship *Bounty*. Your carelessness in losing the first shipment of breadfruit plants not only caused you to return to Tahiti but it saw you additionally jeopardize the safety of your ship and the interests of the stockholders by employing this scoundrel and traitor. I suggest you exercise more care, sir, as your performance and judgment in my estimation has not been that of an officer entrusted with the command of one of His Majesty's vessels."

By this time a large crowd had gathered, many of them muttering among themselves. Both of *Assistant's* longboats had reached the wharf and Brown and Goodwin were standing nearby equally confused over my arrest.

With panic shooting through me I again pleaded with Captain Bligh, but he would have nothing of it.

"Captain Forsythe, I want this man confined in your brig, in irons. I think rather than wait until we reach England I shall see the governor and arrange for this villain's court-martial here, at Vale Royale."

"You can't do that!" I protested, nearly freeing myself, but two more soldiers dashed in to subdue me and I quickly had my hands bound behind my back.

"Captain Forsythe, it will be upon your head should this man escape, now take him away," Bligh finished.

Captain Forsythe was shocked and I know saddened over these startling events, but he had no choice but to order Midshipman Brown, who was standing nearest to him, to escort me to *Assistant's* brig. I felt doomed as a disbelieving Brown called for additional hands to see me into the ship's launch and to my confinement.

"I'm sorry, Mr. Matthews," Brown said as one of the men unlocked the brig's heavy wooden door and pulled it open with a grunt.

That's alright, Brown," I managed, "but untie my hands, will you." Brown unhesitatingly withdrew his knife and cut my bonds, but one of the men reminded him that I was to be put in irons.

"Drop it, Hatcher," Brown warned the man with confidence and maturity.

Never had I felt so doomed since the last moments of the Hirondelle, but this was worse… the interminable waiting for probable execution in the most sickening and foul conditions.

Assistant's brig was below the waterline, and the stench from the bilges and the human waste within made me choke and vomit moments after hearing the door shut behind me. There was little air, which made matters worse, and it was hot and dark inside. I began sweating and became nauseous all over again. All I thought of was that I was going to die, either hanging from a yardarm or through being left to rot in here.

I saw some movement as my eyes became more adjusted – it was a rat scurrying past me.

"You'll be seeing more of them," a familiar voice spoke. My eyes strained to see John Sims sitting against the wall. Irons were clamped around his ankles from chains made fast to ringbolts in the stone barrier.

"Who *are* you?" he asked, unable to make me out.

"It's Matthews, Sims," I allowed him. He immediately began to laugh, reminding me that *I had it coming*.

The stench and lack of air made me weak and sick yet again and I found myself prone in the corner, trying to rest in what I hoped might be a cleaner spot.

"Don't worry, Matthews, you'll get used to it," Sims said.

The noise of the brig's door being opened awakened me from a sickly sleep. I got up from the corner and saw Brown standing at the entrance. Two sentries were outside having been posted to special watch.

"Some food is being brought, Mr. Matthews," Brown said.

"Thank you, Thomas, but I don't think I can manage it."

"Take it, sir, Captain Forsythe himself is sending it; it's from his mess, it'll help keep your strength." I agreed to take it, then I asked Brown how long I'd been confined.

"About ten hours, sir," I was startled to hear. "Look, Mr.

Matthews," Brown continued, "Captain Forsythe asked me to tell you that Captain Bligh went to see the governor not long after he had you brought here; he's asked the governor to authorize your court-martial for mutiny right here in Kingston."

"What did the governor say?" I asked. Brown answered that word had not yet been sent to Captain Forsythe regarding the governor's decision.

"But I'll let you know as soon as the captain tells me, sir," he said. Just then a man carrying my tray of food came to the door. "Take it, Mr. Matthews, it isn't half bad," Brown urged.

"Hey! What about me!" Sims called out.

"Regular time, Sims," Brown reminded him; then he ordered the door shut and I was left once again to my wretched state.

I ate Captain Forsythe's food, which was a fresh cut of beef with potatoes, peas, bread, and cheese. Captain Forsythe was even good enough to have me provided with a jug of water, which I drank and also used to rinse my face.

The passing of time was agonizingly slow. It was as though life had come to a complete standstill but consciousness continued on, bringing me ever closer to a mental breakdown.

After an eternity the door creaked open once again. This time it was Captain Forsythe himself.

"Captain, am I glad to see you. What's happening? Can you get me out of this? I'm completely innocent of all Captain Bligh's charges."

"Matthews," the captain said, "the governor has agreed to Captain Bligh's request for a special court-martial, the charges are mutiny on board His Majesty's Ship *Bounty*. The governor is going to appoint three judges, and the trial will begin before the week is over." I protested half heartedly, knowing that I was probably better off coming to trial here and now, rather than trying to survive six months at sea in the brig en route to England. I nevertheless was certain I had already been convicted so the only thing I could possibly put any hope on was escape, but that looked totally impossible. "I shall attend your trial, Matthews, and I shall bear witness to your character. Captain Bligh was my commanding officer for the duration of the breadfruit mission; the mission is now complete and he is no longer my superior, we are of equal rank and I'll be bound if he is to be allowed to bully me or lay conviction upon you without cause, and such cause I know is not to be found. You shall have my full support, Matthews."

CHAPTER 17

Vale Royale was the official residence of the governor of Jamaica.

After almost a week of confinement I was escorted under heavy guard to the place of my trial. The trial of one of the notorious *Bounty* mutineers was on the lips of many a man in Kingston, evidenced by the crowd gathered outside the splendid two-story building.

Leg irons impeded my stride and added to my humiliation as several marines with fixed bayonets saw me inside Vale Royale.

I was taken into the building's library, which was of such size to comfortably hold several tables and chairs. The furniture had been arranged to accommodate my trial with the largest of the tables aligned to seat the judges.

The mantelpiece clock ticked loudly. It was a dismal ticking... a monotonous sound surrounded by hopeless silence. It was exactly half-past nine when the master-at-arms put his hand on my shoulder telling me to be seated. Captain Bligh and Captain Forsythe walked into the room and seated themselves at separate tables. Captain Forsythe went directly to his seat while Bligh stopped for the briefest moment and looked me squarely in the eyes as though to warn me of what was to come.

The trial was open to the public and at this time the room had become filled with a crowd of perhaps a hundred men, some seated in what chairs had been made available, while others stood only too glad to be witness to such proceedings.

A double-door opened and the members of the court entered. At the order of the master-at-arms those seated rose, and when the judges were at their table, all were seated again.

My life was in the hands of the captains of three men-of-war presently anchored in Kingston Harbour... Captain Courtney of HMS *Tigress*, Captain Allison of HMS *Unconquerable*, and Captain Beard of HMS *Brunswick*. The governor had appointed these senior officers as my judges and jury. I had not even been permitted the services of a lawyer or advisor; it was left to me to conduct my own defense. When I looked at the court's austere faces my heart sank deeper, if that were possible.

My name was called and I was made to stand before the judges while the charges against me were read. Hearing the charges of conspiracy to commit mutiny on board His Majesty's armed vessel *Bounty*, and of actively participating in the mutiny by issuing arms to others culpable made me shout my innocence.

"The accused will hold his tongue; he will be given the

opportunity to speak in his defense," Captain Courtney, the senior justice snapped.

"Captain, I was not a member of the *Bounty*, I was living in Tahiti while the vessel was anchored there, but I was never a member of its crew, and I never had anything to do with the mutiny… this whole trial is a sham!"

"One more outburst and the court will have you gagged, now be seated," Captain Courtney said, directing his angry words and unsympathetic eyes right at me.

Captain Courtney made reference to Captain Bligh's sworn statement at Portsmouth in the 1792 trial of those taken into custody by the *Pandora*. The *Bounty's* former captain was then called to present further testimony to his original statement. I was seated between two marine guards as he approached the court. He stopped directly in front of Captain Courtney, who was flanked by Captains Allison and Beard. Captain Courtney was tall and of slender build, and I would guess he was in his fifties. He instructed Bligh to inform the court of the circumstances concerning my involvement with the *Bounty*. Captain Bligh turned and gave me a glance, then proceeded to accuse me of conspiracy and mutinous conduct.

"The night preceding the mutiny I came on deck during the middle watch and saw Fletcher Christian, the perpetrator, in conversation with this man, Peter Matthews. Neither man observed me in the darkness, although I had no impression at this time that their conversation was of such a dastardly account. As I approached them still unseen I clearly heard this man say to Christian, *You can count on me*, to which Christian replied, *Excellent, that's settled*. At that moment they discovered me and immediately broke off their talk. I have no doubt that this conversation was the foundation of the forthcoming mutiny." I very nearly protested at these absurd charges but I restrained myself, knowing it would bring no good.

"Do you have anything to add, Captain Bligh?" Courtney asked.

"I do indeed, sir, this man was also a willing and active participant in the mutiny; not only did I witness him issue muskets from the armory to Christian's accomplices, he was one of several who forced me into the ship's launch along with as many other innocent wretches who would fit." Again I wanted to protest, but I left myself to sit quietly and shake my head in disbelief.

It was strictly Bligh's word against mine. There were no witnesses and he had no proof. I actually felt I had a chance. If this thrown-together court had any sense of justice they would surely acquit me for clear lack of evidence. How could they convict me when they never even had access to the ship's register? The most they could do, I speculated, was take me back to England to stand an honest trial where they could produce the official register naming the crew, and I could at least call for former crew members to swear upon my innocence.

Captain Courtney spoke at the end of Captain Bligh's testimony.

"You said that you saw the accused issue muskets to those taking part in the mutiny, and bearing in mind, captain, that we do not have the ship's register available to us which would confirm the accused's status or non-status, how can you recall this to be accurate after more than three years?"

"I shall never forget his face. He unlatched the door to the armory and distributed the weapons."

"Is it not possible you could be mistaken?" Courtney

then asked.

"Impossible, it was he."

Captain Beard, a hard looking man with twenty years service spoke next.

"Captain Bligh, you say that the accused was one of several who forced you into the launch; how can you swear to this?"

Again Bligh answered emphatically.

"His face – I shall never forget his face behind the musket he carried." I had had enough at this point and asked the court if I could direct my questions to Captain Bligh.

"The accused may question the witness, and I remind the witness to address his answers to the court," Captain Courtney responded. I got up and tried to walk towards Bligh, adjusting my leg irons as I moved, but Captain Courtney quickly saw me back to my place.

"The accused will present his questions while seated."

"Captain Bligh," I said, "when you had me seized right here in Kingston and accused me of being one of the mutineers on board the *Bounty*, I told you I was not a member of the *Bounty's* crew, nor was I ever at sea on the *Bounty*, and when I asked you my name you did not know it; how is it, sir, that you freely accuse me of participating in this mutiny on the high seas when you do not have the ship's register to verify my status and you never even knew my name before this trial?" Bligh turned from me and faced the court to present his answer.

"I do not require the ship's register to tell me whether or not the prisoner was on my vessel or whether or not he participated in this mutiny; I witnessed his willful participation; and nor do I need to know the name of every man serving under my command."

"Captain Bligh," I followed, "you said you saw and heard me talking to Fletcher Christian the night before the mutiny and you accuse me of conspiracy as a result of this conversation, yet the only words you say you heard exchanged were me saying to Christian, *You can count on me*, and Christian responding, *Excellent, that's settled*; I submit to you, sir, that those few words could relate to any innocent subject and that your accusation of the conversation being a mutinous plot is nothing but speculation which carries not a shred of proof." Bligh did not answer.

"The witness will respond to the accused's statement," Captain Courtney said. Bligh turned slowly from me and faced the court.

"I do not speculate, I clearly heard the prisoner agree with Christian when he said *You can count on me*; in my mind it could mean nothing other than his agreement to aid Christian with the mutiny which followed just a few hours later."

It was Captain Allison who spoke next. The junior of the three officers posed his question to Bligh.

"Captain Bligh, for such few words you heard, do you not think it even remotely possible that the accused was referring to something unrelated to the mutiny?"

"I highly doubt that, sir," Bligh answered.

"Please answer the court's question with either a *yes* or a *no*, and if your answer is no, please qualify it," Captain Courtney challenged. Bligh was thoughtful and appeared surprised at the extent of the court's cross-examination. He finally responded.

"Yes, I suppose it is possible, but…"

"Thank you, Captain," Courtney cut him off. This examination by the court gave me some momentary hope, and I asked the court if I could continue my questioning.

"The accused may proceed," Courtney obliged.

"Captain Bligh, I said before and maintain still that I was never a member of your crew or was ever at sea on the *Bounty*; the man you saw and heard speaking with Fletcher Christian the night before the mutiny was Midshipman Peter Heywood, whom you testified against at the Portsmouth trial in 1792, and who was acquitted by the court at that trial. You are mistaking me for Midshipman Heywood. You recognize me from Tahiti – while you were there collecting the breadfruit plants. Captain Bligh, you are incorrectly connecting me to the unpardonable act of mutiny which took the *Bounty* from your command, do you not see this, captain?"

Bligh turned to the court.

"I do not know how the prisoner can say I mistake him for this midshipman; I tell the court as God is my witness that it was this man, Matthews, I saw and heard with Fletcher Christian plotting the mutiny, and it was this man who issued muskets from the armory, *and* it was this man who willfully forced me into the Bounty's launch!" A prolonged silence followed Bligh's refute.

"Does the accused have anymore questions for the witness?" Captain Courtney asked. Though I presented my case well there was nothing more I could ask Bligh; it was still strictly his word against mine. I was afraid the court was ultimately going to take the word of an officer of His Majesty's Navy over that of an accused mutineer, even though there was no evidence, so I decided to make a special plea to the court. I stood up and addressed the three men.

"I have no other questions for Captain Bligh, but I respectfully assure the court that I am completely innocent of these charges, and I ask the court to consider that there is no evidence to substantiate my complicity or involvement in this mutiny, or relationship with the *Bounty*, and I am willing to be taken back to Portsmouth where examination of the *Bounty's* register will prove my non-status, and the questioning of any and all former members of the ship's crew will attest to my non-involvement and innocence in this mutiny."

The court listened with interest to my impassioned summation then Captain Courtney conferred privately for a moment with Captains Allison and Beard. At the conclusion of their conference Captain Courtney addressed the court.

"If there is no other testimony the accused will be returned to confinement. This court will be adjourned for deliberation." As the officers were about to rise, Captain Forsythe spoke.

"If it please the court I would like to speak on behalf of the accused." Bligh, who was still standing in front of the court, wheeled around at Captain Forsythe's surprise request and stared angrily at his fellow officer.

"You may step forward and state your name; Captain Bligh, you may be seated," Captain Courtney directed. Forsythe and Bligh brushed past each other as they were changing places, and again Bligh scowled at Forsythe for his perceived disloyalty.

"My name is Edward Forsythe, captain in His Majesty's Navy, and presently commanding officer of His Majesty's Ship *Assistant*."

"Make your statement, Captain Forsythe," Captain Courtney said.

"I wish to tell the court that although I cannot say whether or not the accused was associated with the *Bounty*, albeit there appears to be no evidence that he was…"

"Captain Forsythe – I caution you not to make such judgments, that is for this court to decide," Captain Courtney admonished with a raised voice; "you may continue."

"Thank you, sir; I did not intend to be presumptuous. Peter Matthews signed on my vessel in Tahiti requesting to earn passage to England. As occasion had it, I found it not only appropriate to sign him on, but to be in the best interests of my command to elevate Mr. Matthews to the rank of master's mate, and I am proud to say that I would welcome him in my command at any opportunity. He more than proved his loyalty and bravery to the Crown, and I pray the court consider my words favorably while weighing all that has been presented today."

"Is that all, Captain Forsythe?" Captain Courtney asked.

"Yes sir."

"Very well, captain, thank you; you may be excused." Captain Forsythe gave me a nod and a hint of a smile when he returned to his seat. Captain Courtney then said, "If there is no more testimony or evidence the court will be adjourned for deliberation." Before rising with Allison and Beard, Captain Courtney instructed the marines to return me to *Assistant's* brig where I was to spend another interminable period awaiting the court's verdict.

My leg irons were removed before I was ushered into my holding place. I strained to see when the door shut behind me but there was no sign of Sims, he had been moved to God knows where pending his own trial for the death of Lester Bottomly.

I could barely endure the heat and stench after relishing the fresh air, and as the hours crept by I again could not distinguish between night and day.

Eventually the door opened and my meal was brought in. This time it was rancid pork and stale bread with a cup of water. I had hoped that Brown or Goodwin would have arranged a plate from Captain Forsythe's table for me as I bit into the pork, but my earlier good fortune was not repeated. I debated if perhaps Bligh had arranged through his sinister influence to keep Captain Forsythe and all visitors from me. Suddenly I spat the pork onto the floor along with several maggots that I felt in my mouth. Beads of sweat settled on my forehead as I almost gagged at the lingering and slimy movement of the insects. I threw the portion across the cell and fell into a state of self-pity, wishing for the hour to come when I would know my fate one way or the other.

Sleep was impossible in this infested cell. Then even had I been in the most comfortable of quarters, sleep would still be impossible under such circumstances.

I had no concept of time. One hour could have passed or ten hours.

I sat with my back against the wall with my arms resting on raised knees. The sound of the door opening made me turn my head. Another slab of rotten pork, I thought.

"Come on, Mr. Matthews," a marine spoke. I was placed in the center of four guards, two in front and two behind, and I again had irons clamped around my ankles.

The relief of fresh air was unspeakably welcome as I labored up the ladderway to be ushered onto a longboat waiting to take me ashore.

I felt strangely detached when I made my way into the courtroom; it was as though I was in a walking dream from which I expected to awaken... perhaps.

The master-at-arms directed those in attendance to rise

as Captains Courtney, Allison, and Beard came through the double doors.

I looked at the mantle clock behind the judges' table; it was exactly eleven o'clock. My heart started to race. It pounded when my name was called. I was escorted to the center of the judges' table by a lieutenant with drawn sword and two marines with muskets. I was left directly facing Captain Courtney. The murmuring of the spectators stopped when Captain Courtney spoke.

"Peter Matthews, Article Nineteen of the Naval Articles of War states: *If a person, in or belonging to the Fleet, shall make, or endeavour to make, any mutinous assembly, upon any pretence whatsoever, every person offending herein, being convicted thereof by the sentence of the Court-Martial, shall suffer death.*" I went weak as Captain Courtney continued, "Having heard and weighed the evidence produced in support of the charges made against you, said charges being, one, conspiracy to bring about mutinous acts against His Majesty's armed transport *Bounty*; and two, discharging mutinous and piratical seizure of His Majesty's armed transport *Bounty*, and having heard and weighed your defense of said charges, this court is of the opinion that there is insufficient evidence to bear out your guilt of conspiracy; however, this court is of the opinion that the charges of carrying out mutinous and piratical seizure of His Majesty's armed transport *Bounty* have been proved against you. It doth accordingly judge that you shall suffer death by being hanged by the neck on board such of His Majesty's ships of war at such a time and such a place as shall be directed by this court."

My gasp at the verdict could be heard over the renewed murmuring of the spectators.

"The prisoner may retire," Captain Courtney said as I

struggled in both mind and body.

"This is ridiculous… it's madness… I was never *on* the Bounty! Bligh is *lying*!" I insisted in wild defense. I was quickly held firm by the guards and pulled back from the judges' table.

"I said the prisoner may retire," Courtney repeated. As I was being removed a voice was heard from the back.

"May I be heard, with the court's permission?" The voice came from Thomas Brown.

"Step forward and identify yourself – the prisoner may be seated," Courtney said.

As Brown came forward I was pushed back into my chair.

Thomas Brown stood proud before the court in his blue midshipman's coat and white cotton breeches, and smart three-cornered hat, which he held under his arm.

"My name is Thomas Brown, Midshipman; I am assigned to His Majesty's transport *Assistant*."

"What is it you wish to say?" Captain Courtney asked.

"Although the court has pronounced its verdict and sentence, I wish to remind the court that sentence may only be carried out at such a time and place as directed by the Commissioners for executing the office of Lord High Admiral of Great Britain and Ireland."

"What are you attempting to say, midshipman?" Captain Courtney asked with annoyance in his voice.

"*That*, sir, the only body authorized to conduct a trial against members of His Majesty's Fleet is the Admiralty itself, and such trials may only be conducted in Great Britain and Ireland, and only then and there can a verdict be handed down and sentence carried out." There was a stunned silence when Brown finished his bold speech.

Brown's effort to protect me was admirable, but he was careful not to further test the patience of the court with his personal opinion regarding my guilt or innocence.

"Midshipman Brown," Courtney responded, "it is only for your lack of years and pitiful ignorance that this court does not find you in contempt. You need not state the law to me sir, now get out of this courtroom!" Brown bowed respectfully to the judges, turned smartly, and marched out of Vale Royale, having very clearly made his point. His stunning declaration and Captain Courtney's reprimand set the audience chattering to one another, and it saw Allison and Beard lean close to Courtney, evidently questioning Brown's assertion. Captain Courtney shook his head; he would not let an impertinent midshipman sway him.

"The court has found the accused guilty of mutinous and piratical seizure of His Majesty's armed transport *Bounty*; sentence stands, now let the prisoner be removed, this court is dissolved," Captain Courtney finished, and with that, he, Allison, and Beard rose and strode through the double doors whence they came.

Thoughts of how I might escape went chaotically through my mind after realizing the finality of the sentence, but there was nothing I could do with irons clamped around my ankles and chains so short that I could not take normal steps.

Once again I was returned to *Assistant's* brig, this time to wait out my execution. I hadn't eaten in I think two days, declining more of the rotten pork that was just brought to me. If my life was truly over why bother with food? Why be at my physical best to face the ignominy of being hanged, I rambled.

In time I recaptured my composure and accepted my unjust fate. I was determined that if I had to go to my death

I would stand proud, with my head held high.

Sleep did not come even though I was physically exhausted, and once again I didn't know if it was day or night after several more hours in this abominable place.

I continued to sit against the wall, thinking, wondering what time it was. The time *did* matter because I knew that on all British ships the hour for administering punishment was eleven o'clock in the morning.

My thoughts turned to Tiare. How I longed to be with her. I wanted to hold her and be held by her. Suddenly the door opened and I jumped to my feet.

"Outside, Mr. Matthews, if you please," a marine said.

"What time is it?" I asked.

"Half-past ten," was the answer.

I shielded my eyes from the sunlight as this time eight marines escorted me up the ladderway and onto the main deck. Before making my way down the rope ladder and into the waiting longboat I recognized the flag that had been run up on Captain Courtney's ship, *Tigress*… it was the signal for punishment.

The midshipmen in charge of the longboat gave orders to push off after I had been seated between the marines.

The longboat came from the *Tigress* and was now being steered back to her.

Several boats from other vessels in the harbor were ahead of us; the men in them, all members of His Majesty's Fleet, were being sent to the *Tigress* to witness my execution.

There were two marines at each side of me and four facing me, and just ahead was the *Tigress*. I looked at her lofty yardarms and saw a rope slung over the lower yard above the upper deck. I went weak.

The short pull from *Assistant* seemed endless. I had no

escape, but with thoughts again running through my head I decided I would not face the degradation of being hanged; if I was to die then it would be with honor. I would plunge overboard and let the sea have me, or be shot in my attempt to get away.

I was well aware that the fools escorting me had failed to cuff my hands or place irons around my ankles, which should make my attempt less difficult.

I studied the guards then noted the distance between the longboat's sides and myself. I leaned forward with my hands prepped just above my knees. I was ready to spring.

"You bloody incompetents!" the captain of the guards screamed, "you didn't cuff the man! Bind his hands! *Now!*" My lingering cost me my only chance. All hope went away when a guard bound my hands behind my back with a scarf taken from one of the oarsmen.

The longboat rounded *Tigress's* stern and pulled up to her gangway. A rope-chair was dropped down the side. The guards, making sure my bonds were firm, secured me in the chair and signaled to the men on deck. I was then hoisted up.

I was pulled out of the chair and made to stand directly below the yardarm, and the rope, which was to end my life, limped beside me.

I felt amazingly calm as I looked upon Kingston's buildings set under the blue sky. The deck was amassed with officers and men waiting to witness punishment. Opposite me stood the judges – Captains Courtney, Allison, and Beard, and beside them was William Bligh. I stood tall and looked straight ahead.

"Peter Matthews, you have been tried, convicted, and condemned to death for the piratical seizure of His Majesty's armed transport *Bounty*. You are here and now compelled to suffer the extreme penalty prescribed by His Majesty's just laws. Have you anything to say before sentence is carried out?" Captain Courtney said.

"God bless you, Mr. Matthews!" a voice called. It was Thomas Brown.

"God bless you, Thomas!" I called back. "And God help you! *All* of you!" I said to Courtney, Allison, and Beard, and not least of all, Bligh.

"The boatswain's mate will carry out the sentence," Courtney said. Just then a cannon let go a thunderous roar and a cloud of smoke billowed from the ship. It was the signal that punishment was imminent.

The boatswain's mate took the noose in his hands and was about to place it around my neck.

"Bless my soul, what is that?" Captain Courtney exclaimed looking right past me.

"My God in heaven!" Allison followed. I turned my head and saw in all its power and splendor the aura shimmering in a wide circle near the ship's gangway and once again within the rings was an extraordinary turbulence.

I lost no time – I sent the boatswain's mate crashing to the deck and charged over the side, falling hard into the water.

"Get him! Shoot him! Don't let him get away!" I heard Bligh scream.

I kicked powerfully towards the aura, hearing musket shots smacking into the water after me, but I managed to thrust myself over the rim and dive deep.

CHAPTER 18

I held my breath as long as I could while watching the golden waters bubbling above me. Finally, after my lungs could take no more I burst to the top gasping for air.

I heard a shout.

"Hey, look over there man! Where did *he* come from?"

The aura had carried me to within a few yards of the embankment. I lunged to the wharf where two burly men lifted me out of the water.

"Man alive! Where did *you* come from?" one of them said. I lay on my back looking up at the sky.

"Untie my hands, will you," I said as a crowd began to gather. I felt the scarf being cut from my wrists then I was helped to my feet.

"What's going on here?" a policeman said who had been drawn by the commotion.

"He was in the bay man, with his hands tied," one of the

rescuers answered; "we pulled him out."

"And how did you get into the bay with your hands tied?" the policeman asked. I looked around; there was no sign of the *Tigress* or any other vessels of His Majesty's Navy. An increasingly loud roar came from above. I looked up and saw an airliner climbing towards the clouds.

"I asked you a question mister."

"It's alright, really; some bastards robbed me... I'm okay."

"Who are they? Can you recognize them?" the policeman asked.

"No, I wouldn't know them if I saw them again; just let me be on my way, I'm okay." The policeman eyed me distrustfully, but decided to let me go.

I was left standing alone, soaked to the skin and dressed in nothing but the pair of trousers and white ruffled shirt that was given to me by Captain Forsythe shortly after leaving Tahiti.

I can't say I looked too out of place, though, even without shoes and socks, as the men around me were mostly dressed in shorts and colored tee shirts, and some of them were also shoeless.

The sight of another jet climbing high made me impatient to know the date.

I found myself on the main thoroughfare. Reggae music played from the street corners, and bars and betting shops jostled with the churches while Kingston's ambitious youths hawking their goods added to the bustling atmosphere.

I found a newsagent and stepped inside, brushing past one or two customers. The date printed on the *Daily Gleaner* read Wednesday, April 10th, 2013 – about nine months after the Hirondelle had sunk!

I left the shop wondering how I was going to get to England without any money or clothes, or a passport. I couldn't think anymore; I was weak and hungry from my confinement on the *Assistant* and from my incredible escape from the *Tigress*. For the first time in more years that I could remember, I wanted to sleep in a real bed.

Ingenuity was necessary if I was to have food and shelter, *and* money, so I went to the docks to see if I could find some work.

"None here man," was the answer every time I inquired.

I returned to the wharf and asked the men working on the boats, but nothing was offered. I then decided to ask around a section of drab looking offices nearby.

"Get out o' here man, there ain't no work here!" was the answer from the person in the first office. I walked along the shabby, dimly lit hall contemplating whether it was worth trying the others. At that moment a door opened and a man in a dark, wrinkled suit came out. His salt and pepper beard made him look to be about sixty.

"Mister, do you have any work? I need some food and a room," I said.

"I ain't got no work, man," he answered, walking right past me. As he was about to open the door to the street he stopped and turned around. He looked me over for a moment then said, "None that's square, that is."

"What?"

"I said I got a job but it ain't square, if you know what I mean. You interested?"

"Maybe."

The man walked back to his office and unlocked the door.

"Come in; sit down. What's your name?" he asked after

closing the door and sitting behind his cluttered desk.

"Matthews."

There wasn't much to his office. Florescent lights inadequately lit the room; a bookcase stood on the worn and dirty carpet, and a small table was placed between me and the other chair at my side. The telephone rang.

"Yeah?" he answered as he switched on a green glare-shielding lamp at the edge of his desk. "I'm workin' on it, right now in fact; you gotta be patient, man. You'll know when it happens, alright?" There was silence while he listened to the caller. "I found you three quick enough didn't I? Trust me, man, I'll get you more – you know I like the coin. Okay, I'll let you know… if there's time." He hung up and looked at me. "What did you say your name was?"

"Matthews," I said again.

"Alright, Matthews, I'll give it to you straight – I want a boat torched. I'll give you five hundred dollars… U.S."

"Where is it?"

"Along the wharf, east end."

"Why do you want it torched?" I asked.

"That ain't your concern, mister, now do you want the job or don't you?"

"Look, I don't want to do anything illegal, not if I can avoid it anyway; I just want enough money to buy some clothes and get back to England. But if this is the only way… I'll do it for the cost of a ticket to London and some clothes, and a room for a couple of nights."

This unconscionable businessman studied me while he took a cigar out of his desk drawer and lit it.

"You say you want to go to England?"

"Yes."

"You look a sorry sight, mister, but you don't look

the type goin' around torchin' boats. I'll tell you what, Matthews, there's a freighter – the *Jamaica Star* – due to sail for Newcastle tomorrow afternoon, you can work you way and make a few dollars on top of it."

"That'll suit me just right."

"Good. Meet me here tomorrow, one o'clock; I'll take you to the ship and get you signed on."

"I don't know your name," I said.

"You can call me Gilbert."

"Alright, Gilbert, can you advance me some money? I need a room and some food, and I've got to get some clothes, this is all I own," I said, holding my arms out as if asking for understanding. I could tell this shady fellow liked me, and lucky for me he did. He counted out two hundred American dollars.

"I don't know why I'm doin' this, it's against my better judgment," he said as he handed me a one hundred dollar bill and five twenties. "You just be here tomorrow, I want this back from the *Star* and the commission on you."

"Gilbert, I need another hundred, I've got to get some clothes… I need a jacket and trousers, and boots… and a bed for the night." He gave me a stony look.

"You believe in pushin' your luck, don't you mister?"

"I was never one to be shy. Look, Gilbert, you're being straight with me, I appreciate that, but I need the other hundred, I won't let you down, I'll be here tomorrow – you know I have to get to England." He pulled two more twenties and a ten from the wad he carried in his trouser pocket.

"That's all you get; you just make sure you're back here tomorrow," he said again, giving me the fifty and pointing a deliberate finger at me. I got to my feet and extended my hand to this unsavory yet likable character.

"Thank you, Gilbert." He took my hand with a short resigning smile.

I was amazingly lucky to have two hundred and fifty dollars fall into my lap along with working passage to England. My only remaining concern would be how to disembark at Newcastle without a passport, but I could at least worry about that on English shores.

Still early afternoon, I found a cut-rate clothing store and fitted myself with a pair of jeans and a couple of shirts. I also bought a sweater and jacket along with the essential boots, socks and underwear to see me through the voyage.

With more than enough money left over I found a hotel by the waterfront that offered an adequate room.

I shaved off my straggly beard with the razor and soap I also bought then filled the bath with steaming hot water.

After wallowing in the tub and scrubbing myself clean I got dressed and brought back some hot food from one of the wagons parked at the wharf, and after my first meal in several days I lost myself in a long, restful sleep.

CHAPTER 19

I met Gilbert at one o'clock and we left at once for the docks and the *Jamaica Star*.

He parked his old Corolla close to the cargo ship and set the pace to the ship's gangway.

The dock was bustling with men and equipment at work. Containers and crates were being lifted and swung about for workers to load onto outgoing freighters and onto waiting trucks.

Gilbert nodded to one of the men as we boarded the ship.

"The cap'n's expecting us."

"You'll find him in his quarters, you know where it is?"

"Yeah, I know the way."

Gilbert walked directly to the captain's quarters below deck and knocked on the door; he opened it before being invited in. The captain was reading the newspaper at his desk when we entered.

"I have your man, cap'n, you have my money?" The captain looked over the top of the newspaper then put it on the desk. He sized me up with a stare.

"What's your name?"

"Matthews."

"First name."

"Peter."

"Hmm, okay; I'll have someone take you to the bay."

Gilbert held his hand out and rubbed his thumb and forefinger together, motioning payment.

"Oh, yeah," the captain said before reaching into his wallet and counting out several large notes of American money.

"I advanced him three hundred dollars, I want that as well."

"Don't try and con me, Gilbert, you wouldn't advance your mother a penny, never mind three hundred dollars to a stranger," the captain said.

"Hey, Sims, I gave the man three hundred dollars, I want it back – you take it out his pay man!"

I spoke up before things became too heated.

"He advanced me two hundred and fifty, captain; give it to him, it's okay, take it out of my pay."

Gilbert shrugged his shoulders.

"I meant two hundred and fifty; did I say three hundred?"

"Get out of here, Gilbert, before you bleed me," the captain said giving him the money. Gilbert tucked the notes into his pocket along with his commission on me.

"Good doing business with you, cap'n," he said turning to the door, "stay in touch. Don't get into any trouble,

Matthews."

Gilbert left me with the surly Captain Sims, a very familiar name indeed. He had me taken to the crew's quarters, which was an open bay with about thirty bunks. I stowed my small bundle by my bunk and was briefed on various duties.

There appeared to be nothing unusual about the cargo – sugar, bananas, and Jamaica rum. There was also an assortment of pipes and fittings with which Captain Sims seemed unduly concerned.

After a time I began to suspect something was out of place with the cargo of pipes, particularly when I was put off limits to it after looking it over. But I didn't care; my only concern was getting to England as quickly as possible, contraband or no contraband.

I kept to myself throughout the voyage while doing various jobs. At most I engaged in some brief conversations during the evening hours, but I never included myself in the card games, or darts or dominoes; quite simply, the less I knew the better I felt things would be.

Eventually we entered the North Sea. The ship approached from the southern coast and steamed north beyond London's Tilbury Docks towards Newcastle.

Captain Sims kept the vessel well beyond the coast, which again I thought was a little odd as we were so close to our final destination.

It was time for me to think how I was going to disembark without a passport. It seemed I'd have no choice but to say I'd lost it and hope to be let ashore after appropriate citizenship confirmation, but just how easy or difficult that would prove to be I had no idea.

It was late afternoon when I was taking a break, leaning on the railing.

"What're you gonna do if they suspect?" I heard one of the crew say to Captain Sims. Both men were standing at an angle and had their backs to me.

"I don't know. I've done this run enough times, they shouldn't suspect anything." I was still unseen by the two men and listened closer to this intriguing conversation.

"What about them navy boats that tailed us off Brighton – they know something's up; maybe we'd better pitch the stuff."

"I'm not pitchin' anything," I heard Sims respond, "there's too much dosh involved; besides, I do that and I'll be pitched myself, right to the bottom of the Tyne."

"Same luck as your grandfather, eh?"

"Nah, before him. Anyway, he didn't drown, he was hanged for killing some officer; shit, maybe the luck runs in the family. But I'm *not* pitchin' it. We may have to offload it before we get to Newcastle. I'll radio Waring, maybe he can pick us up off Skegness at dark; it'll be easier for him to bring it in from there in his thirty-footer."

I was right, there *was* contraband on board. I walked unseen from my hidden spot guessing that the mysterious cargo was concealed in the pipes.

I thought about the situation as dusk came. I could not afford to be on the ship if it was boarded, which could well be the case if the *Jamaica Star* was already being watched. If Sims was going to pull in close to offload the stuff to this Waring character, it might be near enough where I could drop over the side and swim to the beach. That would solve the passport problem and it would also clear me from the ship in case it was taken in tow.

Sims brought the freighter to within a couple of miles of the coast after nightfall. It was about ten o'clock when I looked on the shore lights.

"The cap'n's pulled us off Skegness," one of the crew commented, joining me at the railing. "I dunno why he's stopping here," he grumbled. I didn't answer, I just shrugged my shoulders and continued gazing at the line of hotel and arcade lights stretching along the resort's coastline.

Midnight came and we were still drifting about two miles offshore. The crew who had no knowledge of Sims' illicit cargo muttered among themselves over the delay.

With no sign of movement I decided to take the chance and make a swim for it. As long as I wasn't seen or heard going over the side I was confident I would step ashore undetected.

I went below to the bay and took a laundry bag belonging to one of the crew. I put my jacket and few other clothes in it along with my remaining cash and returned to the deck, still unseen. It was very still and quiet except for the sound of water lapping against the ship's hull; and it was very dark, almost black. I stood by the starboard railing and put the bag down. I looked around; I was alone. I had no idea where Sims was, I could only guess he was looking out for Waring's boat from the bridge.

I was as hidden as I would ever be, so I removed my boots and socks and put them in the bag. With the cord looped over my head and made snug under my arm, I prepared to drop.

I lifted myself onto the railing and dropped feet first into the water. I wanted to get as far from the ship as possible before turning inland so I swam just below the surface parallel to the coastline.

When my air was spent I came to the top and swam towards the beach with long, easy strokes. I took my time in a thankfully calm sea and fortunately did not tire too badly. When I did need to rest I stopped and treaded water until I caught my breath.

Finally I stepped onto the soft wet sand. I was in total darkness except for the hotel lights, which were recessed probably a half-mile from where I stood. I used the lights as a marker to guide me to the rise lining the beach.

The grassy hill was not very high and its angle was easy to scale.

I looked at my watch, which I had also bought in Kingston. It was twenty minutes past one. I didn't think I had enough money left for a hotel *and* train fare into London, so I chose to rough it for a few hours on the rise. I laughed to myself for thinking that I actually considered a few hours on the front a hardship after so many tortuous days of confinement in *Assistant's* brig.

As cold and wet as I was, I made myself comfortable on the grass, hidden from all directions in the dark.

I watched the *Jamaica Star*, wondering if Sims would continue to wait for his accomplice or would carry on to Newcastle. I didn't have to wait long to find out… a powerboat approached from the freighter's stern with searchlights aimed directly at the ship.

Sims made way when he saw the searchlights but he was too late, the boat was already close and the voice on the loudspeaker warned the captain to stop engines and prepare to be boarded. Sims had no choice but to comply and within a couple of minutes the patrol boat had pulled alongside. I saw no cause for the authorities to come ashore at this juncture, but I took no chances and slung the bag over my shoulder and set off for the center of town where I would wait out the remaining few hours until the first London train was ready to depart.

I managed my way to the bus station where I made myself comfortable on one of the benches. There was still a lot of activity about with the holidaymakers enjoying the all-night arcades and coffee houses. This allowed me to blend in somewhat without appearing to be a vagrant who was trying to shelter himself for the night, and to make sure I wasn't ushered away from the station I occasionally walked around.

It was a few minutes after seven when I got up from the bench to stretch my aching limbs, made so by my still wet clothes. I took my remaining cash from the laundry bag. I had put the money inside a biscuit tin to keep it dry during the swim to shore, and now, before I could buy my ticket I first had to change the dollars to pounds.

I left the bank with English notes just after nine o'clock – plenty of time to make the nine-thirty train.

CHAPTER 20

The train pulled into Kings Cross in the afternoon. It was amazing to me that nothing was different; here I was fifteen years older but it was only about nine months since I was last in these surroundings. The mental adjustment was more difficult than I thought it would be as I looked on the commuters blindly rushing to and from their trains. I suddenly felt stranded. I wanted to get away from this twenty-first century chaos.

"Sorry," someone said after bumping into me while I stood in front of an oncoming crowd.

"'Scuse me," said another after brushing against my shoulder.

"Make your mind up, Jack!" still another said while trying to side step me. I was engulfed; the crowd swept through me on their way to their platforms. I was left standing alone with the laundry bag at my feet, then the loudspeaker came on and a voice echoed some arrival and departure information.

I went outside into the bustling city streets. People were rushing in all directions, getting on and off buses and hailing taxis; horns were sounding and traffic was chock-a-block. I was confused; I didn't know which way to turn. Here, in the center of London during afternoon rush hour I didn't know what to do or where to go.

"You alright, guv?" a voice spoke. A newspaper seller had noticed my state.

"Yes, yes, thanks; I'm just a bit lost…"

"Where d'ya wanna go?"

"Er… Horsley," I remembered.

"*Horsley?* Blimey, you've got a way to go, guv. You know how to get there?" I shook myself out of my confusion and concentrated on the man.

"No, I don't think so…"

"Your best bet's the tube to Waterloo, then get the Horsley train."

"Right, okay."

"You sure you're alright?" he asked again. I nodded and went back inside the station to the underground. I had become totally overwhelmed by this transition, but I snapped out of my bewilderment and oncoming depression. With renewed confidence I took the escalator to the trains now knowing exactly where to go.

I bought the ticket with my last coins and jostled with the crowd on the platform. Everything became familiar and unchanged, and for an instant it felt as though I had never been away.

I reached Waterloo and connected to the Horsley train already at the platform.

Finally, I arrived. The suburb was still very beautiful with its quaint shops and quiet, tree-lined streets. I approached 51 Springfield Road not knowing what to expect. I could picture the shock on my father's face when he realized that his thought-to-be-dead son was standing in front of him, aged fifteen years in the span of nine months.

The door opened just as I flipped the latch on the gate. It was Mrs. Ryder, the housekeeper.

"Hello, Mrs. Ryder, is Mr. Matthews in?"

"No, 'e's not," the frumpy cleaning woman answered. She looked at me as though she knew me but wasn't sure. "Do I know you?"

"Yes, you do, Mrs. Ryder. Don't be alarmed... it's Peter. I didn't die; let's just say I got older."

"Cor, strike me!" she exclaimed grasping her chest, "it *is* you! But..."

"I know, I've changed," I smiled, putting my hands on her shoulders in a move to calm her. "Do you mind if I wait for him?"

"You can, but 'e's gone away," she said, still with a hand on her chest.

"Oh, do you know where he went?"

"Canada 'e said; 'oliday I 'spect."

Mrs. Ryder looked back at me as she turned down the street, shaking her head in amazement.

I looked around the house and found some of my old clothes. I also found some cash and credit cards sealed in a plastic bag in the master bedroom, and conveniently written on the signature strip of one of my father's cards was the PIN.

I decided to go into the office the next morning to see if I could find out more about my father's trip and when he would be back. For now, though, I was going to enjoy a hot bath and a good night's sleep. As I turned to the bathroom something caught my eye beside the dressing table. It was a small chest. I knelt beside it and lifted the lid. It was heavy and opened stiffly. I looked inside and found my passport along with some other personal items. I had no idea how the passport had been retrieved, but there it was in a very strange chest.

The office was locked when I arrived the following morning so I went into the accounting firm next door to see if either of the partners could shed some light on my father's activities.

"He took a few days to go to Canada, Vancouver I think," Reginald Wentworth told me. "Something about looking up a chap who was with his son when he died." *Heinrich Werner*, I remembered.

"Did he say when he'd be back?"

"He wasn't sure, he said a week, perhaps two; why, are you his brother? Or a relative?"

"No, just an old friend." If only Reggie knew, I laughed to myself; known me for so many years and he takes me for my father's brother! As I was about to leave a young clerk approached us.

"Excuse me, Mr. Wentworth," the clerk said, "Mr. Matthews telephoned Mr. Chalmers yesterday and asked him if he would keep an eye on things a bit longer because he wasn't sure when he was coming back."

"What do you mean?" Reginald Wentworth asked.

"I think Mr. Matthews told Mr. Chalmers that he was going to Tahiti from Canada, something about looking for his son."

"That's odd, Leonard didn't tell me. Oh, well, I suppose he forgot."

First Canada, then Tahiti. There was something very curious about my father's movements. He had evidently found Heinrich Werner, but how? And how would he have connected him with me? I was stumped by these strange events. Before leaving the accountants' office I spoke with the other partner, Leonard Chalmers, who took the call from my father. Leonard indeed confirmed that he was leaving Vancouver directly for Tahiti because he had evidence that his son may be alive and living there.

I went home and thought about what I might do next, not that there was much choice but to wait for him to return from Tahiti. I was sure he would come back after three or four weeks; he couldn't search for me indefinitely, and he *did* have a law practice to run.

While I sat watching television for the first time in fifteen years I pictured my father walking the streets of Tahiti looking for me. Then my thoughts turned once again to Tiare, and Tommy and Neolani. How I longed for Tiare and wanted her with me. I wonder how she would have taken to this world…

As I enjoyed the memories of my family I had a compelling thought – what if I went back to Tahiti and looked for my father? It was a small island; we might just find each other. I had the credit card for an airline ticket, and I had a valid passport, even though there was a change in my appearance opposed to the passport's photograph. I decided to do it. I would go into Thomas Cook's in town in the morning and make arrangements for the earliest flight available to Papeete… and my wife and I would again walk the same ground together, only we would be separated by some two hundred years.

MICHAEL BRIAN BRUSSIN

CHAPTER 21

Once again I was traveling back in time, but in mind only as the plane touched down at Papeete's airport.

I was booked in the same hotel where Sarah and I had stayed nine months earlier, or do I say fifteen years before?

The Maeva Beach Hotel brought instant recollections when I registered that evening. I recalled some of the events that preceded the squall; I reflected on the friendship that Sarah and I had struck up with Heinrich and Ursula Werner, and I relived my life-changing encounter with the aura.

Now that I was back in Tahiti I didn't really know how to begin the search for my father. I could walk the streets and look for him, and ask at different places. As small as the island was I realized it would still be like looking for a needle in a haystack. This was *not* a good idea after all; I should have remained in London and waited for him to return. But it was a moot point now so I planned to set out after breakfast and spend the day in Papeete and around Mahina in a general search.

I took a taxi to downtown Papeete and spent until early afternoon walking about with the unrealistic expectation of success.

Papeete was just as I remembered it – flowing with traffic and busy with tourists and street vendors.

I went in and out of the shops and restaurants looking at all the faces.

After a search along the harbor and waterfront I took a taxi to Matavai Bay.

I asked the driver to wait while I reminisced at Point Venus. Once again I came upon the lighthouse and the monument marking the landings of Captain Wallis, Captain De Bougainville, and Captain Cook. I knew I wouldn't find my father here, but I was happy just standing on the same ground as Tiare and my children. I looked up at the ridge where my house would be. I wanted to go up there, but it made no sense, it would be like trying to catch the wind.

After running my hand over the monument as though making sure it was really here, I walked over to that piece of land I remembered so well, the strip that jutted into the lagoon on which I had the most amazing sensation of déjà vu. It was so vivid recalling poor Sarah trying to snap me out of my trance. This was where it all began, and now I wanted to go back.

"Monsieur, do you still want me to wait?" the taxi driver asked.

"Yes, please, I'll just be a few more minutes." The driver went back to his car while I stood looking, and waiting…

I returned to the hotel at about four o'clock. A cup of tea, I thought, and then a nap.

The desk clerk gave me my key and an envelope with my name written on it. I took the items and went to the lounge where I sliced open the envelope and read the note. The message didn't make any sense… something about meeting the doctor at six-thirty. I took the note back to the clerk and told him he had misdirected it.

"Oh, pardon, monsieur," he said, "this is for Monsieur *Jack* Matthews; I put it in your box in error – two names the same, forgive me." A rush of excitement engulfed me.

"You said *Jack* Matthews?"

"Oui, monsieur, he is staying here with a colleague, Doctor Werner. The doctor asked me to give him this message," the clerk explained.

"Can you tell me where Mr. Matthews *is*?"

"He left after lunch, monsieur, I do not think he has returned yet, but I believe you will find Dr. Werner at the lagoon."

"Thank you, thank you very much!"

I crossed the pool area and headed towards the lagoon while looking out for Werner. What would I say to him? How would he react?

I stepped onto the sand and continued to the water's edge with my eyes peeled. A strange wave splashed over my feet and I jumped back; it was strange, that is, coming from a still lagoon. Another one caught me and I danced backwards again. Suddenly I saw a familiar figure. It was Werner.

"Heinrich!" I shouted. As he turned around I was knocked off my feet, this time by a powerful wave. High, swirling waters threw my stunned body down again after I had lifted myself up. I managed to get to my feet and saw Werner looking in my direction through the lagoon's arching waves. But I could not move, I was trapped inside a circle of glowing rings.

The aura disappeared and the lagoon returned to its own fluent state, rippling serenely under the sun's reflection.

I was soaked from head to foot and was shaken from the brute force of the waves that threw me into the air.

I turned towards the hotel, but it was not there. Nor were the beach chairs, or the people, including Heinrich Werner. I was alone on a desolate stretch of beach.

I walked for several minutes without seeing a soul. I hurried inland. There was no road. I eventually spotted some houses in the distance; they had a familiar shape about them, all similarly rectangular. I focused on some people standing near the houses.

"Manu!" Where did you come from?" I heard somebody call. I turned and saw a fisherman I knew breaching his canoe. I saw other canoes approaching the shore, and then I saw several people walking towards me. They were dressed alike in white tops and kilts. As I came closer to them I heard a woman's voice.

"Manu! You *didn't* go!" I turned to see Tiare running towards me.

"No, I *didn't* go," I whispered when Tiare threw herself into my arms. "I will *never* go."

The aura had returned me to the very day that the *Assistant* departed. The vessel had sailed on the morning tide and I reappeared that afternoon. Six months of harrowing exploits had occurred in the span of those few hours.

CHAPTER 22

Not long after my return I again became intent on writing an account of everything that had happened to me from the day I left England for my Tahitian holiday. The coming of the British store ship, *Daedelus*, gave me the opportunity to acquire the necessary writing materials.

I made myself known to Captain New of the *Daedelus*, who was quite surprised to hear my perfect English, and being curious about my western features under a deep Indian tan he invited me to dine with him on board his vessel.

Captain New received me in his quarters that evening.

"I'll warrant it's been a long time since you tasted a cut of good English beef," he said.

"Not as long as you may think, captain."

"Oh," he muttered, then added, "don't you feel rather strange in those togs?"

"Captain, I have lived here for many years, I am naturally

comfortable in the mantle and kilt."

"Of course," he patronized, settling into his meal. "Tell me, Mr…"

"I am called Manu, although my English name is Matthews, Peter Matthews."

"Tell me then… *Manu*, how did you come to live so long in Tahiti?" I pondered my answer, listening to the somber creaking of the ship's boards while the vessel swayed slightly from side to side. Finally I told him I was a crewmember on a ship that went down in the Tuamotus and had managed to make my way to Tahiti where I decided to settle.

My time spent with Captain New was stimulating. He shared some of his experiences with me and told me of his present assignment to Australia. Before the evening concluded I asked him for whatever writing material he could spare for my autobiography. Being fascinated he graciously gave me a stack of paper and quills, and a sufficient supply of ink for the project.

After the crew had stored fresh water and food for their onward journey, the *Daedelus* weighed anchor. And I began writing this manuscript.

It gave me a great deal of pleasure documenting my experiences, even though it became arduous at times using the unfamiliar quill and liquid ink. My foremost concern was to keep the papers safe from the elements; but I was fortunate to come by a small chest complete with padlock and key, for which I had bartered with one of the Indians who had previously obtained it from a member of the *Daedelus'* crew.

CHAPTER 23

Four years were to pass before another foreign vessel called at Tahiti.

Now sixteen, Tommy had long overcome the terrible injury he sustained in the hunting accident. Although he would bear an angry scar for the rest of his life, he was able to walk normally and even run with little evidence of him favoring his weaker leg, and he continued to enjoy the thrill of the hunt, showing no loss of confidence over his encounter with death when he was so savagely gored.

My daughter, Neolani, now eleven years old, had developed the characteristics of her mother and was going to grow into a beautiful woman; and Tiare's beauty and elegance, and ever-present impish charm, remained as enchanting to me as ever before. As for myself, I could not be happier.

Peace between the Pomares and my district of Mahina was maintained during the four years that followed the *Daedelus'* departure, with the tension lessening a little towards the end of this period as something of a political rivalry had developed between the eighteen year-old Otoo and his father. The elder Pomare, having carefully prepared Otoo to be supreme ruler of the Society Islands, had become oddly resentful over the power that his son now commanded.

I was aware during those years that there would be many more ships anchoring in Matavai Bay, and I knew equally well that the arrival of each vessel would bring events which were to establish the destiny of Tahiti and her sister islands.

Knowing I would continue to see history in the making for years to come gave me a further uplift, and watching history repeat itself – particularly the events of which I had prior knowledge – was certain to put me into a state of awe as it did in the case of the *Bounty's* arrival, but never again would I fear the mental impact of witnessing those inevitable future events. Nor would I intentionally do anything that would change an event, which in turn might alter the specific and required historical development of Tahiti.

It was March of 1797 when the *Duff* entered Matavai Bay. The arrival of the *Duff* was to play a prominent role in shifting Tahiti's culture as His Majesty's Ship carried a group of missionaries whose objective was to establish a Protestant mission on the island.

Having prior knowledge of the *Duff's* sailing, I had naturally been anticipating her arrival, but no matter how prepared I was, watching history again unfold before me continued to amaze.

Eighteen men and five women disembarked from the *Duff*, and they were intent on changing the religious ways of the Indians.

These missionaries were so different from any other Englishman seen by the natives they were initially believed not to be English. The Indians had never before seen a white woman, and with their weighty full length dresses they were looked upon with curiosity and amusement, and the men were hardly any less unusual with *their* unfamiliar wardrobe. Notwithstanding the peculiarity of it all, Hitihiti and Otoo cordially received the missionaries when they came ashore.

After presenting the chiefs with gifts of cloth and trinkets, the missionaries were taken to a large house on the westerly side of Point Venus, which was specially built for visiting dignitaries.

I followed the evangelists to their new residence, picking up pieces of conversation along the way. The first English words I heard in four years came from one of the women.

"Henry, I never conceived how heathen these people were," she whispered cautiously. "Look at them, they're *naked*; and the women – have they no shame?" This nervous missionary was particularly referring to the bare-breasted women.

"Now, my dear, let's not fret ourselves; we have God's work to do and we must go about it with strength and not be afraid of what we do not understand." These soft-spoken words came from the woman's husband, who himself appeared uncomfortable at the fierce appearance of the men and nakedness of the women. I could not help being amused at what I heard, but then I found myself resenting the missionaries for intending to impose their ways on the people of Tahiti. *What right had they?* I asked myself. However, after looking inward I suspected it was I who was being intolerant, recognizing the fact that this event was a necessary chapter in Tahiti's development.

The day following the *Duff's* arrival, Hitihiti and Otoo

hosted a feast in honor of the missionaries. The evangelists planned to use this occasion to talk with Tahiti's two most powerful chiefs of ending sacrificial rites to false gods, and of recanting the order of infanticide. Meanwhile, I made myself known to the ship's captain.

Captain Wilson took quite a turn when he heard my fluent English. I told him the same story I had presented to Captain New of the *Daedelus*, that I was shipwrecked off the Tuamotus some twenty years earlier and made my way to Tahiti.

Once I was comfortable in the presence of Captain Wilson I asked him if he would kindly deliver my chest with the manuscript locked inside to the Admiralty, whom I trusted would do whatever possible to see that it reached its ultimate destination.

I had also made myself known to the missionaries and volunteered my services as translator during their stay. The Englishmen could not have been more pleased to have someone available who spoke both Tahitian and English.

The missionary leader, a portly middle-aged gentleman named Henry Jefferson, was most emphatic when he directed me to tell Otoo and Hitihiti that human sacrifices and killings of blemished or malformed newborns had to stop.

"I will, Mr. Jefferson, but remember, I shall only act as translator for you and nothing more; do not ask me to use my influence to achieve your ends."

"*Mr. Matthews,*" came the pastor's stern reply, "it is your duty as a God-fearing Christian to see that my associates and I fulfill what we have been sent here to do. These savages must stop killing innocent men in sacrifices to false gods, and they must stop the murder of helpless infants at birth because they are malformed or carry a blemish; these little ones should be loved all the more. We must turn the people of these islands into Christians, Mr. Matthews."

"Although I am in agreement with your motives, Mr. Jefferson, you must understand that I have lived with these people for more than twenty years; this is my home, and I will tell you again, sir, do not ask me to lecture for you. I will translate your words and no more."

By limiting my role in this way I was satisfied that my involvement with the missionaries would not impair the natural course of Tahiti's development.

A few days after her arrival the *Duff* set sail with eight of the missionaries to the Friendly Islands where that group was to undertake their gospel endeavor. In the meantime, Otoo and Hitihiti had summoned the dignitaries of Tahiti to yet another feast to be held in the honor of Henry Jefferson and his remaining party.

The citizens of Pare received Hitihiti's presence coolly as Mahina and the Pomare followers were still in part holding onto a tenuous peace, but any tension was soon lost amongst the spirit of the evening. I sat with the missionaries and opposite Otoo and Hitihiti during the feasting, still in the role of translator.

"Mr. Matthews," Jefferson said as the servants brought out lavish quantities of roast pork and placed it on a mat that had been spread on the grass, "please tell our hosts that we are most grateful for their hospitality, and that it is our hope that we can in kind show their people the way of God." I translated these words to the chiefs exactly as Jefferson had spoken them. "But tell them that before God can look lovingly upon them they must first stop these barbaric sacrifices and shameless killings of their marked newborns." One could feel the emotion in Jefferson's voice as it grew louder and trembled before he finished speaking. While deliberating on the translation I caught sight of some disturbing activity nearby. "Well, Mr. Matthews?" Jefferson prodded.

"Mr. Jefferson, I'm afraid that you and your associates are unaware that an offering to Oro is going to occur at this moment." There was a frozen silence.

"What? Now?" Jefferson panicked. "For what purpose? They can't do it! Matthews! Stop them!" He then stood up and looked around wildly as though searching for someone to intervene. At that moment, in the flickering shadows of the evening, a man of low rank was brought to an altar away from the assembly area. He was carried in a spread-eagle position with his wrists and ankles tied to the corners of four poles that had been knotted together with sennit cord. The executioner then thrust his knife into the stomach of the upright victim and ran the weapon up and then down, slicing the wriggling body open. Some of the missionaries ran with their hands over their mouths while one or two others passed out at the gruesome spectacle.

"Matthews, this must be stopped," Jefferson cautioned in a whisper as he slowly sat back down.

The limbs of the corpse were detached by Otoo's servants and given to the young chief as a token of respect. This ugly exhibition caused the remaining missionaries to leave, and when Jefferson himself stood up I discarded my principle of not interfering with the course of events and suggested to the Protestant leader that he and his group stay for the dinner as their abrupt departure would likely put them in disfavor with the chiefs. He reluctantly took my advice and managed to persuade the others to remain.

"Eat, Mr. Jefferson," I encouraged, "I understand your feelings, but it will be better for you if you stay and eat; *then* we can talk, and I will be happy to translate everything you wish to say." Jefferson and his party looked at me with pale, appealing faces.

"Thank you, Mr. Matthews," Jefferson responded, touching my arm.

Henry Jefferson endured the evening and spoke afterwards to Otoo and Hitihiti of abolishing the two most brutal and disturbing religious and cultural practices. Otoo, now Tahiti's most powerful chief and speaking for all the others, including Hitihiti, was receptive to Jefferson's request, but not without wanting something in return. The young chief stipulated that before any such abolishment could be considered, Jefferson first had to deliver rifles and ammunition to him. Now, before sailing to the Friendly Islands, Captain Wilson gave strict orders to the crew who remained behind not to give muskets or ammunition to the Indians, and Jefferson could not undo this command, nor would he want to. Jefferson promised Otoo nothing but boldly told him that if he persisted in continuing the present inhuman rites he and his people would face eternal hell. Because he did not understand the meaning of *eternal hell,* Otoo simply remained adamant about the muskets and ammunition before he would consider Jefferson's request.

The evening concluded with neither person conceding. If anything the relationship between Jefferson and Otoo became strained. Hitihiti, however, was pleased over Otoo being denied the firearms, as it would have all but stripped Mahina's leader of his remaining power.

Jefferson and his ministers maintained a low profile during the days following their ineffectual evening in Pare; but in time, and with me still translating, Jefferson once again spoke with the island's more influential citizens of the Christian way. Whenever the benevolent gentleman felt or received a promising response his balding head became flushed with excitement and he talked faster, often causing me to fall behind with my translation.

Although Jefferson was taking a more careful approach with his conversion methods, Otoo remained angry over his failure to lay claim to the muskets he dearly wanted. Finally, in a display of frustration he ordered a party of warriors to ambush two of Jefferson's men while the Englishmen were en route to meet with a group of potential followers. The missionaries' absence from the rendezvous led me to set out after them, but just as I left the borders of Mahina, the two men, beaten and stripped of their clothes staggered towards me.

"In the name of God, what happened?" Jefferson exclaimed when I assisted the men into the village.

"Otoo's men…" one of them said in obvious pain. "They attacked us… they kept beating us… I thought they were going to kill us."

"The heathen!" Jefferson said angrily, gritting his teeth. "This is his way of trying to make us give him the muskets," he realized, referring to the conniving Otoo. Jefferson and I then helped the men onto a pair of sleeping mats where they could have their wounds tended.

The missionary leader later spoke to me about his concern over the possibility of further attacks by Otoo's men, and confessed that he was at a loss as to how the situation could best be handled. Because of the friction between Otoo and his father I gambled that the best course of action was to fight fire with fire, so to speak, so I sailed to Moorea the following morning to talk to Pomare about his son's cowardly attack on the missionaries.

Being loyal to Hitihiti I was met cautiously by the people of Moorea.

I told Pomare of the unwarranted attack on the two Englishmen by his son. Knowing that Pomare had a liking for the missionaries, I was not surprised at his anger over Otoo's violence, and since he was now willing to put political pressure on his young son, I was also not surprised by his promise to take action against Otoo over the attack.

Jefferson welcomed the news of Pomare's intervention.

"It is strange, Matthews, that the enemies of your own district are the ones we must rely upon for our protection," he remarked.

"It's an unusual political contest between Otoo and his father, Mr. Jefferson; although we're at peace with them – as precarious as it has been over the years – there's such a rivalry between these two men that whatever one does the other disapproves; that's why we can use their personal conflicts to our advantage."

With Otoo heeding his father's warning, the missionaries became more at ease as the days went by. They still had to rely upon my translation, but considering their relatively short time on the island they were gaining the people's confidence at a promising rate.

Apart from being men of the cloth the missionaries were also skilled tradesmen. Their construction of a longboat was of particular interest to the Indians, and the Indians were also intrigued by the missionaries' blacksmith shop; the curious natives would step backwards with a start whenever the blacksmith immersed his scalding iron in water, causing a loud hissing and a rush of steam.

The *Duff* had been gone almost four months before she was again seen approaching the familiar entrance to Matavai

Bay. I calculated that the vessel would stay for no more than a week, as Captain Wilson needed to remain only long enough to store food and water for his voyage home to England, and that week would give me adequate time to complete this manuscript and secure it in its well suited chest.

Once Captain Wilson had settled back on shore I asked him for some of his personal stationery. I explained that I wished to write a letter to the Admiralty requesting the chest be kept safe until sometime after the year 2012, at which time it was to be opened and the contents removed. Captain Wilson was puzzled at this odd request but nevertheless agreed to accommodate me, and he was additionally kind enough to put his endorsement to my letter notarizing its importance.

I have now almost completed this narration of my twenty years as Manu. Not since the first year of my journey back in time have I had any regrets over my destiny. I still hold to the idea that Peter Matthews is a reincarnation of an Indian who lived many years before the discovery of the island by Captain Wallis, and I am still certain that my passage through the time barrier was preordained to keep Tahiti's development on course through the means of not only my spontaneous interventions, but also through my day-to-day activities.

I look back in amazement at seeing history repeat itself with the landing of the *Bounty*, her pursuit by the *Pandora*, the coming of the *Providence* and *Assistant*, and of the coming of the *Duff* and the missionaries; and I look back at how I prevented Captain Bligh's assassination, and in so doing assured that the mutiny would occur which in turn established the future generations of the *Bounty's* crew and their Indian women. And I still marvel at my trial in Jamaica and amazing escape from the hangman's noose.

I had often thought it odd that not since the day I awoke in that strange hut did I ever have another sensation relative to my soul's past. After evaluating these thoughts I concluded that the déjà vu feelings I encountered occurred for the single purpose of preparing me psychologically for my new life as Manu.

It is with conviction that I believe the human mind is not nearly developed to the degree where it can use its conscious recollections of previous incarnations to a positive end. I believe our soul has more than one entity, but not for eons will our minds be able to cope with the conscious awareness of our previous lives. Such awareness today will create mental chaos, or perhaps better stated, perpetual madness. I can recall my emotions and behavior when I realized that Peter Matthews was a reincarnate of an earlier Tahitian warrior; I was dangerously close to a mental collapse. Man is simply not ready to handle such conscious and veritable images.

CHAPTER 24

As I sit under the shade of a tall tree writing these closing words I can see Tommy and Neolani riding the breakers beyond the reef, and Tiare swimming leisurely in the lagoon's rippling waters.

"Manu! Stop making those marks and come swim with us!" Tiare called.

She had always been fascinated by this curious method of communication; still she could not understand my desire to document my life on the island and send these papers to my father in a strange, distant land.

I am optimistic that this manuscript will reach its ultimate destination, but I ask myself how this could ever reach you – my father – when as I last saw you it was 2012, so how can 2012 come around again? I cannot begin to search for the answer, even though I have myself crossed the barrier of time. I can only trust that the navy will find the chest sometime during or after 2012 – the year of my arrival on this island in the eighteenth century – and will do what they can to see that you receive its contents.

As I envisage the *Duff* sailing into the future with my papers safely on board, I feel that I have been handpicked to fulfill a special task, as though I were selected by a supreme being with whom I feel a wonderful and exhilarating closeness.

"Manu!" Tiare called again. "Stop your dreaming and come and swim with us!"

CHAPTER 25

Jack Matthews put the manuscript in his briefcase when the aircraft began its descent into Vancouver.

After clearing immigration and customs he got into one of the waiting taxis and left for the forty-five minute drive to the suburbs and Heinrich Werner's residence.

Jack suddenly felt uneasy when the taxi stopped outside an attractive Tudor house, which shared a tree-lined street with similar homes. He was nervous over calling on Dr. Werner without at least phoning him from the airport. Jack watched the taxi drive away before he walked up the garden path. He rang the doorbell and waited. A tall, husky man soon greeted him. Heinrich Werner still sported the thick but neat black beard that Peter had described. The doctor was visibly surprised to see a stranger on his doorstep holding a suitcase so early on a Sunday morning.

"Yes?" he inquired, adjusting his dressing gown and

wiping his wet hair with a towel.

"Dr. Werner?" Jack asked.

"Yes."

"I'm terribly sorry to disturb you, doctor, I'm Jack Matthews, I talked to you about my son, Peter; I called from London... England..."

"Yes, of course," Werner said, remembering their conversations. "I'm sorry for appearing a little surprised; I wasn't expecting you so directly."

"I apologize for calling on you without ringing first, but I came straight from the airport. I have so many questions about my son that are unanswered, I had to see you as soon as possible to try and clear up this quandary behind his disappearance." Werner took another moment to study Jack.

"Please come in," he finally said, escorting Jack into his living room and offering him a seat.

"I'll just be a few minutes while I get dressed and make some coffee, then we can talk." Jack settled himself on the sofa and looked over the nicely furnished room before picking up a magazine and thumbing through it.

Jack felt comfortable with Dr. Werner even though he was received with some uncertainty over his unexpected and rather presumptuous calling. He sensed the same warmth from Werner that Peter had enjoyed.

Jack put the magazine down when Werner came back into the living room.

"That's better," Werner said, tucking a sports shirt into his slacks. "The coffee will be ready in a couple of minutes." Jack again apologized for his intrusion but Werner shrugged it off.

"Don't worry about it. Now... Jack, yes? What is it exactly that I can tell you?"

"How did Peter die?" Jack asked him bluntly. Werner thought for a minute.

"It was very odd. Peter and I were the only two left alive after the boat went down. I would say there was about fifty meters between us, perhaps more; yes, I remember, we tried to get closer to each other but could not, the sea was too rough. All we could do was hold onto the bits of wreckage until help came."

"Go on, *please*," Jack said when Werner got up to bring in the coffee.

"I could not believe it when he drowned," he continued, returning with the pot. "Please help yourself to milk and sugar. Peter kept shouting that canoes were coming but I could not see them, then when I looked back in his direction he was gone. I could not believe it."

"Was there anything unusual about the way he drowned?" Jack asked.

"I don't think so, I couldn't really tell, I was looking the other way."

"What about the wreckage he was holding onto? Did it remain afloat?" Werner again characteristically stroked his beard.

"I don't remember, I suppose so; it *has* been several months," he said. But after some careful thought he changed his mind. "Wait a moment! That's right! The box was gone! But how could this be? How could a wooden box sink just like that?"

"Doctor, think again, did you notice anything strange about Peter just before he drowned? Think carefully, no matter how insignificant it may seem to you." Werner strained to remember.

"Other than the fact that he seemed so in control of the

situation I would say there was nothing unusual." Werner refilled their cups then deliberated for a moment.

"Wait a moment," he recalled, "there *was* something."

"What was it?"

"When I turned around to face Peter I saw the faintest outline of him; it was like he was hollow or transparent but I could still make him out, then he was gone. It was as though he faded from my sight. I remember now, I thought I was hallucinating, I... I was so exhausted."

"That's it," Jack said to himself. "Heinrich... may I call you Heinrich?"

"Of course."

"I brought the manuscript with me – that Peter wrote; I told you about it on the telephone. You'll understand the reasons for my questions once you've read it."

Both men felt a genuine friendship developing during the short time they were together. Jack began to feel at home and intuitively refilled their cups; he then picked up his briefcase and very carefully removed the manuscript.

"This is what I received from Peter," he said, handing it to Werner. "Be careful, it's very brittle." Werner picked through the pages taking care not to damage any. "It was given to me by the Home Office a few days ago. They don't know where it came from; they said it just appeared in an old archival building that was being torn down, that's all they could tell me."

Werner turned another page and broke off a corner.

"Scheisse! Das ist sehr alt."

"I'd like you to read it before I go back to England... would you mind?"

"Of course, I will be happy to read it; it has my curiosity. You are certain this was written by Peter?"

"Yes, it's definitely Peter's handwriting."

It was midday and Jack thought he should arrange for a hotel, so as he flipped open his mobile phone to get a hotel listing, Werner asked him where he was staying.

"I came directly from the airport, I was going to ask if there was a hotel nearby – I'll be in Vancouver for two or three days." Werner considered for a moment and then responded with a touch of enthusiasm.

"Why don't you stay here? There is plenty of room and I shall be glad for the company." Jack couldn't have been more pleased.

"Are you sure?"

"Of course; now come, fetch your suitcase, I'll show you your room – the bed is already made."

Heinrich and Jack went out for lunch and took the opportunity to get to know each other better. When they returned Werner settled down to read the manuscript at the dining room table while Jack occupied his time watching golf on television.

Jack occasionally turned from the golf to browse through a magazine while Werner continued to read, carefully setting down each completed page.

Jack's composure shifted to one of edginess each time Werner made a remark to himself. Jack was tempted to ask his host what he was commenting on, but he withheld his questions until Werner set down the final page late into the night.

"This is incredible," Werner said, stretching himself. His initial reaction was a desire to believe Peter's story, but logic would not permit it.

"Well, it is obvious he did not drown. If it was not for the fact that the paper *looks* two hundred years old…"

"You think he made up the story?" Jack asked.

"Of course, there is no other explanation. If he wrote this manuscript he must have survived the squall, unless he wrote it *before* he went on his holiday, but then he could not have predicted the ferryboat sinking. No, I am so inclined to think he is living right now in Tahiti – today – but in a world of his own creation. No one can go back in time. Life cannot repeat itself," Heinrich Werner concluded in his characteristic German accent.

Disappointment lined Jack's face after hearing Werner's theory. He knew he could not expect him to believe such a story, but he refused to discard the possibility of time travel and embarked on a debate with Werner over how one might enter another dimension.

Jack reminded Werner of Peter's strange and sudden disappearance, which to him was evidence of the time change.

"And what about the aura? You were in it; couldn't that have been the source of energy behind a thrust into another dimension?" Jack suggested.

"It was unusual, that is for sure," Werner agreed. "I remember, it was strange the way the water raged inside of the aura even after the storm had passed, yet *outside* the water was calm. It was very strange. But how can anybody travel back in time?"

"Maybe Herr Einstein was right," Jack implied.

"The theory of relativity?"

"Precisely."

Again Werner thoughtfully picked at his beard.

"Alright… so, I can see perhaps being thrown into the future, but to go *backwards* – into the past? No, this is not possible… there is no logic to it."

"Why not?"

"Because things cannot *repeat* themselves. If a specific event has already happened, it cannot happen again," Werner attested. "I can see possibly traveling into the future because such an event would not yet have occurred, but to travel into the past... *no*, I am sorry."

"Alright, let's say that it's possible to be sent into the future by increased velocity, why then can't it be possible to be sent into the past through the same velocity?"

"Because the past has already *happened* and the same things cannot happen again, this is what I am telling you!" Werner stressed.

"Look, assuming Einstein was right and you attain a certain acceleration, the speed of light in this case, and you come back to the point of origin, say twenty-four hours later, you would have actually returned several years in the future; so by using the same rationale," Jack aggressively continued, "if a person can reach that necessary acceleration in a forward dimension, why can't that same degree of acceleration be reached in a reverse dimension, as in the pull of a catapult; you know what I mean, before the catapult is actually slung forward, a state of regression – or a journey back in time – would exist. I think it was something like this that happened to Peter in the aura."

Werner assessed Jack's theory.

"We are trying to answer questions that may never be answered," Werner said, not committing himself one way or the other to Jack's theory.

"Then what about Peter's behavior?" Jack asked. "What about his belief that he was a Tahitian warrior in a previous life, what do you make of that? And what about him believing that a divine power sent him back to keep Tahiti's development on its proper course?" Jack added before Werner could respond to his first question. The psychiatrist said nothing but stared into Jack's eyes and shook his head in a display of inconclusiveness. "Also, what about Peter's belief that his familiarity with the Polynesian culture – supposedly caused by his soul's previous life – and his déjà vu sensations were necessary means of preparing him for his transition?" Jack finished enthusiastically.

"I know what you are trying to say, Jack, but I cannot agree with you without more exacting evidence."

"Then you still think he made up the story?"

"I'm sorry, I see no other explanation."

"Look, we know he couldn't have drowned if he wrote about the boat sinking and everyone else on board drowning. If he died in the storm he obviously couldn't have written about it. If he *did* die it *wasn't* in the bloody storm; and if he *didn't* die where the hell *is* he? You didn't see him rescued or see him swim to shore, did you? You saw him fade from sight, back to the eighteenth century!"

After a measurable silence Jack felt he might have had Werner convinced, or at least open to the possibility.

"And don't forget, the Home office said the navy found the manuscript in an old building that was being torn down, and even *they* said they didn't know how it got there. I doubt if Peter wrote it before he went on holiday and sent it to them to try to authenticate a conjured up story," Jack concluded.

"Isn't it possible he wanted to escape from an unhappy life and, and dreamed up the entire thing after somehow making his way to shore… then… then it developed to the degree where he could not tell fact from fantasy?"

"I don't think so, Heinrich, you said you didn't see him swim away. You said he *faded* away."

The two men continued to sift through the facts and

theories in search of a mutual conclusion.

Jack again tested Werner's memory when he asked what Peter had said to him about the subject of reincarnation.

"He asked me my thoughts on the matter, just as he said in the manuscript. I remember how disturbed he was over the déjà vu experience and his unaccountable knowledge of the native culture, and particularly the incident when he spoke Tahitian in his sleep. I put it down to the psychology of perception – that his experiences were created by an intense desire to escape to that sort of lifestyle."

"Can the mind actually do that?"

"It can indeed. You see all behavior occurs in an environmental context with stimuli and events preceding and following them." Jack looked puzzled. "Let me clarify… I assume Peter was always interested in the Polynesian islands and had done a good deal of reading about them… their history, their culture; now, I can also assume that over the past few months – or perhaps even years – he had been largely dissatisfied with his life, including his marriage; this could have caused him to escape to a place that would be the most appealing to him – Tahiti, circa the 1700s." Jack listened hard to Werner's hypothesis, making sure he understood everything the psychiatrist was saying. "Once Peter arrived in Tahiti on his holiday all of the things he had read about and seen in pictures became real, and because his desire to escape was so intense he mentally associated himself with the way of life, even to the extent of subconsciously speaking a few words of the language.

"What about his belief he was a reincarnate of a Tahitian warrior? *You're* a psychiatrist – surely you must give some credence to the subject."

"Just because I am a psychiatrist does not mean I have to

believe in reincarnation. I have an open mind, yes, but I tend to think we have one life and that is it; when it is over, it is over. I think people want to believe in reincarnation because it is a way of trusting they will have another opportunity, a hope that when their present life is over, they – or their soul – will return in another body and then they will *have* that chance as a different person." Jack was quick to disagree with him.

"People don't just believe in reincarnation because it's a way of convincing themselves they'll always have another go around, they also believe in it because it's *logical*; alive once, why not twice? And so on until we learn all there is to know through the rebirth of our soul into new bodies. Look at all the people who have been hypnotized and have gone back in time to their former entities, how do you explain that? And how is it that when under hypnosis subjects have been known to speak in foreign languages and describe the lives and times of their previous incarnations right down to the smallest details?"

"First of all, it is theory; good sound theory, nevertheless theory; secondly, going back through hypnosis may seem remarkable to some, but I still believe it is the result of an extensive and inspired knowledge of the subject matter which causes these individuals to suggest they have lived more than one life, as in the case of Peter."

Jack was forced to consider the possibility of his son being mentally unbalanced. He obviously didn't like the idea, and now after hearing Werner deliver a persuasive analysis of Peter's behavior, he listened to the psychiatrist sum up his view of the manuscript.

"Look, Jack, I have found myself believing one thing then another, but *somehow, some way*, without me seeing, Peter made his way to shore, and at this moment – in *our* century – he is living in Tahiti in his own make-believe world."

Jack fidgeted with the manuscript, straightening one page then another. He heard Werner say again that he wanted to believe Peter's story.

"I would like to, Jack, I think you know this." He then took one of the musty pages from the stack and studied it. "It certainly *does* look two hundred years old," he confessed with a sigh.

"Damn!" Jack exclaimed, jumping to his feet. "Why didn't I think of it before?"

"Think of what?" Werner reacted.

"I left a page at a laboratory to be dated – *they* can tell us if he made the bloody thing up!" Jack said, brimming with excitement. "Let me call London, I have the receipt in my wallet." While Jack rummaged for the receipt Werner reminded him that it was ten past seven in the morning in England.

"*Blast*, that's right," Jack realized.

The pair spent the remainder of the evening watching television, resting their minds from the taxing debate while waiting for one o'clock and the usual 9:00am opening hour of most businesses in England.

A few minutes after one Werner telephoned the laboratory. When he heard the ringing he handed the phone to Jack. The receptionist connected Jack to a technician, and after talking with him for a moment and referencing his receipt he was left to wait.

"They're checking," he said to Werner, moving the mouthpiece away from his lips. "Come on…" Jack mumbled after a long time. "Yes. Yes, that's right," he said to the voice back on the line. He listened carefully. Werner's eyes were fixed on Jack. There was a long silence. Finally, without saying a word, Jack aimlessly replaced the receiver. He stood expressionless. "He said it's two hundred and thirty years old… give or take…" Jack said in a soft voice, feeling his way to the sofa.

Two or three minutes passed before either of them spoke or even made a move. Werner eventually got up and went to the liquor cabinet and brought out a bottle of schnapps and two glasses.

"Here, shock treatment," he said, handing Jack a glass. "There is something I find puzzling," Werner said.

"What's that?"

"Why didn't the Home Office give you the manuscript *before* the ferryboat sank? If the manuscript was in the archives since the *Duff* had returned to England in 1800, why didn't the navy find it *sooner… before* the ferry sunk?"

"I know what you're getting at, Heinrich, and I think the answer is apparent. The fourth dimension is a space-time continuum, and I think the manuscript became lost in that continuum upon Peter's birth into our dimension. In other words, once it was there, it ceased to exist during Peter's presence in our dimension. It couldn't have existed because while he was in our dimension he had not yet gone back to the eighteenth century, meaning his life as Manu had not yet begun and the manuscript had not yet been written; but the moment he went back the manuscript came out of that continuum – or dimension if you like – and reappeared in the archives, which was in actuality two hundred and thirty years after Peter's reported death, and that was when the navy discovered it – when they were tearing down that old building."

As complicated as Jack's theory was, Werner understood

what Jack was driving at.

"So what you are saying is that the manuscript became non-existent at some point after it was placed in the archives because, through some law of physics, it could not exist in the same dimension as Peter – the dimension *before* he went back in time, but the moment he was in the eighteenth century – the *other* dimension – it reappeared in the archives, and only then could it be found."

"Exactly!" Jack confirmed with a slap on his thigh.

Though Jack had always sensed the truth, the impact of seeing it authenticated by scientific analysis still left him stunned.

Managing only a couple of hours of sleep Jack got up at dawn and sat alone in the living room with his thoughts still tormenting him.

"How long have *you* been up?" Werner asked when he ambled downstairs at six-thirty.

"Before the roosters, I think."

Werner made some coffee then called his secretary at home and told her to cancel his appointments for the day.

"You're not doing that on my account, are you?" Jack asked.

"No, no, I just don't feel like seeing anyone today, that's all… not after last night and all that has happened."

The two men had become firm friends, and with Werner canceling his appointments he suggested showing Jack a little of Vancouver.

After a cruise around Victoria Island Jack and Heinrich enjoyed afternoon tea at the elegant Empress Hotel.

They were greeted by the delicate sound of knives and forks against bone china when they entered the dining room. Several paintings adorned the plush room, including one of

Queen Elizabeth to add a patriotic touch.

Shortly after being escorted to their table a waitress dressed in a traditional black and white uniform brought them a pot of tea along with a tray of tempting pastries.

"What are you going to do with the manuscript?" Werner asked, pouring the tea.

"What do you mean?"

"What are you going to do with it? Are you going to give it to the government, or to a medical or scientific agency?"

"I don't know, I hadn't thought about it."

"Do you know we could turn the world on its head if we made this document known?" Werner remarked.

"Yes, I suppose we could," Jack agreed, "but I doubt if it would ever be revealed."

"And why not?"

"Do you think for a moment that any government or scientific body would divulge the truth behind the manuscript? People couldn't handle it. I believe Peter was right when he said the human mind isn't developed enough to consciously cope with such sensational self-knowledge. I think the manuscript would be treated the same as if an alien landed on Earth and was captured… the government would cover it up out of fear of panic."

"You don't even think man could handle the knowledge of extraterrestrial beings?" Werner asked a little surprised.

"Oh, I think most people could handle it, but I think there would still be too many who would either mentally panic or even be openly terrified over witnessing other intelligent beings in the universe. I think it could even create confusion and outcries from the religious extreme."

"This is an interesting thought," Werner said, touching his napkin to his lips. "How is it we got on to extraterrestrials anyway?"

"I used it as a correlation. Don't you see, if people would have trouble accepting the existence of extraterrestrials, how do you think they would react to the reality of reincarnation and time travel? I'm telling you, we're not ready for anything so traumatic."

Werner mulled over their exchange.

"I think people could deal with extraterrestrials," he said boyishly to himself.

Jack became pensive, turning his thoughts back to Peter.

"When will you return to England?"

"I've been thinking, Heinrich; I know the manuscript is two hundred and thirty years old, and I know Peter wrote it, but something's missing."

"What do you mean?" a puzzled Werner asked. There was a silence.

"*Damn* it, Heinrich, what if Peter *is* in Tahiti? I mean *now*, and… damn!"

"He could *not* be," Werner assured him, "the laboratory cannot be wrong… unless he got hold of two hundred year old parchment and wrote it on that – in the last year or two if you know what I mean. But the ink… no, this is not possible."

Jack pushed his cup and saucer aside and took a deep breath.

"Heinrich, I'm going to Tahiti."

"What! What for?"

"I've got to find Peter, either find *him* or find his grave." Werner studied him.

"You want to find his grave?"

"I want to either find Peter alive or find Manu's tomb,

yes."

"When will you go?"

"I think in a day or two." Jack then leaned forward and focused his eyes on Werner's and assured him with a smile that he would let him know the outcome. Werner stared back at Jack.

"What would you say to some company?" he proposed.

"You mean come *with* me?"

"Why not? I can close the office for a few days, it is only a matter of rescheduling my patients' appointments; anything serious can be referred to a colleague. I can show you the island; trace some of the routes that Peter took."

"Are you sure?"

"Look, my dear Ursula is gone. I have no family here, they are all in Germany; believe me, I am as curious as you."

Jack was delighted over Werner's offer and shook his hand firmly. He then called for the waitress.

"Two brandies, please, Miss."

"A toast to our enterprise?" Werner smiled.

"A toast to our enterprise."

CHAPTER 26

A cool south sea breeze followed Jack and Heinrich when they walked from the tarmac to the terminal.

"Where to from here?" Jack asked, looking up at the starlit sky, a little in awe of being on the island.

"Maeva Beach — that is where we met Peter and Sarah. It is hard to believe, almost one year," Werner said.

The thought of searching for his son on this famous island sent a rush of excitement through Jack.

"Monsieur?" a voice inquired.

"Yes?" Jack looked up, collecting himself.

"Votre passeport, s'il vous plait," the official said.

"Oh, I'm sorry," Jack realized as he fumbled for his passport.

Jack and Heinrich left the concourse and went to the taxi stand.

"The Maeva Beach Hotel, please," Werner instructed the

first driver in line.

Following a few hours of welcome sleep the two men got up at mid-morning and discussed the day's activity over breakfast.

"This is where we met your son and daughter-in-law. Ursula and I were sitting somewhere over there when I invited them to sit with us," Werner said, pointing in the general direction of their table. "You see, I met Peter earlier in the day at the Blowhole of Ara… whatever it is called. In fact, it is here that Peter told me about the odd things that had happened to him and asked me my thoughts on the subject of reincarnation."

"Hmm, yes, that *is* how he put it in the manuscript. So, how do you feel about hiring a car and going into Papeete?" Jack posed, sipping his coffee.

"You are wondering if we might find Peter there, yes?"

"Well, that is why we're here, isn't it?" Jack chuckled.

Papeete was busy with vacationers when Jack and Heinrich reached the town center. Just as Peter had described in the manuscript, old ladies lined the pavement showing off their jewelry and trinkets to the passing tourists.

After sliding the car into a parking space the men walked along the sidewalk on the far side of the quay.

"Bit dingy, isn't it?" Jack remarked.

"Yes, but it is much nicer once you go beyond Papeete."

Both Jack and Heinrich wore complementary sports shirts over their slacks, yet even this casual attire made them appear overly dressed compared to the majority of tourists and locals who went about in shorts and open shirts, or no shirt at all.

Jack was constantly looking around him. He was studying the young men in the crowd, always on the alert for

Peter's familiar face. Werner noticed the anxiety in him and watched him jump when he spotted a tall, blond young man walking along the quayside. Jack crossed the street, signaling the traffic to give way, and approached the man for a closer look.

"It *did* look like him," Jack said after Werner caught up to him.

They remained on the quay and looked over the array of boats tied up along the wharf.

"Look, this is where the ferry sailed from," Werner said, pointing at a vessel docked ahead of them. "In fact it looks like the same boat."

A group of men were at work loading sacks and boxes onto the boat for transportation to Moorea. The vessel also carried passengers to and from the neighboring island, just as the Hirondelle had done.

"She's going to Moorea," Jack confirmed. "They must be taking that stuff to the hotels and stores. What do you say we sail over on her, Heinrich? We can go to the hotel where you stayed."

"I don't know…" Werner hesitated, remembering the deadly squall that sunk the Hirondelle.

"It'll be alright," Jack assured him, realizing that Werner was reliving the terrible events of the past. "I don't think we're going to find anything in Papeete, we might as well look over Moorea and see if we learn anything there." Jack then turned to one of the workers who had taken a moment to wipe the perspiration from his face with the scarf he removed from around his neck. "What time does the boat sail for Moorea?" he asked.

"Pardon, monsieur?"

"What time… Quelle est l'heure de le bateau pour

Moorea levee, s'il vous plait?"

"Douze heure."

"Merci. Twelve o'clock – half an hour. How about it Heinrich?"

This boat, the Moineau, was the vessel that had replaced the lost Hirondelle.

Just as Peter had so vividly narrated, tourists were seated both on the upper and lower decks waiting for the hour-long crossing.

"This makes me sick," Werner said after he and Jack climbed the stairs and seated themselves at the forward section.

"Come on Heinrich, nothing's going to happen."

"It is not that; it is that Ursula should be with me now; it feels as though if I turn around she will be there."

"I'm sorry," Jack said, recognizing that this was a very difficult moment for his friend.

As a member of the crew collected fares another took orders for beer and soft drinks.

"How about a beer?" Jack suggested, at the same time motioning the crewmember to bring him two bottles.

Before long the Moineau was in the open sea chugging towards Moorea. Werner didn't say much during the crossing. Understanding his emotions Jack let him stand by himself at the railing and watch the swells slap against the side of the boat. Occasionally Werner would look up at the sky as if to make sure there were no storm clouds gathering. In time, Jack joined him at the railing.

"How are you doing?" Jack asked.

"I'm fine. Look, here come the porpoises… just like last time."

"Well, no rain, no gale, and no squall," Jack said as the

343456789

boat passed through the opening in the reef and entered the lagoon.

"And no Peter," Werner said, still staring into the water.

"Yes. You know, we should plan our approach; I mean we've walked around Papeete, we're now headed for Moorea, but what *exactly* are we looking for?"

"We are looking for Peter; or his tomb."

"*Right…* or his tomb," Jack repeated. "Could it be possible, Heinrich? Could it really be possible to find his grave? Manu's grave?"

"I think we must search for it," Werner said with a deliberate look in his eyes.

Jack and Heinrich arrived at the Moorea Lagoon Hotel with a group of other visitors who rode one of the island's rickety buses with them. The two men went directly into the dining hall to order lunch and establish a plan. The vast room remained familiar to Werner. The tables were spaciously set apart from one another and there was still very little décor to the area.

Jack led the way to a window table overlooking the beach.

"So, what do you think?" he said.

"Well, it certainly has not changed. There is nothing of it to change really. Shall we order?"

A few minutes later a pretty young waitress dressed in the traditional pareu took their order.

"Where do you think we should start?" Jack asked.

"I think we have time to look over most of the island and still drive to the tip to Club Mediterainee and see if we might come across Peter there; you know… in case the manuscript is a fake."

"Right, a two hundred and thirty year-old fake," Jack

replied.

"We *are* going to stay the night, aren't we? I think the boat will leave for Tahiti before we return to the hotel. Tomorrow we can go to the burial grounds and see if we can find any evidence of Peter's tomb."

"You mean *Manu's* tomb," Jack corrected.

"Yes, Manu's tomb. Perhaps he was buried here and not on Tahiti."

"No, I doubt that," Jack deliberated; then he pushed his empty plate aside and agreed on getting a bungalow for the night and renting a car.

Jack and Heinrich drove to Vairapu Bay where they parked and strolled amongst the tourists and residents.

"Peter and I swam out to that islet when we were here," Werner recalled pointing to the reef.

"Didn't he tell you about the underground ovens there, and how the natives cooked their food and all that?"

"Yes, he did, how did you know this?"

"From the manuscript, remember!" Jack laughed.

"*Scheisse* – of course. I remember thinking he had an extraordinary knowledge of some very detailed customs."

"As though he had lived here before," Jack commented.

"I suppose this is possible…"

"Damn! If only there was something more conclusive," Jack cursed.

"I suppose finding his tomb *would* seem to settle it. Come, we go back the other way, to Club Mediterainee. Perhaps there will be something waiting for us there; we don't find anything if we keep going south."

Jack and Heinrich returned to the hotel in the evening, tired and disillusioned. They learned nothing at Club Med. They found the resort filled with holidaymakers. They saw snorkelers and sunbathers, people playing cards and back-gammon, and people sipping drinks and talking at the bar. But they didn't find Peter.

"Like to have a nightcap?" Werner posed when they entered the lobby.

"Sounds good."

"They took a table in the cocktail lounge where they settled down and listened to the music of a lone guitarist.

"Well, tomorrow we can find out where the burial grounds are located," Werner said.

"I still think we're better off searching the maraes in Tahiti, that *is* where Peter lived."

"You mean Manu," Werner corrected him this time.

"Right… *Manu*," Jack smiled.

"Look, we are already here; if we don't find his tomb in Tahiti we will only have to come back here to look for it, so why don't we do it tomorrow," Werner argued.

"Let's get that drink, we can decide in the morning," Jack said rubbing his eyes with the palms of his hands.

A young waitress caught Werner's wave and came to take their order.

"Monsieur…"

"Whiskey for me, please, with a little water,"

"Apfel schnapps… you have schnapps?" Werner asked.

"Oui, monsieur." The waitress stared at Werner for a moment before going to fetch their drinks.

"Think she fancies you?" Jack joked.

"Ha! I don't think so – there is at least twenty-five years between us."

"And?"

"Ach!" Werner went, waving his hand to sweep the idea aside.

The waitress returned a few minutes later and placed their drinks in front of them.

"Allo, monsieur," she said, finally remembering Werner. "You 'ave come back for another 'oliday?"

"Excuse me?" a surprised Werner answered.

"You remember me, monsieur? Denise, we meet about one year ago I think."

"Denise! Yes, of course! Of course I remember you!"

The young woman hadn't changed; she still wore her hair cut short and she frequently showed her captivating smile.

"You are here with your wife and the English couple, monsieur? Peter… n'est-ce pas, and his wife?"

"No, they are not here, I'm afraid they died when the ferryboat sank in that storm. You remember that storm, don't you?"

"Oh, mon dieu, oui; we 'ear about it, that everybody drown, je suis vraiment desole. But you?"

"I was the only survivor."

"Did you know Peter?" Jack asked.

"Oh, I'm sorry, Jack, this is Denise. Peter wrote about Denise in the manuscript."

"Yes, I gathered that. Denise, I'm Jack, Peter's father."

"Enchente, monsieur."

"Je suis heureux de faire votre connaissance, Denise. Could you join us for a drink? I'd like to ask you some things about Peter."

"I do not finish work for another hour, but we are not so busy, perhaps for a few minutes; un moment, I will come back."

"So *that* is why she was staring at me," Werner realized. "*Verdammen*, I should have recognized her."

"Finally we've found something – someone who knew

Peter," Jack said.

"But of what help can Denise be?"

"According to Peter's manuscript she had some sort of insight into him."

Denise returned with a cup of coffee, and with the guitarist still strumming in the background Jack asked her what she knew about his son.

"What exactly do you mean, monsieur? You see I did not know 'im so well."

"Did he at all behave in a strange way whenever you were with him?"

Denise thought hard, wrinkling her nose in a cute expression of concentration.

"Non, monsieur. 'is wife was perhaps a little, er… jalouse when I danse with 'im, but that was all."

"Did my son appear to be attracted to you, Denise?"

"Oh, oui, monsieur, we were attracted to each other," she answered candidly.

Jack was careful to not directly ask her if she felt any unusual emanations from Peter, rather he was hoping she would volunteer that detection.

"What was it that attracted you to him?" Jack asked.

"'e was very 'andsome, monsieur. But there was also something different about 'im, je ne sais pas ce que c'est. Although 'e was anglais, 'e 'ad the characteristique of a native of the island."

"What sort of characteristics?" Jack prompted.

"Je ne sais pas… I do not know, I just felt it. When we danse at the tamaaraa I can see a naturel way about 'im. I feel the special, er… sensation, if you know what I mean."

"Yes, I think I do," Jack said more to himself than to Denise.

Jack turned to Werner but said nothing. His expression suggested that the information presented by Denise left remarkable possibilities, at least in his mind, of Peter having a previous life as a Tahitian native.

"Denise, have you ever seen Peter at all since the day we left?" Werner asked.

"Non, monsieur. 'ow could I? Did 'e not die in the storm?" she asked, quite mystified, looking at Heinrich and then to Jack.

"Yes, he did," Jack answered.

"Then what is the purpose of such a question?"

"There were just some things we needed to know, Denise. We do appreciate you talking with us; now, can we buy you a drink?"

"Non, merci, monsieur, I should go back to work now. I am sorry about your son and 'is wife, and your wife, monsieur," she said as she stood up to leave. Jack again thanked her and offered her a gratuity.

"Oh, merci, monsieur, but that is not necessary. Bonne nuit."

Jack let out a sigh and drank the last of his whiskey.

"So, we know she never saw him after the boat had sunk," Werner affirmed.

"Yes, that was a good question. It never occurred to me to ask it. Heinrich, I don't think we're going to find him here, or on Tahiti."

"Then we look for his grave," Werner responded with a dramatic overtone.

"I don't want to look for it here, Heinrich. If it exists it'll be on Tahiti. We should find the location of all the burial grounds in Mahina first and start there. He lived in Mahina so the chances are he was *buried* there."

Jack and Heinrich boarded the Moineau shortly after one o'clock the following afternoon for the return crossing to Tahiti, and once again the boat was filled with passengers.

It was another beautiful afternoon with a blue sky stretching as far as the eye could see.

"This is what it was like before the squall," Werner remarked as he and Jack leaned against the upper deck railing.

"Don't worry, it's not going to happen again," Jack said.

"You have made sure of this?" Werner cynically responded.

Porpoises met the Moineau when she entered the ocean, and the mammals again escorted the boat for about a half a mile before they dived one more time and disappeared.

There was an element of nervousness about Werner during the crossing, which seemed to rub off onto Jack. Both men found themselves looking up at the sky and then down at the swells that rolled the boat with increasing measure.

"For God sake, Heinrich, this is ridiculous! Nothing's going to happen! Look at the sky, there's not a cloud *in* it and we're already halfway across."

"You are right," Werner conceded after looking at the passengers basking in the sunshine. "But I am telling you… that storm… it came from nowhere."

A feeling of relief nevertheless passed through Werner when a member of the crew tossed a rope to a hand on the wharf who in turn tied it firmly around one of the curled iron bars fixed in the concrete.

"I don't think I shall ever get used to sailing again," Werner said as the boat gently bumped her nose against the quay before shifting herself alongside the dock. "So where to now?"

"Let's find out where the burial grounds are; they'll be able to tell us at the hotel."

"Is there more than one in Mahina?"

"I don't know; it doesn't matter, we'll go through as many as we have to."

"What if we don't find his grave or any evidence of him in Mahina?" Werner posed, stopping at the car and unlocking the passenger door for Jack.

"Then we'll look through the burial grounds *outside* Mahina."

"Did it occur to you that he might have left Tahiti? Perhaps he was buried on another island; or perhaps he died in another country," Werner suggested as he pulled away from the curb. Jack considered the possibility.

"Then we'll have to go home, won't we?"

Once back at the hotel they picked up some literature that outlined various tourist attractions throughout the island. Included in the pamphlets was information about the Mehiatea Temple, the only ancient burial ground in Mahina.

"Point Venus!" Jack said with authority, tapping his finger on the box marked on the map. "It's about twenty miles from here; we have to go back through Papeete."

"You don't intend going there *now*, do you?" Werner said.

"Of course, why not? It's still early."

"If you don't mind I would rather stay here for the rest of the day and make a fresh start in the morning."

"Too tired, eh? You're getting old," Jack kidded, but then said, "I suppose we could go in the morning, but I think I'll go back into Papeete for another look around."

"Alright; I'm going to have a drink and sit by the pool.

I'll see you later."

After an uneventful walk around Papeete, Jack returned at six-thirty and found Werner in the cocktail lounge.

"So, did you find anything interesting?" Werner asked.

"No. I suppose I didn't expect to. Anyway, how about an early dinner?"

"Yes, I think so – I'm hungry."

When the desk clerk saw Jack and Heinrich going into the dining room he said to Werner, "Dr. Werner, did Monsieur Matthews find you?" Werner stopped while Jack kept walking.

"Of course he did," Werner answered, looking over at Jack and appearing a bit mystified. He stared at the clerk for a moment, who also seemed confused, then he caught up with Jack.

"Oh, Jack, there was a very strange occurrence in the lagoon while you were in Papeete; it was almost like a miniature storm if that makes any sense," Werner said after they had been seated in the dining room.

"What do you mean a storm in the lagoon?"

"I was walking along the beach and there was turbulence in the lagoon. It lasted perhaps a minute; it was like a giant wave that would not go down, and other waves hit against it; it was in the lagoon but also on the beach. If I did not know better it could have been the aura, but I did not see any glowing rings."

Jack's eyes lit up.

"How long did it last?"

"Only a minute. The big wave that was like a wall was already up when I turned around. It did not go down right away. It could only have lasted for a minute, if even that long; then the lagoon went back to normal – very calm. I wish you could have seen it."

"Strange…" Jack muttered. "You didn't see any rings or colors?"

"No, nothing, just that wave that hung like a wall."

"Did anyone else see it?" Jack asked.

"I don't know, probably, there were others on the beach."

"Hmm… you didn't see anyone inside it?"

"No, I couldn't, it was a solid wall of water."

"Oh, well, we might as well order," Jack concluded. But seconds later he slammed the palm of his hand on the table and jumped to his feet, causing the china and cutlery to rattle loudly and several heads to turn.

"What? What is it?" Werner reacted.

"*Damn!*" Jack swore. "*Damn!*" he swore again.

"What is it? Tell me!"

Jack sat back down and held a hand to his forehead.

"What bloody fools we are!" he realized. "He was *here*, right here with us! That wave you saw was the aura, and Peter was in it!"

"What? How do you know?"

"Because he bloody *told* us!"

"How? When?"

"*In the bloody manuscript!* Oh, what idiots we've been. All we had to do was sit here and wait for him," Jack said, thoroughly distraught and angry with himself for not picking up on something so obvious.

"Ach, nein!" Werner finally caught on. "How can we have missed this? He tells us everything and we read right through it! Scheisse und verdammen!"

"He said he was here looking for us, and all we had to do was wait for him! And now he's gone back! Heinrich – how could we have been so blind?"

"Mensch, I don't know. But, Jack, perhaps there is something more powerful that has control over this."

"What do you mean?"

"It was so obvious from the manuscript that all we had to do was wait for Peter to appear and keep him away from the lagoon, it seems to me that perhaps the Good Lord saw to it that we would not see the obvious because it was Peter's destiny to return to the eighteenth century and there was nothing we could do to prevent it. It is like Peter said in the manuscript, you cannot change history, or what was it… the end result."

The two men sat mostly in silence through their dinner, eating little, too disappointed in themselves to say much.

Finally over coffee Werner spoke.

"I suppose it is not worth going to the burial grounds now. I think we should go home."

"No… I don't think so," Jack responded.

"Why not?"

"If Peter returned to the eighteenth century his tomb should be in existence in *our* time because Manu will have long been dead. No, we'll continue tomorrow. We're going to find his tomb."

CHAPTER 27

When Jack and Heinrich arrived at the Mehiatea Temple they were instantly taken by the three hundred foot altar and the dozen fifty foot tiers spaced across it. They became caught up with a group of tourists who were listening to their guide explain that the altar was used for such things as wedding ceremonies and human sacrifices.

"Look over there," Jack said, pointing to a cave abutting the courtyard. "Do you think there could be tombs in there?"

"There could be," Heinrich responded, "do you want to have a look?"

"Let's go."

"Do you think we can get inside?" Heinrich questioned when they stopped near the entrance.

"It doesn't look like it," Jack said, nodding to a sign at the opening that read *TABOO*.

"Come on," Jack whispered, touching Werner's arm.

"Wait, that man is looking at us; I think he is the caretaker." Jack studied him.

"No, he's just one of the crowd; come on."

To the surprise of the watchful custodian Jack and Heinrich entered the darkened crypt and began feeling along the walls for evidence of tombs.

"We need a flashlight in here," Werner said.

"Yes, we do, damn it; we'll have to come back with one."

"Messieurs! S'il vous plait! Les Tombeaux est prive!" the custodian called to them. The men ignored his warning and continued to feel along the walls within the cavity's dim confines.

"Look! It feels like etching!" Jack said squinting at what were graves. "It is! You can see it, Heinrich! There are markings under each tomb!"

"Gott, Du hast Recht!" Werner gasped.

"Messieurs! Vous devez partir le caverne immediate-ment!" the attendant again warned, this time causing the tourists to focus their attention on the cave. Still Jack and Heinrich paid no notice.

"How the hell are we going to translate this?" Jack said.

"We must come back with someone who can read it, we have no choice."

As the intruders turned to leave two uniformed policemen followed by the hesitant custodian entered the cave.

"Messieurs, we must ask you to leave this sanctuary at once. You have violated sacred grounds, we must insist you do not enter the resting place of our ancestors again," came the stern warning from one of the officers.

Jack was buzzing with excitement when he and Heinrich

were ushered past the curious tourists.

"Heinrich, we've got to get back in there! We've got to find someone to translate that writing!"

"It will probably cost some money; you know the people are superstitious. They will not go into a crypt, they are afraid of disturbing the spirits."

"The police went in."

"It is one thing to step in the entranceway, but going right inside is a different matter, except perhaps for the police."

"Look, I don't care *what* it costs; I want to find someone who's more interested in money than is afraid of bloody ghosts, now where are we going to find that person?"

"Probably not here. Perhaps if we ask around Papeete we might find somebody," Werner suggested.

"Let's go then."

Werner wasted no time behind the wheel. He sped along the winding path and quickly made the connection to the main road leading into Papeete.

After parking along the front they looked over some of the men employed on the wharf.

"Who are we going to ask?" Jack posed, turning from one group of men to another.

"They all look likely enough, how about *them*?" Werner said, pointing to three hardy individuals doing some work on a boat.

The men welcomed the opportunity to wipe the perspiration from their faces and rest for a moment when Jack and Heinrich approached.

"Messieurs, est-ce que vous parlez anglais?" Jack asked.

"I speak," one of them answered, bearing the same grim face as his co-workers.

"Good, we're looking for someone to translate some old

Tahitian writing into English for us. We'll pay well for it."

The spokesman took a drink from a soda bottle and wiped his mouth with the back of his hand.

"I will do it," he said.

"You'll have to come with us to see the writing."

"Why can't you show it to me here?"

"Because the writing is on the cave walls at the Mehiatea Temple," Jack explained. There was a shocked silence before the stranger responded.

"Non, monsieur! I do not go in there! Les tombeaux est sacre! Non monsieur, adieu!" In an instant the spokesman's arrogance was displaced by fear. The rugged worker, visibly frightened by the thought of entering the cave, translated Jack's request to his friends who reacted similarly and eyed both Jack and Heinrich with extreme caution before turning away.

"What happened?" Heinrich asked.

"He just got very nervous when I mentioned the cave."

"I told you, they are afraid to go into the caves."

"Maybe if I show them some money. Jack re-approached the men, this time waving several notes in his hand, but before he could say a word the spokesman pushed Jack's hand aside.

"Monsieur, l'argent ne pas important. I do not go inside the cave." Jack turned from the man and walked back to Werner.

"Not even money. I could be holding a million bloody francs in my hand and he still doesn't want to know," Jack complained, waving the cash in Werner's face.

"Perhaps a taxi driver might help us find somebody who will do this," Werner suggested.

"Yeah… let's try a taxi driver. Damn superstitious

lot…"

"Messieurs! I will 'elp you!" a voice unexpectedly called to them. Jack and Heinrich stopped and looked at each other before turning around. When they faced the man they saw a tall, well-built islander probably in his mid-forties standing with his hands on his hips.

The native was dressed in a pair of cut-off trousers and a lightweight shirt buttoned half way up. He was deeply tanned and spoke English with a distinctive French accent.

"What did you say?" Jack asked as he and Heinrich approached him.

"I 'ear you talk to those men," the stranger said, pointing to the laborers. "I work with them; they are afraid of les caverns, they are all afraid."

"And aren't you?" Werner asked.

"That is my business, monsieur. Maintenant, you want somebody to go inside and er… traduire…"

"Translate," Jack prompted.

"Oui, translate… translate the writing inside, on the walls, n'est ce pas?"

"That's right. Will you do it?"

"Oui, but you will pay me fifteen thousand francs."

"Yes, alright," Jack agreed, "but we can't go until after dark, we were thrown out by the police before."

"Because it is against the law to enter les tombeaux. It is better we go after midnight when the watchman is not there." Jack found himself oddly fascinated by the cocky way the stranger had about him.

"Alright, we'll meet you right here… two o'clock."

"Don't forget, we have to buy a couple of flashlights," Heinrich said.

"I know, I haven't forgotten."

"What about my money?" the stranger said, tapping a cigarette out of an opened pack and lighting it.

"Don't worry about your money, Monsieur…"

"My name is Thierry."

"Don't worry about your money, Thierry; we'll pay you when we're inside the cave."

CHAPTER 28

The night was still alive with activity from Papeete's bars when Jack and Heinrich pulled up along the quay a few minutes before two. They crossed paths with some hungry men stopped at the catering wagons that were lined along the embankment.

"Smells good," Heinrich remarked, sniffing the aroma of fowl and seafood floating from the wagons.

There was no sign of Thierry when they reached the boat on which he had been working the previous afternoon. Jack became agitated. He panned the darkness for the stranger and muttered under his breath.

"It's almost two-thirty," Heinrich said.

"I know."

"Do you think he will come?"

"I don't know; damn it, he'd better, he seemed interested enough in the money."

Three o'clock came and Jack continued to pace while Heinrich stood by the boat's stem. With still no sign of Thierry, Jack motioned to leave.

"Wait a minute!" Heinrich jumped, "that may be *him*." Jack peered along the quay and saw a tall, silhouetted figure.

"May… be…" he said as the form drew nearer.

"'Allo, messieurs," Thierry said.

"Where *were* you?" Jack asked, "we've been here since two o'clock."

"It *is* two o'clock; what is the problem, monsieur?" Thierry said, pointing to his watch.

"You're an hour slow – it's *three* o'clock," Jack argued.

"Never mind, Jack, he's here now. Let's get going," Heinrich advised.

"Do you 'ave my money?" Thierry asked.

"Wait a minute – let me see that watch," Jack said, taking hold of Thierry's wrist, only to have the stranger pull his arm back and look menacingly at Jack. "That looks like Peter's watch… where did you get that?"

"It is *my* wristwatch," Thierry insisted.

"Just let me look at it, I won't take it," Jack said, using a softer approach in the hope that Thierry would at least let him see it up close. At further prompting from Jack, Thierry held his wrist out and Jack looked at the face and touched his forefinger to it. "Would you let me hold it – I *will* give it back to you, I promise." Feeling less threatened, Thierry undid the strap and handed the watch to Jack. Jack studied it then turned it over.

"*He's here… on the island, Heinrich; look!*" Jack exclaimed, showing the back of the watch to Werner.

"I do not believe this!" Heinrich gasped. He read an

inscription to Peter from Sarah; she had given Peter the watch for his birthday. "How do we find him? Where do we look?"

"I don't know; Thierry is going to have to lead us to him – if he will tell us where he got Peter's watch. Thierry, will you tell us who you got this watch from? Can you take us to him? We'll pay you well."

Thierry looked suspiciously at Jack and Heinrich. He didn't say anything; it was as though he was thinking carefully over what he should do.

"I take you," he finally said. "You drive car; I take you."

The men hurried to the car, which was parked at the center of the embankment. Jack and Heinrich were mindful of the nighttime breezes and had dressed appropriately, with Jack wearing a windbreaker zipped up over his shirt and Heinrich sporting a khaki jacket with a sewn-on belt buckled at the waist, while all Thierry needed was a frayed long sleeve shirt tucked into his trousers.

With Heinrich again behind the wheel Thierry directed him to leave the island's main road and turn onto the path leading upward to the temple. Heinrich downshifted and accelerated to manage the incline.

"This is the way to the temple," Heinrich realized.

"Why are we going to the temple?" Jack asked. "You said you would take us to the man who gave you the watch."

"I take you; you drive car to temple, I take you."

The entire area was pitch black except for where the light from the car's headlights shone.

"La!" Thierry said, pointing from the back seat as Heinrich recognized the turn leading to the temple's quadrangle. Heinrich pulled up near the altar and stopped the engine, but left the headlights on. "You come, I take you.

You have light?" Jack gave Thierry his flashlight and he and Heinrich followed their guide to the cave entrance. There was not a sound to be heard; the macabre presence of their shadows only made the silence more intensifying.

"I don't like this, Jack," Heinrich confessed when they rounded the altar and approached the cave entrance; "something does not feel right."

"Come on, don't go wobbly on me now," Jack whispered.

Suddenly Heinrich stumbled over a rock and fell to his knees, causing the birds to flutter in the darkness.

"Scheisse!"

"Shh… come on."

The cave was damp and cool inside and it appeared to be an endless catacomb. Jack and Heinrich found it difficult to focus their eyes on the tombs as the beams from the flashlights danced about erratically in the confines.

"You say you want me to translate, monsieur," Thierry said.

"I wanted you to read the names that are inscribed on the tombs, but you said you were going to take us to the man who gave you the watch," Jack responded.

"You tell me why you want to know the names of the dead," Thierry replied.

"Jack, as long as we are in this verfluchter platz let him translate the names on the tombs, just to eliminate the possibility… you know…"

"Alright. Go ahead and read the markings," Jack directed Thierry.

"You 'ave not told me why you want to know the names of the dead, monsieur; and you 'ave not paid me my money."

"Look, I'll pay you now, but never mind *why* we want to

know the names – you just read them to us."

"D'accord, you give me the money when we are finished in 'ere," Thierry said. He then edged to the first tomb and strained to see the etching in the flickering light while Jack and Heinrich looked over his shoulder. Thierry read a long Tahitian name, which meant nothing to Jack or Heinrich.

"Go on," Jack said.

Thierry edged sideways to the next tomb and shone the light on it. Again Jack and Heinrich peered over his shoulder and listened to him read another long name.

"No, go to the next one," Jack directed.

"How many tombs do you think are in here?" Heinrich put to Jack.

"Il y a vingt-huit," Thierry answered.

"How do you know that?" Jack asked

"Il y a vingt-huit tombres, monsieur; *je sais.*"

"How many?" Heinrich asked, turning to Jack.

"He says twenty-eight."

"He seems to know a lot about this place."

"He must have counted them," Jack said.

"Not tonight; he did not count them tonight – he has been in here before."

Thierry stood with his back to the third tomb looking deeply into the men's eyes. Heinrich glanced nervously towards the cave entrance, then back to the mysterious islander.

"I know what you are looking for, messieurs." Jack and Heinrich cringed when they heard this. Before Jack or Heinrich could question his defiant statement Thierry said, "Come with me, I take you to the man who give me watch." Thierry then walked to the end of the chamber and waited for them to follow.

The men walked slowly, almost in a reluctant shuffle to where Thierry stood. Jack perspired in anticipation while Heinrich's skin crawled in unbounded fear.

When they reached him Thierry shone the flashlight on a tomb embedded in the cavity's back wall and near to the ground.

"Voici." He then took Jack's hand and ran his trembling fingers over the tomb's carved inscription. Jack's voice quivered.

"What does it say?"

"It say *The body of Manu the Englishman rests 'ere.* See the bird." Thierry then pointed to Peter's namesake – the carving of a bird in full flight.

"*Mein Gott,*" Heinrich whispered.

Thierry moved to his right, still crouching.

"The body of Manu's woman, Tiare, lies beside 'im." Jack took the flashlight from Thierry and ran his hand over the inscription. A carving of a flower followed Tiare's name.

Jack stood up and looked at Heinrich in a state of shock. The first hint of dawn had come which reflected just enough light to allow the men to see each other's own amazed expressions.

"I feel as though I am dreaming," Heinrich said.

Jack again went to one knee and examined Manu's and Tiare's tombs.

"Thierry, how did you know what we were looking for?" Jack asked after getting to his feet. The stranger said nothing but stared at the two men in a proud silence. "Thierry, what is it?" Why are you looking at us like that?"

"My name is not Thierry," he finally spoke, throwing out his chest. "I am Teura-Kanokoa," and to prove his identity the Indian ripped open his shirt and displayed a striking tattoo of a boar carved boldly across his chest. Jack and Heinrich stared in astonishment at the warrior.

"This is too much," Heinrich shuddered. He then turned and ran to the cave entrance, which had become visible from the dawn's light.

A long, clinging silence dominated while Jack and Teura-Kanokoa stared at each other.

"You knew my son," Jack said after taking hold of himself.

"Manu was your son?"

"Yes."

"I know 'im well, and Tiare – 'is woman, and 'is children."

"When did he come to Tahiti? Where did he come from?"

"'e was found in the water. 'e come from an etrange land; 'e say 'e fly from 'is land to Tahiti, so we call 'im Manu."

Jack had a never-ending number of questions to ask Teura-Kanokoa.

"How is it that you are still alive? It's been two hundred years since Manu died," Jack tested the Indian.

"Well you know, monsieur, that I come this time the way your son come my time. I do not understand 'ow. Je ne sais pas. When we return to Tahiti from the island of Aki Aki our boat pull into strong water. This water 'ave a, er... etrange color around it; it was like a, a... arc-en-ciel."

"A rainbow," Jack translated to himself.

"Outside of the colors the water was still, but inside... ce'etait une mer demontee. I think the boat go, er... underneath. I fall into the water. Manu cannot 'elp me, but I manage to swim to the land, et alors, I find myself in a different, fantastique world."

Jack found himself grasping the warrior's shoulders in an emotional show of gratitude and admiration. Indeed, Jack's actions dramatically expressed his most inner feelings, having come face to face with the one man who knew his son so well in a world so fantastically far away.

Suddenly Heinrich burst back into the cave.

"We have to get out of here! The police are coming!"

"Damn! Come on!" Jack warned Teura-Kanokoa, "we were thrown out of here once; if they catch us again we're in trouble!"

Jack and Heinrich ran from the cave and jumped into their waiting car just as two policemen swung open the doors of their vehicle.

"Komm! Mensch, du schwein! Komm!" Heinrich swore when the engine wouldn't start. "Es ist das verdammte Licht! We had the lights on too long! Komm…"

"Where's Teura-Kanokoa?" Jack said as the policemen cautiously approached them, "we can't leave without him."

"We cannot leave at all if this scheisse auto does not start!" But then with another crank the engine turned over and idled safely while waiting for Heinrich to put it into gear. "Richtig! Heraus!"

"Not without Teura-Kanokoa!" Jack insisted.

"No, Jack! They will arrest us if we stay!" Heinrich then put the car into reverse and backed up.

"Not without Teura-Kanokoa I said!" Jack ordered this time, putting his hand on the steering wheel to stop Heinrich.

"Sortez la voiture, s'il vous plaît, messieurs," one of the policemen directed after opening the driver's door, but before Heinrich or Jack could get out of the car Teura-Kanokoa appeared and threw the officers to the ground.

"Allons!" the Indian said, climbing into the back seat.

Heinrich immediately turned the car around and sped out of the quadrangle.

"Where were you?" Jack snapped at Teura-Kanokoa. The Indian did not respond. Jack could only speculate that he wanted to remain in the temple that he knew so well but had a change of mind when he saw their impending arrest.

As Heinrich pulled the car onto the road winding down and away from the grounds, a second police car passed them on the way to the reported intrusion.

"Scheisse!" Heinrich swore when the second vehicle turned into the quadrangle.

"It's okay," Jack said, "they've gone into the grounds; let's get back to the hotel."

"Damn it! They haven't!" Heinrich cursed again; "they are behind us!" Heinrich raced the car along the descending road, screeching its tires and hugging the curves.

The sun had just risen when the car came nearer to the main road paralleling the shoreline. Jack looked behind him, and then Teura-Kanokoa did the same.

"There's *two* of them now!" Jack alerted Heinrich. "Damn it! Lose them, Heinrich!"

Both police cars stayed close behind as the vehicles sped along a short straightaway. Heinrich tried desperately to lose them but the piercing sound of the sirens would not go away.

As Heinrich negotiated another curve the leading police car accelerated and pulled alongside in an attempt to force the car into the hill, but the road narrowed unexpectedly when the car came abreast. The next few seconds were an eternity to Jack and Heinrich as they and the unruffled Teura-Kanokoa stared into the terrified eyes of the two policemen next to them. In an agonizing instant the car flopped over the unguarded edge and crashed to the bottom, exploding into a ball of flames. Terror swept through Jack and Heinrich when they watched the policemen plunge to their death, while Teura-Kanokoa, showing no emotion, passed it off as the price of battle.

Heinrich swung the car onto the main road and sped along the waterfront with the remaining car in close pursuit. Suddenly two loud cracks rang out.

"They're shooting at us!" Jack shouted.

"We are not going to lose them! I'm going to stop before we get killed! We should have given ourselves up at the temple! Donner und holle!"

"Drive, damn it! They'll throw the lot at us if they catch us now! Don't you realize we're responsible for those men's deaths!"

Heinrich pulled himself together and punched the accelerator only to see the pursuers do the same.

Another loud crack sounded over the sirens and this time the bullet found a rear tire. The speeding car skidded uncontrollably along the road then veered onto the sand and rolled over before coming to a rest back on its wheels.

"Get out before it explodes!" Jack shouted, kicking open the wedged passenger door. "Come on!" he yelled, pulling out the shaken Werner. Teura-Kanokoa quickly followed, and the three men, all miraculously uninjured, found themselves watching the police car pull up behind their disabled vehicle.

"Go behind the rock!" Teura-Kanokoa ordered, pointing to a tall rock formation in the sand. "There is an opening between the rocks, go in there!"

The policemen got out of their car and began walking

towards the fugitives.

"Courez!" Teura-Kanokoa shouted to Jack and Heinrich, who still had their eyes fixed on the advancing men and yet another police car that was speeding down the hill towards the main road. The pair then ran towards the rocks, leaving Teura-Kanokoa to face the two officers.

Jack and Heinrich could not believe the enormity of their situation. They were desperate over not surrendering when they had the opportunity, where they would have probably faced minor charges, but now they found themselves hunted men, responsible for the deaths of two government officials and looking at potential murder charges, considering that the policemen's deaths were the result of them resisting arrest.

Teura-Kanokoa turned to face his adversaries when Jack and Heinrich disappeared behind the rocks. The policemen stopped a few yards from the Indian sensing that he was one to be reckoned with. Teura-Kanokoa, standing with fists clenched at his sides, saw their caution. When one of the men drew his gun and made the sand fly at Teura-Kanokoa's feet with a warning shot, the Indian screamed savagely and threw himself on the two men and sent them to the ground with a flurry of blows.

Teura-Kanokoa's bronze body glistened in the morning sun as he stood over the unconscious men, still looking every bit of the warrior that Manu had known. He then turned and ran for the rock formation to join Jack and Heinrich as the other police car swung onto the main road. The sirens again pierced his unaccustomed ears as he rounded the rocks.

Teura-Kanokoa stopped in full stride when he saw Jack and Heinrich standing frozen in the sand staring out to sea. Just beyond the reef was a bright, shimmering aura whose colors danced above the water.

"L'arc-en-ciel!" Teura-Kanokoa cried out, and saying no more he ripped off his shirt and threw it to the ground in what appeared to be a long awaited display of defiance against the twenty-first century. He then ran into the lagoon and swam powerfully towards the reef.

Jack and Heinrich stood with their eyes fixed on the aura. They knew they were about to be arrested and ultimately charged with the deaths of the two policemen. They stared at each other in silence; then they watched the other police car turn from the main road onto the sand. The men inside got out and approached their fellow officers who were now staggering to their feet. Jack turned to the turbulent waters inside the aura; then he looked at Heinrich and smiled.

"I'm going," he said. There was another moment's silence between them.

"So, come then," Heinrich smiled back, "what are we waiting for?"

Teura-Kanokoa was approaching the reef when Jack and Heinrich plunged into the lagoon.

"Wait! Wait for us!" they shouted when the warrior lifted himself onto the reef. Their shouts reached his ears and he urged them on while the policemen watched from the water's edge.

Jack Matthews and Heinrich Werner climbed onto the reef, and with Teura-Kanokoa leading the way the three men dived into the ocean and swam towards the aura's beckoning glow.

WITH COMPLIMENTS

A special acknowledgement is extended to H. G. Wells (*The Time Machine*), Douglas L. Oliver (*Ancient Tahitian Society*), Albert Einstein (the theory of relativity), and Charles Nordhoff and James Norman Hall (*The Bounty Trilogy*), whose ideas, theories, and works were used for reference in the writing of this novel. And to remind us how refreshing and important it is to maintain a sense of humor, recognition is given to Mark Twain who told us that, when he was a boy of fourteen, his father was so ignorant he could hardly stand to have the old man around. But when he got to be twenty-one, he was astonished at how much his father had learned in seven years.

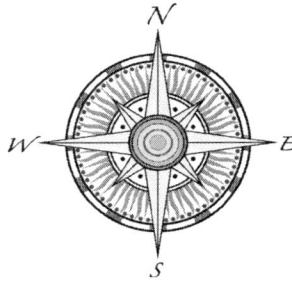

About the Author

Michael Brian Brussin was born in England and moved to Los Angeles in 1967. In addition to *The Aura of Destiny*, Michael has written a series of children's stories called *Stories of Old Ned and his Animal Friends*, and he has also completed a combination autobiography-fiction called *Lola and me and the Dairy of a Thirteen Year-Old*. Michael and his wife, Lola, returned to England in 2000 where they enjoyed their time living in Leicestershire in the East Midlands before returning to Los Angeles in 2003. Michael is an ardent soccer fan, having played throughout his youth and through his thirties, and enjoys following the English and European leagues. Michael and Lola presently reside – with their two parakeets, Jake and Sophie – in Shasta County in Northern California.

Also by Michael Brian Brussin

Stories of Old Ned and his Animal Friends

Lola and Me and the Diary of a Thirteen Year-Old